"From the opening line to the terrifying cliffhanger ending, this is an adventure readers won't soon forget!"

—*RT Book Reviews* (Top Pick!)

"Larger-than-life, full-to-the-brim, jump-off-the-page, made-of-awesome *good.*"

—*Rabid Reads*

"HOLY FRACKING HELL!!! THAT is how you end a book! . . . Jenn's voice is superb."

—*Yummy Men & Kick Ass Chicks*

"This series has managed to get infinitely better with each new story. . . . A jaw-dropper of an ending."

—*Sweet Tidbits*

"Bennett's spectacular urban fantasy series has earned her a spot on my favorites shelf. . . . Her writing is crisp, imaginative, capped with witty dialogue."

—*Paranormal Haven*

"This is one of those books that you want to devour in a day but wish you hadn't when you turn the last page."

—*Romancing the Dark Side*

SUMMONING THE NIGHT

Nominated for the *RT Book Reviews*
Reviewers' Choice Award

"Bennett quickly establishes that her terrific debut was no fluke, delivering another riveting tale. . . . A series for your keeper shelf!"

—*RT Book Reviews* (Top Pick!)

"I can't find enough superlatives for the enjoyment each of Bennett's books has brought. She has won a lifetime fan in me."

—*Fresh Fiction*

"Cady, Lon, and Jupe are my new favorite crime-fighting, magic-wielding Earthbound family unit. More, please."

—*Reading the Paranormal*

"Jenn Bennett has created another amazing novel filled with strong characters, magical surprises, and quirky humor."

—*Tynga's Reviews*

KINDLING THE MOON

"The talent pool for the urban fantasy genre just expanded with Bennett's arrival. This is an impressive debut. . . . Plenty of emotional punch, not to mention some kick-butt action. . . . Bennett appears to have a bright future ahead!"

—*RT Book Reviews*

"Without a doubt the most impressive urban fantasy debut I've read this year. . . . The writing is excellent, the characters are charming, and the romance is truly believable. . . . Flawlessly original!"

—*Romancing the Darkside*

"The perfect blend of action, intrigue, tension, and the supernatural."

—*Reading the Paranormal*

"Fun and original. . . . I can't think of one thing I didn't like about the book."

—*Urban Fantasy Investigations*

JENN BENNETT

BANISHING THE DARK

POCKET BOOKS

New York   London   Toronto   Sydney   New Delhi

Pocket Books
A Division of Simon & Schuster, Inc.
1230 Avenue of the Americas
New York, NY 10020

This book is a work of fiction. Any references to historical events, real people, or real places are used fictitiously. Other names, characters, places, and events are products of the author's imagination, and any resemblance to actual events or places or persons, living or dead, is entirely coincidental.

First Pocket Books paperback edition June 2014

POCKET and colophon are registered trademarks
of Simon & Schuster, Inc.

For information about special discounts for bulk purchases, please contact Simon & Schuster Special Sales at 1-866-506-1949 or business@simonandschuster.com.

The Simon & Schuster Speakers Bureau can bring authors to your l ive event. For more information or to book an event, contact the Simon & Schuster Speakers Bureau at 1-866-248-3049 or visit our website at www.simonspeakers.com.

Cover photo illustration by Tony Mauro

Manufactured in the United States of America

10 9 8 7 6 5 4 3 2 1

ISBN 978-1-4516-9509-0
ISBN 978-1-4516-9512-0 (ebook)

To Mr. "Freaky Deaky" Squeaky

1

Jupe crouched in the shadows, watching a pair of nurses stroll down the hall. Cartoon horses on the female nurse's scrub pants stretched over a pretty good ass. Good enough that he considered following her. After all, he'd analyzed forty-three nurses over the past month. Only two of them even remotely qualified as hot, and one of those was a guy.

But right now, he had more important things to do than accept the depressing likelihood that hot-nurse fantasies were a sham. So when the pair sauntered around the corner out of sight, he pushed to his feet and scrambled across the hall.

A taped-up sheet of plastic, two trash cans, and a warning sign might keep stupid people out of the construction area, but anyone with half a brain could see how easy it was to squeeze through. The display downstairs in the lobby said the new hospital wing cost three hundred million dollars. Maybe they should have spent some of that on a few pieces of plywood if they were serious about keeping people out until it was finished.

He'd been sneaking out to the sixth-floor glass walkway stretched between the old and new hospital wings off and on for a couple of weeks. On one side lay a silent parking lot. On the other, a couple of people smoked cigarettes at tables in an outdoor pavilion. He was too far up for them to notice, but he wanted to make sure no one heard him through the plastic. So he sidled around a pallet of boxes and strode down the carpeted walkway to the far end.

At least they'd had enough sense to lock the doors to the new wing. He pressed his forehead against the glass and squinted inside. All clear.

Chain clinked against his thigh as he dug a black wallet out of the back pocket of his jeans. Thumbing past his GTO Club membership and an ATM card for his savings account, he found the laminated piece of paper. It took him a couple of seconds to roll his tongue around the inside of his mouth, working up saliva, but when he was ready, he held out the card and spit on the magick sigil in the middle.

Bull's-eye.

"Priya, come," he commanded.

The air shimmered, and a ball of light appeared. He stepped back to give the guardian room to land and watched as two enormous black wings flapped into view. The boy's body soon followed. No shirt. Weird-ass gray skin. Mass of black spiky hair that looked like a Brillo pad that had been chewed up by a garbage disposal. (He should know; it had taken him an entire month of lawn mowing to work off the debt of repairing the disposal when he'd not so accidentally dropped one down the sink.)

The Æthryic guardian shook the walkway when he landed. His wings made a snapping sound as they folded into place behind his back. He looked pissed. Sounded it, too. "I told you not to summon me unless it was vital."

"And I told *you*, Cady said I could summon you whenever I damn well pleased."

"I feel quite certain she said no such thing. But now that I'm here, get on with it, and tell me why you called. I am busy doing important work."

"*Pfft.* Like what?" Jupe flicked a look toward the creature's bare chest. "Getting some sort of nuclear tan?"

Priya growled, flashing a row of pointy silver teeth. "I grow weary of your verbal puzzles, Kerub."

God, what a douche. Worst servant ever. He didn't understand why Cady put up with him. Then again, if the creature hadn't come to Jupe a month ago to tell them what had happened with Mr. Dare in Tambuku, Cady might be dead. Grumbling to himself, Jupe bent to wipe Priya's sigil card on the industrial carpet. It only moved the spit around on the laminate. He gave up and wiped it on the leg of his jeans. "Cady's awake."

Anger drained from the creature's face. "When?"

"Last night."

"Why didn't you summon me immediately? Is she well?"

"She's in and out of consciousness. They said it was normal. Might take a couple of days for her to shake it off. But . . ."

"But what?" Over his bare shoulders, the tops of Priya's wings shifted anxiously.

"Doctor said best-case, they'd still have to keep her in the hospital for a week. Longer if she can't walk."

"She will walk. She is very strong. What of her mother? Has Enola been communicating with her in her dreams?"

Jupe shook his head. "No idea. She hasn't mentioned it, but she's having trouble remembering things. She's pretty doped up, so I'm not sure if she really knows who I am. And we're not supposed to talk about anything upsetting or stressful in front of her. Dad's been trying to get in touch with Dr. Mick— that's the Earthbound doctor who healed—"

"Yes, yes," Priya said irritably. "You have spoken of this healer many times."

Whatever. "Anyway, Dr. Mick is the one who can release Cady. Dad wants to get her home ASAP."

"Your father needs to get her into a protected place immediately."

"That's what I just said. ASAP—it means as soon as possible." God, this guy was as dense as a brick wall. Were all Hermeneus spirits like this or just him?

"Then your healer should release her into Lon's care," Priya said. "A-S-A-P."

"Aren't you listening to me? Dr. Mick's mom died. He's at her funeral. In Australia."

"Where is this? Can you go there?"

"Australia? Are you kidding? It's a billion miles away. My dad's flown there before for work, and it takes an entire day on a plane. You do know what an airplane is, don't you?"

The creature snapped his wings open like one of those dinosaurs that spreads its frill to make it seem bigger than it really is. As far as intimidations went, it was a good one. And it was at times like this that Jupe wished like hell he had his father's ability to transmutate. A couple of bad-ass demon horns would really come in handy.

Priya pointed a long finger in Jupe's direction. "Listen to me, Kerub, and listen well. Arcadia's mother is scouring the Æthyr for a demon capable of sending her back to this plane. If you care anything at all for Arcadia—"

"More than you."

"Then tell your father to get her to a warded place immediately. I do not know how long she will be safe. A few days. A week. Possibly a fortnight."

Jupe opened his mouth to ask what the hell a fortnight was, but Priya flashed a mouthful of crooked silver teeth. Kind of creepy. And Jupe could already see the static erupting over the creature's skin; Priya seemed to have less and less power to keep himself solid every time Jupe summoned him.

"Arcadia must seek protection," the creature said.

"She must find the spell her mother used during Arcadia's conception and uncover a way to reverse it, or her mother will cross the planes to claim her."

"I've told you a million times, Cady will fight her mom," Jupe said confidently. "Besides, nothing that crosses the Æthyr can live on this plane permanently. You said so yourself. I mean, look at you. You can't even stay here five minutes."

Priya's eyes narrowed as he leaned closer. "Enola Duval wants to cross the planes permanently. She seeks old, irreversible magick that will bond her soul to Arcadia's so that Enola will occupy her body."

Jupe stilled. "Earthbound," he whispered in shock. "Cady's mom wants to be one of us?"

"In a manner of speaking, yes. And do you know what happens to souls when a new one possesses their physical body?" Priya struck a fist against his palm, causing Jupe to jump. "If Enola takes Arcadia's body, Arcadia will become nothing but a sack of energy existing to keep her mother alive. She may as well be dead."

2

Blurry memories of my hospital room rearranged themselves like frames of film spliced out of order. Nurses. Doctors. A painful catheter being removed. Being walked to the bathroom, my legs too weak to support my weight. Everything smelled funny. I wanted a real bath. I wanted my ribs to stop hurting.

And I wanted my brain to work better.

Pain meds slowed everything down. Made me dream crazy things. But I wasn't dreaming now. I was awake.

I gazed up at an enormous circle of sigils painted on the ceiling. A circle inside a circle. Two spells. One that prevented magick from being used. The other was magick to hide something. The same ward we'd seen on the boat Lon chartered last fall.

"It's to keep your mother out," a kindly female voice said.

I craned my neck to see the haloed head of one of Lon's housekeepers, knitting in a chair by the fireplace. This wasn't the hospital. I was home.

"Mrs. Holiday."

"Hello, Cady, darling," she said, tucking her needles and yarn into the chair cushion. "You with us this time?"

"Yes, I think I am."

"Good. Lon gave you something to clear out the medicine. He said it would take you an hour or so to wake. He'll be back from the store any minute. How does a bath sound?"

"Heavenly."

What I really wanted was half an hour in Lon's luxury steam shower, but I was too weak to stand by myself. Still, the tub was nice. Once I'd sloughed off a few layers of dead skin cells and brushed my teeth until my gums bled, the Holidays got me back into bed and left the room, and when they returned, Lon was with them.

His expectant face brightened when he walked into the bedroom, dressed in a thin brown leather jacket and jeans. Green eyes squinting, he strode through a patch of sunlight to pull a chair over to the side of the bed while Mrs. Holiday set down a tray of food. The Holidays left us alone, pulling the door shut behind them.

He sat down and leaned close. He had a full beard, a darker shade of his honey-brown hair, with two streaks of silvery gray at the chin—gray I'd never seen when he had it trimmed down to the pirate mustache. Had it always been there, or did my time in the hospital cause it?

Gray or not, beard or not, he was divine to look upon, painfully handsome and oh-so-serious. At that moment, I felt as if I hadn't seen him for months.

"Oh, Lon."

"Thank God," he mumbled, dropping kisses over my eyes. "I couldn't sense anything through the morphine. Damn, it feels good to hear you again." It took me a second to realize what he meant: he could "hear" my feelings with his demonic knack. "You scared"—he kissed one cheek—"the living shit"—he kissed the other cheek—"out of me."

When his lips pressed against mine, I threw my arms around his neck and pulled him close, crying a little. Drowning a little.

He pulled back and wiped my face with trembling fingers as I wiped his. We both laughed at ourselves. Then he sat back down and slid one warm hand around mine. "Christ, I've missed you."

"How long was I—"

"You've been home a day."

"What about the hospital?"

He ran his fingers over the damp hair near my ear, sending pleasant shivers racing across my skin. "Three days since that first night you woke up. Do you remember that now?"

Barely. It was all so . . . confusing. "I remember dreaming you were some crazy mountain man coming to kill me. What's all this?" I raked my fingers through his beard.

"Laziness."

"Hides the tic in your jaw," I teased. "How will I know when you're mad now?"

"Don't worry, I'll shave it."

"It's sort of sexy."

"You won't say that when it's scraping sensitive skin."

"Don't tease me when I'm feeble and debilitated. What's the date?"

"February fifth."

February . . . I'd been in the hospital an entire month?

"Are you in pain?" he asked.

"Everything aches. My ribs hurt when I bend a certain way."

"Then don't bend that way."

I smiled. "What did you give me?"

"Ginkgo biloba and the detox medicinal you gave Bob when he quit drinking. They had you on morphine after you woke, because Mick wasn't there to tell them no. You were pretty out of it."

"Mick. Your Earthbound doctor friend?" One of the best surgeons in La Sirena, Lon had bragged, thanks to a crazy-strong healing knack.

"He did most of your work. Do you remember?"

The faces of several doctors and nurses blurred in my mind.

"Do you remember Mick telling you anything before he put you under for healing?"

"Like what?"

"Something very important. Think, Cady."

Whatever he wanted me to remember, he was super-intense about it, so I tried harder. Something finally came into focus inside my head. Yes, that's right. I remembered Mick in the hospital. Remembered his bright blue halo and his handsome smile. But he wasn't smiling when I was hurt, was he? No. I was remembering meeting him before I got hurt. The night before—

"I killed Dare," I said, suddenly sobering. Not just Dare but also his thugs, the ones who beat and punched and kicked my body until I nearly died myself. "They trapped me, Lon. Dare knew I could be trapped in a binding triangle. He knew, and he . . ." I inhaled a shaky breath.

Lon's eyes narrowed to angry slits. "Don't you even think about being sorry."

Never. I steadied my emotions and concentrated on the here and now. "Do the police know?"

He reached over to the tray and uncovered a bowl of soup. An intoxicating scent wafted from the steam. "Chicken stock. Ginger. Seaweed. Vegetables."

"You made it?"

"Same thing I make when Jupe's sick. Plus a few other things." When I began to ask what those "things" were, he cut me off with a stern look. "Just eat it."

"Yes, sir." Thank God for Lon's cooking skills. It tasted a thousand times better than the hospital's canned soup. Between spoonfuls, I said, "See, I'm eating. Now, tell me. Am I going to jail?"

He shook his head. "I paid someone to collect

the ash and bone from Tambuku before anyone else showed up."

"Who?"

His eye twitched. "Someone Hajo works with when he's death dowsing."

"Oh, God."

"No one knows what happened but you and me." He squinted one eye closed. "And Jupe. And Priya—your guardian appeared to Jupe to tell us what happened. That's how we found you."

"I sent him to get help," I said, remembering. "But what about Tambuku? The bodies?"

"I took the bones to Dare's wife, Sarah. Told her a version of the truth, that he was looking for the person who'd leaked his bionic knack drug. Do you remember all that?"

"The red liquid that amped up demonic knacks. Tambuku was robbed . . ."

"And Dare used a magician to manufacture the drug until he realized someone had stolen it and leaked it to the general public. So I told Sarah that Dare had traced the leak to the magician, and some Earthbound's juiced-up knack went haywire and burned them all. It wasn't that far from the truth, and it kept the whole thing out of the papers. She announced that he'd had a heart attack; their money and influence prevented any further investigation. The funeral was two weeks ago."

It was overwhelming, how much I'd missed. And my foggy memories made everything feel surreal. My brain felt broken. "I hate that you had to lie for me." He never lied. Loathed lying, in fact. I was the professional liar; he was a walking lie detector.

"I'd do it again in a heartbeat," he said very seriously.

"What about Kar Yee?"

"What about her?"

Good question. Why was I so worried about her? "We had a fight," I said, reaching for the details. "I told her who I really was. Who my parents were. She got angry with me for keeping it from her all these years. I tried to go after her . . . that's why I went to the bar. To find her. She hates me."

"She had Bob drive her to the hospital several times a week to see you, and that doesn't seem much like hate to me."

No, it really didn't.

Before I could get too sentimental about it, he added, "But the two of you will have plenty of time to sort things out later. Right now, you eat. Need to get your strength back."

I continued to feed myself spoonfuls of soup, starving but impatient to finish and ask Lon more questions. After I'd finished most of the bowl, he set it back down on the bedside table as I glanced at the painted sigils on the ceiling. "You did that?"

He nodded and picked up my hand again, rubbing circles into the pad of my palm with his thumb. "It's why I wanted you home. You're safer sleeping here. Your mother . . . do you remember?"

That I did remember, unfortunately. My mother, Enola Duval, infamous occultist and former member of the highly esteemed Ekklesia Eleusia esoteric society (or E∴E∴, as it's known in occult circles), one of the Black Lodge Slayers, number 37 in a set of American Serial Killer trading cards, on the FBI's Most Wanted list.

After finding out the truth—that they weren't framed for the Black Lodge murders, as they'd always claimed—last year, I'd commanded a primordial demon to take her into the Æthyric demon plane with my father as payment for crimes they committed, assuming they'd been killed.

Never assume.

My mother not only survived, but she'd found a way to tap into me when I was sleeping and use me like a puppet. Under her control, I'd nearly stabbed Lon with a knife. She swore she'd take over my consciousness and kill everyone I loved. And she was demented enough to try.

"Priya told me I wasn't safe," I said to Lon. "He said I needed to find the spell she'd used to conceive me and try to reverse it. That I should seek refuge at the E∴E∴ temple in Florida." I put down the soup spoon. "Go to my godfather."

"I'm sorry, Cady. The caliph passed."

I stilled. "The caliph . . . died?"

Lon nodded. "Two days after you went into the hospital. Jupe sent Priya to tell him what had happened to you. But when he tried to find him, he couldn't. I e-mailed around until I got in contact with his assistant. Heart failure."

Fresh tears welled. "He was only in his seventies. He was in decent shape last time I saw him." In San Diego, when he'd come with Lon to help me escape from my parents' attempt to sacrifice me.

"They'd already had the funeral by the time I found out. I guess that was about three weeks ago. His oldest son, Adrien, will take over as the new caliph."

"Jesus." After the initial shock passed, I pulled myself together and focused on the reality that lay before me. The caliph was my advocate. A few people in the order knew I was still alive: the caliph's assistant, one of the other magi at the main lodge, and the grandmaster of the local lodge and her assistant. But the caliph was the only one with the power to rally all of them. He was the one they respected.

"What am I supposed to do now?" I said. "I have to find asylum somewhere. Priya said you weren't safe around me."

"Cady, I don't think I've been safe around you since the moment we met. That never stopped me before, and it's damn sure not stopping me now. You're not going anywhere without me, and that's all there is to it."

I hadn't realized how tense I was, but when he said that, it felt as if a weight had been lifted from my shoulders. Maybe it was because I felt physically frail and secretly wanted help. Or maybe because I'd learned that asking for help didn't equate to weakness.

I slumped against the pillows, mulling over everything he'd just told me. Wondering if I should try to contact the E∴E∴. It seemed pointless, now that the caliph was gone. My troubled thoughts turned to my new abilities, and I began to remember more about that last night before I ended up in the hospital.

"What is it?" Lon said.

"Dare. Before I . . . incinerated him. He told me things he found out through an investigator."

"What kinds of things?"

I struggled to recall what Dare had told me. "He said I had a brother, and that my parents tried the Moonchild spell on him first. But it wasn't successful, so they drowned him when he was eight years old. He said it was their first kill."

"Christ, Cady." His hand stilled on mine. "Maybe he was lying."

"But why make that up?"

"Because the man was the fucking devil!" Lon shouted, making me flinch.

Well, he wasn't wrong. But Lon rarely let his emotions get away from him. He tried to pull his hand away, but I stopped him, threading my fingers through his.

When he was coolheaded again, I said, "He knew he could trap me in a binding triangle. And he knew something about the mythology of the Moonchild that no one has ever hinted at—not anyone in the E∴E∴, not my parents, not any other demons I've summoned."

A small line formed in the middle of Lon's brow. "What?"

"I have all demon knacks."

He stared at me, blinking.

"Every knack. I can command every knack."

"Impossible," he said, but I could hear the doubt in his voice.

"Think about it," I said. "I slowed time at Merrimoth's house. I yanked the transmutation spell out of Yvonne. I transported myself thirty miles through thin air."

Lon didn't say anything for several seconds. "You healed yourself."

"What do you mean?"

"In the hospital. Before Mick left for Australia, he said he'd come in to work on one of your broken bones, and it would already be healed. He said he'd never seen anything like it. He said it was the closest thing to a miracle he'd ever witnessed."

That wasn't good. Never trust a miracle.

My mind jumped away from my knacks and focused back on the hospital room and the doctor. I vaguely recalled Mick's face hovering above mine when I was on death's doorstep. Some strange, hazy memory tried to poke its head above water in the back of my head. Something Mick was trying to tell me. I just couldn't quite make it out.

Lon exhaled heavily. "If you really do have the ability—"

"To wield every knack known to demonkind?" I finished.

He nodded his head toward this intangible, terrifying *thing*. "If you do, it would explain a lot. And it would also mean that Dare really did have someone who was investigating you."

"Well, we know he already uncovered my real identity."

"Identity is one thing, but if Dare hired someone to find out about the Moonchild spell, that's a whole other matter. Uncovering dark occult secrets isn't your everyday PI work."

"I suppose you're right."

And maybe this investigator opened up my options.

Priya insisted that the only way to stop my mother was by reversing the Moonchild spell, but heading straight to my order in Florida might not be the right move now that the caliph was gone. And really, besides magical protection, what could my order give me? I'd already scoured its libraries for information about the Moonchild ritual when I was still living there in my teens. And I had to believe that if the caliph knew something about the Moonchild spell, he would have told me.

My parents' house in Florida had long been sold, several times, and eventually demolished; new condo buildings stood there now. Nothing I could find there to help me. I could try to track down people who knew my parents, but they didn't have friends. So that led me back to the main lodge.

After I told all this to Lon, I asked, "Am I thinking about this all wrong?"

"No, you're not wrong," he said quietly. "Given everything we now know, I agree that a better tactic would be to track down this investigator."

I gave him a tight smile. "Guess I should've asked Dare for a name before I killed him."

3

No amount of magick or demonic ability could change the past, so there was little use dwelling on what happened with Dare. My mother was the pressing problem. But before Lon and I could piece together a plan of action, a distant door slammed.

"Sorry, but I can't hear you!" a voice called out before a sound akin to stampeding buffalos clambered up the stairs. A few moments later, two things lunged through the doorway: a chocolate Lab and a fourteen-year-old boy with a spring-green halo and a pouf of dark corkscrew curls. The sight of him squeezed my heart.

Jupe skidded to a stop at the foot of the bed. Green eyes blinked at me as he slid his backpack off his shoulders, the straps snagging on monster-movie patches sewn to the sleeves of his Army surplus jacket. "Foxglove!" Jupe protested.

"Hey, girl," I said, dodging the Lab's tongue while Lon grabbed her purple collar to keep her from jumping on the bed.

"Do you know who I am?"

"Aren't you the kid who mows the lawn?"

A whimper buzzed from the back of his throat.

"Kidding," I said. "Do I get a hug or what?"

His shoulders dropped, and a toothy grin spread. "I knew you'd be okay," he said as he pounced on the bed and his skinny arms curled around me.

"For the love of God, don't crush her," Lon warned.

I didn't mind. Unlike his father, Jupe was never one to have problems expressing feelings. His hair smelled pleasantly of chamomile and coconut oil, and when he finally released me, I pushed his frizzy curls off his forehead and studied him. "Missed your face," I murmured.

"Missed you *so much*." He looked as if he might be on the verge of getting too emotional. Just for a second. Then he reeled himself back in and smiled. "I told everyone a thousand times you'd be fine—right, Dad?"

"'Everyone' and 'a thousand' aren't exaggerations," Lon confirmed.

"Man, your halo looks so much better today."

Did it? I wondered just how bad it had looked before and if Jupe had seen me at my worst. But even if he had, I guess he wasn't scarred for life, because he seemed to be his normal high-energy, bright-eyed, Motormouth self. He plopped down next to me on top of the covers and lounged against the headboard.

"Let me just say, I *never* want to step inside a hospital again."

"That makes two of us."

"God, I'm glad you're home. I have so much to tell you."

No doubt.

"Do you remember everything now?" Jupe asked, looking at his father for some sort of confirmation.

"Mostly," I answered.

"Do you remember . . . ?" He trailed off and gave me a probing look, long lashes fluttering nervously as he searched my face. "Remember our fight?"

My mind jumped back to the last time I remembered seeing him. The afternoon I'd been trapped by Dare. I'd confessed my real identity to Kar Yee and Jupe. Kar Yee had left angry. Jupe had stayed, interrogating me, until he found out I was planning to go to Florida alone. He didn't take it well. And he let something slip that he shouldn't have.

Lon had bought me an engagement ring.

"Oh, crap," Jupe muttered, reading my face.

And judging from the way Lon shifted uncomfortably, Jupe must have told his father that he'd spilled the beans about the ring. My cheeks heated. Lon and I never had a chance to talk about it. I remembered that he'd given me plane tickets for Christmas, had wanted to take me to the French Alps. Pretty romantic for someone like Lon. Add on a ring, and you had a big step for two people who hadn't been able to say "I love you" for the first several months of their relationship.

Our French Alps sex vacation was certainly not

happening anytime soon. But did he still want to give me the ring? And did I want it?

"One thing at a time," Lon said quietly.

I nodded and buried awkward feelings while Jupe quickly changed the subject. "Hey, like, you should be sleeping or something."

"I've slept more than enough over the last month," I assured him.

"No, I mean, it's day. You're supposed to be sleeping in the daytime. That's what Priya says. Your mom uses moon energy to tap into you. I asked him if they had the same moon in the Æthyr, and he said they had three moons. Can you believe it? Three! So I asked him if your mom could use their moon energy or ours, and he said ours."

I stared at Jupe for a moment. Then Lon.

"He's been summoning Priya," Lon said.

"So I gather." I looked at Jupe. "How are you two getting along?"

"Someone needs to tell that guy to put a shirt on," Jupe said. "Plus he's kind of a dick."

"That's my guardian you're talking about, you know."

Jupe backpedaled. "It's just that he's *so serious* all the time. I don't think he knows how to smile." He did—it just didn't look like much of a smile with all those pointy teeth. "And he's always trying to boss me around, and he doesn't look that much older than me. When I asked him his age, he said he was only three months old. He told me all about how

Hermeneus spirits can reincarnate into new bodies when they die and that they usually reincarnate into babies, but sometimes they get lucky and can hop a ride on an older body. Which is what he did. Crazy, right?"

"Crazy." And more than I knew about Priya's new body. At least, more than I remembered knowing.

"But I asked him how long he had his previous body," Jupe continued, "and he said he'd only had it for eighteen years. Is that true?"

"I never thought to ask him."

Jupe looked at me as if I were nuts, but I wasn't about to explain how Priya had once been a sexless, subservient projection with the personality of card-board and that most magicians don't make small talk with their guardians. But still, if Priya was eighteen, that meant he'd been all of ten years old the first time he'd attached himself to me. And that weirded me out.

"Priya will tell you almost anything if you ask," Jupe informed me proudly. "And I asked him all *kinds* of shit."

"Clearly."

"Don't worry. I reported everything Priya told me to Dad."

I glanced at Lon. One quirking brow and the flare of his nostrils confirmed that his barely re-strained impatience with Jupe's energetic questions hadn't changed. This made me simultaneously want to laugh and cry. In a good way. Lon's eyes squinted at me in shared amusement while Jupe chatted on, oblivious to our silent conversation on the sidelines.

"Priya says you can't fall asleep at night. Like *Nightmare on Elm Street*. Your mom is Freddy."

But instead of killing me when I dreamed, she'd just puppet me into killing Lon. Or Jupe. Or whomever the hell else she wanted.

"He also says your mom is trying to do some complicated magick ritual in the Æthyr, and—"

"Jupe," Lon said sharply. "Remember what we talked about?"

"I'm sorry."

"What?" I looked at Jupe, waiting for an answer.

"Dr. Mick says not to bring up anything too upsetting until you're on your feet again."

"I'm fine," I said. "Go on, Jupe. What else did Priya tell you?"

Jupe glanced between us before continuing. "She's undergoing some kind of purifying ritual, where she fasts for a week. Like, she only drinks water, and she does some sort of weird meditation. Priya wasn't very good at explaining it," Jupe said, assuring me the communication problem wasn't on his end, which I didn't believe for a second. "Anyway, your mom doesn't know you're awake. At least, Priya's pretty sure she doesn't know."

That was something, I supposed.

"But don't worry," Jupe continued. "Priya figures you've got anywhere from a few days to a couple of weeks before she finishes the ritual and crosses back over to earth to control you. So all you have to do is find the spell your mom used when you were born and reverse it. That way, you'll break your connection with her, and she can't get inside your body. You can do that, right?"

I glanced up at the sigils on the ceiling before giving Lon a look.

We needed to make some plans. And I needed to get better, faster.

"Bring me my box of medicinals."

4

Although I tried several times that night, it wasn't until the following morning that I could finally reach out for electricity and pull it into my body—my benchmark for normal health—and another day before I could walk around the yard for half an hour without getting winded, which was Lon's benchmark. He pushed me hard, forcing me to walk and bend and stretch, and it was worth every bit of frustration. Because when I fell asleep that next day, sore and exhausted, mentally and physically, it was in his arms. I don't think I'd ever appreciated just how good and safe that felt. Maybe that's because I was usually too distracted by the great sex. Granted, somewhere in the back of my mind, I hoped I'd be distracted by that again soon, but for now, it was enough to smell his skin and hear his heartbeat.

He didn't need to adjust his schedule to stay up with me at night, as I discovered; he'd already been doing that in the hospital. Every night. Just in case my mother tried to slip into my brain and do something to me. When he told me this, I broke down. I mean, sloppy sobbing. He just said I'd do the same for him or Jupe.

And I would.

But if I was going to be around long enough to get that chance, I needed to get moving. And on my third night home, despite a few holes in my memories, I was feeling much better. My halo was back to normal, I could kindle Heka and walk without limping, and I was ready to tackle the problem of my mother.

First things first: I had to find the name of the PI Dare had hired to investigate me. And after weighing all the options for procuring it, I settled on something Lon suggested.

Or someone.

Arturo Archard. One of the remaining thirteen Hellfire Club officers who made up the organization's ruling "Body." Since I'd offed both the club's leader and the second in command, David Merrimoth, that only left eleven officers, including Lon. Arturo, Lon assured me, was one who could be trusted. Like Lon, he kept to himself and rarely participated in official Hellfire activities. To Lon, this meant Arturo stayed out of group politics. To me, it meant the guy didn't participate in a monthly hedonistic Succubus/Incubus orgy in the Hellfire caves on the beach. Big points.

Arturo owned a successful vineyard north of La Sirena, and his husband ran a swank wine bar near the center of town. The Lamplighter, much like Tambuku, was Earthbound-friendly. It was also closed on Mondays, and early in the evening of my third night back at home, Arturo agreed to meet us at the closed wine bar.

Frankly, I was just thrilled to be going out into the real world again and would have been satisfied with a trip to the grocery store. But the universe wasn't going to allow me the luxury of domestic bliss, so an interrogation it was.

We parked in a short alley on the side of the building around nine. A handsome Earthbound swung open the delivery door as we got out of the car. "Lon Butler, you've gone native," he said in an amused voice, gesturing toward the beard.

"Itches like hell," Lon said, running his fingers over it. "Arturo, this is Arcadia Bell."

The older man gave a quick glance at my silver halo and inclined his head. He was tan and carried a few extra pounds of bulk. His gray-streaked dark hair was crowned by a dark green halo. "I noticed you at Merrimoth's funeral, but we didn't get a chance to speak. I'm sorry about your recent attack. Reminds us how dangerous the city can be."

Lon's cover-up story: I was attacked by one of the degenerates with amped-up knacks who were committing robberies over the holidays.

"Where are my manners? Come inside." After locking the door, Arturo led us past empty tables and oak barrels into a lounge area of the wine bar, where we sat on a plush couch in front of an unlit fireplace. "The boys are getting restless, Lon," Arturo said as he took a seat across from us. "They want to know if you're going to run the club."

"I haven't decided."

"If you plan to lead, they want a show of strength, or they won't get behind you. And if they smell weakness, someone else will make a play for it. Tomkins or Warner are my bets. Tomkins wants his kid to take one of the two openings. Dare's son is next on the list, then Sharon Wood. But it's no secret that Sharon isn't a fan of the Dare family."

"Question is, are you?"

Arturo settled an arm on the back of the sofa. "You already know the answer to that. But if you want to poke around each other's minds, I'm happy to oblige."

Lon had warned me about Arturo before we came. In the same way Lon could hear feelings, Arturo could see memories. Older ones were only possible if he was transmutated, apparently, and it was easier if you were thinking about them. But, unlike Lon, Arturo required skin-to-skin contact for his knack to work.

No shaking hands with Arturo, in other words. But that was a pretty good rule of thumb when dealing with most Earthbounds, I'd come to learn.

"As you're aware, Ambrose didn't like me getting too close," Arturo said. "Sure, he was happy to use me when he wanted to shake someone down. Which is why I know a little more about the man behind the mask, so to speak. Dare had the Body's allegiance, but he didn't have our love. Half of the Body was sad to hear Dare had died. But it was the kind of sadness you feel when you hear a celebrity has died. You think, *That's a shame*, then you move on, because you didn't really know them, did you?"

"What about the other half of the Body?" I asked. "How did they feel?"

"Honestly? Relieved. We knew too much about his dark side."

"Then why didn't you do anything about it?"

"A fair question," Arturo said thoughtfully. "My husband asked me the same thing many times. I suppose I told myself I was too jaded to care about club politics. When I was your age, it was a little more glamorous. Now I mainly just want to be left alone. And Dare usually complied. As long as I attended most of the meetings and showed my face at the Hellfire caves every now and then, he seemed satisfied. But now that he's gone, I wonder just how strong his knack really was."

Dare's knack was known as Rally: the ability to inspire—or coerce—a group of people.

"Ambrose Dare had us all under his thumb," Arturo added. "Even those of us who should've known better."

Lon murmured to himself.

I twisted the silver double-serpent bracelet on my wrist, a Christmas present from Lon. Maybe the guy was right. I should have known better myself. I mean, I dutifully did magical work for Dare for weeks before I finally had the sense to give him the middle finger. And look what it got me: a whole month of my life beaten out of me.

"Dare was investigating me," I told Arturo. "Did you know that?"

"I heard rumors that he seemed . . . preoccupied with you, shall we say?"

"And what exactly was he telling the Body about her?" Lon asked.

Arturo looked at me. "That you're special. Different. Someone we wanted on our team. He said you might be more useful to the Hellfire Club than a hundred other magicians. But he needed to test you first. He was suspicious of your loyalties."

"Are you?" I asked.

"I'm suspicious of the manner in which Dare perished. But that doesn't necessarily mean I'm going to call for a witch hunt. For the first time in years, I can go to sleep knowing I won't get a phone call at three a.m. telling me to drive out to some back alley and rifle through a guy's memories—only so Dare can put a bullet in his head the second I drive away."

"Dare was using a private investigator to dig up things about my past," I said. "I need to find out who that investigator was."

Arturo held my gaze for a long moment. "Why would I know that?"

"Because people trust you," Lon said.

Arturo shrugged, not denying it. "They know if I really wanted to see what's on their minds, I can brush their fingertips." He gave me a pointed look. "Having a gift is all well and good until people decide they want what you've got."

No truer words . . .

But I wasn't afraid of the Hellfire Club. Not anymore. Arturo said the Hellfire Club wanted to see a show of strength, or they wouldn't follow him. Maybe he'd be more inclined to give me what I wanted if he had a clearer picture of who I really was.

"I killed Dare."

The confession hung in the air like a plastic bag caught in dead branches.

"If it matters, it was self-defense," I added.

"Your 'attack,'" Arturo said softly.

"He had a gun and three men, and he was trying to teach me how much power he had. He might've temporarily broken my body, but I turned them all into ash, just like that." I snapped my fingers.

Arturo flinched and mumbled something I couldn't hear.

"I have no beef with the Hellfire Club," I told him. "Frankly, I just want to be left alone, too. But if I can find out who Dare was using to investigate me, that would make me extraordinarily happy. Please."

Arturo said nothing for a moment. Then he crossed his legs and exhaled. "I saw a memory when I bumped into Dare at a holiday party. He'd been telling someone that he'd just flown back from L.A. And when I touched him, he was remembering sitting outside by a pool talking to an Earthbound named Wildeye. Don't know his first name. All I can tell you is that he looked to be in his thirties or forties and had an aquamarine halo. He was giving Dare a packet of papers that had 'Duval/Bell' scribbled on the outside."

5

Outside the wine bar, Lon and I thanked Arturo and watched him drive away in an expensive sports car.

"He wasn't lying," Lon said before I had a chance to ask. "And we can trust him."

"I figured you would've stopped me if we couldn't. I guess now we'll need to hunt down a PI named Wildeye in L.A."

Lon tapped the back tire of his SUV with the toe of his boot while digging his silver valrivia cigarette case out of his jacket pocket. "We need to be careful. Don't know if this PI is loyal to Dare. We can fly down there tonight if you want. Better to talk to him in person so I can hear his emotions when we question him."

"What about Jupe?"

"He'll be fine with the Holidays. With any luck, we can take care of this in a matter of hours, then turn around and come back home. You feeling all right?"

I nodded. "Can I have one of those?"

He looked appalled that I'd even ask. "Absolutely not." He snapped his valrivia case shut. "Neither one of us needs it."

I frowned. "Meany."

He grunted, pocketing the case. "You still want to drive into the city?"

I'd asked him to drive me to Tambuku so I could see Kar Yee. She didn't know. Lon had called her the day before to tell her I was home but requested she hold off visiting until I was better recovered. "If we're flying out tonight, maybe we should stop by on our way to the airport. Would save us—"

A very distinct familiar feeling stole my attention.

"Cady?" Lon said.

But someone else was talking inside my head. *May I show myself?*

I glanced up and down the alley. No cars. No people. The whole area was fairly dead, and it was dark. "Yes," I told him. "Come, Priya."

"Jesus fucking Christ," Lon mumbled as a ball of white light shimmered in midair. The light flickered violently, and a gray-skinned boy with black wings exploded into view.

We backed up in tandem to give him room to land. A smoky black halo trailed over his haystack black hair as his bare feet touched the pavement. His face lit up when he saw me. "Mistress!" he called out, snapping his wings shut behind his back. "I am so relieved to see you!"

"You, too, Priya." And I was. Despite his physical

and personality changes, he was still the same spirit who had watched my back since I was a teenager.

He grinned with a mouthful of pointy silver teeth and started to reach for me until he spotted Lon and drew back. "Kerub," he said in greeting, inclining his head politely, if not begrudgingly, before speaking to me again. "The demon boy has told me of your progress. You look well."

"Getting there. Has Jupe been summoning you a lot?"

His eyes narrowed before darting toward Lon. Yeah. He still didn't like Lon. And whatever he'd wanted to say, he'd definitely thought better of it. Instead, he made a funny sort of shrug as he gestured awkwardly. "We have been getting to know each other."

Yeah, I'll bet. I was going to have to have a talk with Jupe about using Priya like his own personal chat buddy. "Why are you here?"

"I have urgent news about your mother."

"Let's have it."

"She has killed the demon Lord Chora and fled his fortress with a group of slaves."

"Dear God." Lord Chora, grand duke and commander of two legions of Æthyric warriors. That demon had torn down my house wards, flown away with Jupe, and nearly killed Lon. He was highly skilled with Æthyric magick—not a demon to screw around with. But my mother had killed him? "I thought he was helping her. Jupe said—"

"He was," Priya insisted. "I do not know what went wrong, nor do I know whether she's discovered the magick she needs to cross the planes. But you should assume the worst and be on guard. She could take possession of your body at any time."

"Like right now?" I said, glancing up at the night sky as if she might tumble down.

"Today. Tomorrow. A few days. I do not know. But the sooner you can reverse the Moonchild spell and sever the bond with her, the better. Perhaps it's best you seek the protection of your order until you do that."

I shook my head. It was natural for Priya to assume that a group of magicians could protect me; Hermeneus spirits and magicians had been allies, if you could call it that, for centuries. In Priya's mind, magick was power—and that was true. But magick wasn't infallible, and I couldn't sit around twiddling my thumbs while my order kept me from the inevitable.

"I'm not going to Florida right now," I told Priya. "Lon and I just uncovered a trail we need to follow. Someone who might have information about my past."

"We don't even know if it's safe in Florida, now that the caliph is dead," Lon added.

Priya's brow furrowed. "You should not gamble with her life, Kerub. Your associations got her injured. Put your faith in her own people now."

Oh, boy. I didn't have to look at Lon to know that

the horns were coming out. I could feel the transmutation in my bones like an esoteric platoon of soldiers marching to war. But when I lifted my hand to hold Lon back, something caught my eye: threads of pale light.

I'd seen threads emerging from my hand before but not quite like this. And when Priya leaned closer to have a look himself, the gossamer strings brightened like fluorescence exposed by ultraviolet light. Priya's Æthyric halo was making them visible.

When Jupe had secretly, and stupidly, tattooed my sigil on his body, it created an invisible thread connecting us. One that lit up bright gold when he was in danger, much brighter than it was now. And when I first summoned Priya in his new body, my guardian reestablished our link and created a second thread, a black cobweb that anchored him to my Heka signature, even across the planes.

Two threads. But now there were *four*.

Four wispy filaments of light growing out of my palm, waving in the wind like dandelion tufts. My gaze followed the black thread to Priya. And a second pale gold thread that trailed off beyond the alley: Jupe's.

The third thread was pale green. I followed that . . . right next to me.

To Lon.

I grabbed Lon's hand and saw its endpoint, right in the middle of his palm. Just like Priya's. "What did you do?" I said, confused. Lon hated tattoos. And

I hadn't seen every inch of his skin since I'd come home from the hospital, but he had no reason to want my sigil on him.

His mouth fell open, but no sound came out. I looked back at my palm to the fourth thread: a white line that on first glance seemed to be sprouting from my palm like the others but on closer examination was a little bit different. It splintered from the green thread connected to Lon, and it headed . . .

Down.

To my stomach.

But that couldn't be right. That meant . . .

Goose bumps pimpled my arms as my world tilted. The oncoming rush of memory made me feel as if I were strapped to a railroad track with no chance of escape, watching a train barreling toward me. I remembered Dr. Mick forcing Lon to leave the surgery room. Mick leaning over me, telling me the news . . .

The baby survived. I'm not sure how—you're badly bruised, and your hip is broken. But it showed up in the blood work, and I can detect the heartbeat with my knack.

You're about seven weeks along, I'd guess. Maybe eight.

"Leave us," Lon barked at Priya, his angry voice snapping me back into the moment. "Return when you have news."

"Mistress—"

"Go!" I shouted.

Priya disappeared, and in his absence, the threads

quickly faded until they were invisible. I looked up at Lon, blinking into the fire flaring from his halo. His eyes were wide, his brows drawn together. The shock I felt was mirrored in his face.

"You knew," I whispered accusingly. "Why didn't you tell me?"

"I've been trying, asking if you remembered Mick telling you."

"But I didn't. You should've—"

"I didn't know how you'd react," he said, suddenly becoming animated. "You have *no* idea what I've been through. None at all. When I walked into Tambuku and saw you lying on the floor in a pool of blood, I thought you were dead. You damn sure felt dead in my arms. Your pulse was so weak I couldn't hear it. And even when I got you to the hospital, I didn't know if you'd make it. And if you didn't make it"—his eyes glazed over as grief lanced through his features—"I didn't know if I could handle that," he ended in a broken voice.

"But I made it," I whispered.

"Yes." He blinked rapidly and pulled himself together. "But you had trouble remembering, and Mick said to take it slow. To let you remember on your own, or it might be too upsetting. I just . . . did the best I could."

I heard what he was saying, but it was all just too much. I strode away from him, to clear my head. To breathe and get some perspective.

So . . . I was pregnant.

Fuck.

How the hell had that happened?

I went through the same list of symptoms I'd gone over the first time I'd been told, remembering things I'd ignored over the holidays. All the crying and getting tired at weird times. My breasts getting bigger. I glanced down. *Pfft.* Not anymore. I must have lost it all in the coma.

And oh, God, that's right: my stupid phone alarm. Forgetting to take the Pill. And of course, we pretty much screwed like rabbits—before the coma, at least.

I spun around to face him and nearly shrieked in surprise when I found him inches away. "You bastard!" I said, shoving him back. "You knocked me up!"

"You helped!"

We stood there for several moments, glowering at each other, until I started laughing. His face twisted in confusion. Then I burst into tears.

His arms roped around me, and I fell against him, weeping into his shirt as the distant sound of a speeding car mingled with the crash of the Pacific surf.

"What are we going to do?" I said, pulling back to see his face after I'd gotten a grip on my tears.

He'd shifted back down, no horns, no fiery halo, just Lon, green eyes peering down at me over his brown and gray beard. With the pad of his thumb, he brushed away the tears beneath my eyes. Then he pushed my hair away from my forehead with one warm palm. "I don't know."

"It could be Earthbound."

"Or human."

Or something else entirely. I looked down between us and put a tentative hand over my stomach. How could I not know? Surely that had to make me the worst mother ever already, and I hadn't even started. I pulled up my T-shirt. "I don't feel anything. I'm not showing."

"You're only eleven weeks along, and you just got out of the hospital. But don't worry. That tea I've been making you is a thousand calories a glass—"

"Oh, my fucking God."

"—which you *need*. I can already tell from your face that it's helping."

"But how do I even know the baby is okay?"

"They did sonograms and tests and monitored you. Mick checked everything before he left for the funeral and said it was healthy and normal. That was a day before you woke up."

"I can't believe he told you." I felt a little betrayed. As if it wasn't his business to share. As if they were scheming behind my back.

"He didn't have a choice, Cady. I had to sign the surgery release. He thought you might miscarry."

And how I had managed not to, after what I'd been through . . . I couldn't even think about it. I just couldn't. It was too awful. But in shunning one bad thought, I faced another. "I've been releasing kindled Heka without a caduceus all day."

"I told you to stop doing that!"

"I didn't know why! You didn't tell me I could shock my own baby!"

He took a deep breath and closed his eyes, calming himself. "Electrical tolerance is inherited, so I'm sure the baby is fine. And you saw the threads. They're a supernatural marker, just like halos, and you know how a halo changes when you're sick or unhealthy. But the baby's thread looked as strong as mine, and I'm fine, so I think we can assume that means everything's normal."

"Normal? Having threads in your palm isn't normal."

He grabbed my chin and leaned closer to my face. "They are for you, because you're extraordinary and special, and what you have inside you is, too. Not because of what you are—I don't give a shit if you're a goddamn alien or an average human being. You're mine, and so's that baby. And whatever it is, it's beautiful."

Goddammit. I almost started crying again. Until I had a terrible thought. "Oh, God. My mother—"

"Cannot find out," Lon said firmly.

She could drop down from the Æthyr and possess my body. She tried to kill Lon. What was to stop her from trying to take my baby away? "What if—"

Lon shook his head emphatically and cradled my

face between his hands. "Not going to think about what-ifs. We're going to figure out a solution, and we're going to live through it, just like we always do. You hear me?"

"I hear you," I said in a quiet voice. "And I love you. But I'm very, very scared."

"Me, too," he said, pulling me closer. "All of the above."

6

We drove straight home from the wine bar. I pretended I wasn't quietly panicking while Jupe talked my ear off and watched TV for a while. After Lon sent him to bed, the two of us headed to the covered back patio, where we could talk without worrying we'd be overheard. Where we could make a plan.

Midnight was my new noon. I supposed I was doomed to keep bartender hours from now until God knew when. I shivered under a blanket and pecked at a tablet touch screen.

"Nothing in Los Angeles," I confirmed to Lon. "When I look up 'Wildeye' and 'private investigator,' I get one hit in Golden Peak, California."

"That's a little resort town in Big Sur, maybe three or four hours south of us."

"Robert Wildeye . . . huh."

"What?"

I peered at the screen. "He's got a website. Says he's in Golden Peak and gives a phone number. No street address. No e-mail. No nothing. Just says, 'Private Investigator. Confidential. Twenty years experience. Licensed and insured. Premium rates for premium service.' Oh, interesting. Nox symbol." Two interlocking circles that indicated the business was Earthbound-friendly.

"Any reviews on other sites?" Lon asked.

I backed out of the page and searched again, using the full name. Only scam sites trying to get you to fork over your credit-card number in exchange for a bogus background check. "It's like he barely exists," I said, shivering again.

"Maybe he only exists if you have enough cash." Lon padded over to the control panel to turn on the heating in the cement flooring.

"Luckily, you do. But I think we need to be careful about contacting him. What if he tries to give us the slip? Or what if he was friends with Dare?"

"Dare didn't have friends. The town's not that big, and it's the off-season. Bet we can ask around and figure out how to find him."

He sounded a lot more hopeful than I felt, but at least it was a place to start. One small thing decided. Now there was just the other enormous one to face. I set the tablet on a nearby patio table and sighed.

We hadn't told Jupe the news. Hell, I was still in shock myself. And feeling more than a little foolish. Seriously. Who doesn't know they're pregnant? Even Lon said he'd noticed I had missed a period in November, but he just chalked it up to stress, since

I'd been busy working at the bar while juggling piddly magical jobs for the Hellfire Club in my off time. Then there was that horrible afternoon on the chartered boat. And the holidays spent chasing down the boys who robbed Tambuku while they were amped up on Dare's bionic drug.

Not to mention putting Yvonne in the hospital.

So, yeah. I'd been under a lot of stress. But no use dwelling on the whys and hows. I was pregnant, and that's all there was to it. I had choices, of course, but when I considered whether I was ready for something so life-changing, I knew my situation could be worse. I was an adult in a solid relationship. More than solid. I really couldn't imagine being with anyone else. Couldn't even imagine *wanting* to. Kar Yee joked about all the men she fantasized about. But no matter where they started, all my fantasies eventually led back to Lon.

And maybe I'd never be a domestic goddess, baking pies and arranging tablescapes for dinner parties, but I was pretty good at handling Jupe. Better than Lon sometimes, but that was mostly because he'd been a single parent too long. If I had to raise Jupe alone, I'd lose my shit on occasion, too. All things considered, Lon was a damn good father.

Financially, it wasn't a problem. I had savings. Not a lot, granted, and I hoped Kar Yee wasn't so fed up with me that she wanted to ditch our partnership in Tambuku. No, I couldn't imagine myself slinging drinks with a baby bump, but she could manage just fine without me, at least for a little while.

And Lon was more than financially stable. Maybe he was only rich compared with someone working-class like me, but he didn't hurt for anything, and even if he decided to retire from photography, he had his inheritance.

So, yeah. Logically, there was no reason *not* to have a baby.

And emotionally? God help me, but despite the chaos that seemed to plague my life before and after I'd met Lon, it was our baby. Us. Him and me. We made it together, no matter how foolishly. Hell, yeah, I wanted it. Fiercely.

There was only the small matter of my murderous mother.

"How's that?" Lon asked. "You feel it warming up, or you want me to light a fire?"

"No need. It's much better," I said, holding the blanket up so he could crawl under with me on a wide wicker chaise. When he stretched out and wrapped his arms around me, his warmth chased the last of the chill away.

Lon often lounged out here, reading beneath the cover of the deep roof. From this vantage point, my gaze drifted over the wraparound redwood deck and the green lawn beyond, lush with palms and Monterrey cypresses. Past the cliffs, the moon-bathed Pacific spread out like a never-ending black carpet.

"Eleven weeks," I murmured. "I don't even know what that means."

"It means the baby's the size of a shrimp."

He held up his fingers to demonstrate. This made my stomach flutter nervously.

"We'll find an obstetrician," he said, brushing my hair aside to tuck his chin in the crook of my neck.

"When? Before or after the Moonchild spell deteriorates my humanity? Before or after my mom realizes she's got another living target?" I didn't mean to sound so bitter, but goddamn. It wasn't fair. How the hell was I supposed to find a spell my mother had used in some black-magick sex ritual during my conception twenty-five years ago? One that didn't follow any of the original medieval Moonchild spells?

Priya had alluded to the possibility that my mother had constructed the spell herself, compiled from different sources. What if she was the only one who knew the details? And even if someone else could re-create the spell, it might take years of research, decades of trial-and-error. If they'd tried a different version on my deceased brother and failed, then God knew how many versions they'd experimented with before they conceived me.

She'd murdered an eight-year-old boy.

Her own child.

I pressed my palm against my belly as a slow, hot panic dripped down my spine.

"She can't find out," I whispered.

"We'll go find the PI tomorrow."

What if tomorrow wasn't soon enough? Curled up with my back against Lon's chest, I could easily drift into a lazy daze in minutes. If she tapped into me tonight, would she poke through my brain and see my knowledge of the shrimp-sized baby inside me?

I turned in Lon's arms to face him. "I can't take the chance."

"Cady . . ."

"You're willing to risk it? I don't believe that for a second."

"I would lay waste to the entire state and everyone in it before I'd let anything happen to you or that baby. And I would gladly kill your mother a hundred times over. Should've done it in San Diego when I had the chance."

I shook my head. "It was my choice to give her up to the albino demon. And it was the wrong one."

"No use thinking about that now."

"What if Priya's right? What if she finds a way to cross over, takes possession of me, and disappears with my body and the baby?"

Lon didn't say anything for a long time. He was upset. So was I. And the longer it took him to come up with a logical argument, the more panicked I got.

"We know she can tap into my thoughts," I said, thinking aloud. "I don't know how deep she can go, but when I had those dream conversations with her, you were there in those dreams, lying next to me. And she clearly remembered you from San Diego. She remembered you, and she knew we were together, because she wanted to hurt me by killing you."

"Yes," Lon said impatiently.

"By that logic, we can assume the only reason

she didn't know about the baby already was because *I* didn't—not when she was tapping into my dreams." I sat up in the lounge chair. "She doesn't have some all-seeing omnipotent power, Lon. She could only see inside my head. Like you, when you're transmutated. Or . . . maybe more like Arturo."

"Memories."

"Exactly. So if I don't know I'm pregnant, neither will she."

"But you do."

"But *you* know a way to change that."

Lon sat up, brows drawn together. His eyes flicked back and forth between mine. Then his face fell. "The book of memory spells."

"Yes."

"No. Absolutely not."

"Why?" I challenged. "You've tried two of those spells, and they both worked. You retrieved my lost memories from childhood, *and* you wiped Riley Cooper's memories."

"That was a permanent wipe."

"But there were other spells. Temporary ones. Think about it, Lon. You could remove my memory of the baby just until we have a chance to track down the PI or fly down to Florida or whatever we need to do to stop my mother."

"Those spells are hundreds of years old. What if it wipes your memories for months?"

"Well, you did say the baby's healthy."

"It is, but—"

"And you said you wouldn't let me do this alone."

"I wouldn't."

"Which means you'd be with me, so you could stop me from doing anything that would put the baby in danger."

"But—"

"And it can't last forever. Spell or no spell, I think I'll eventually figure out something's up when my stomach starts ballooning. Hell, if you're afraid I won't remember, you can just tell me about it."

He lifted his chin in reluctant acknowledgment. But he wasn't entirely convinced. "Memory spells are tricky, and you've just recovered from major trauma. You had multiple concussions. I could fuck something up. Turn you into a vegetable."

"If we're weighing risks, better that than endanger the baby. Plus, you said that I healed myself— miracle, remember?" I tried to smile, but neither of us was in the mood for humor. Something else crossed my mind. "Maybe the reason I didn't remember I was pregnant until I saw the threads in my hand was that my body was trying to protect the baby from me."

He made a small, miserable noise and pushed himself off the chaise. I watched him pace the length of the patio, bare feet arching beneath the hems of his jeans. When he made it to the deck, he leaned against the railing and stood there for several minutes, looking out at the dark, glittering ocean. Thinking.

I was thinking, too.

I didn't want to be wrong about this. But when I considered other options—not doing anything, trying to hide myself with portable magick, summoning unknown Æthyric demons until I could barter with one who was brave enough to take out my mother in the Æthyr—it still seemed like our best shot.

Dare was gone, so Jupe would be safe if we had to leave him in the Holidays' care until we sorted this out. And surely if the shrimp inside me weathered a brutal beating, it could tolerate a little more magick.

Surely?

I wondered if the baby had a halo and what color it would be—a thought that nearly sent me into another fit of weeping. Jesus. We had to do something, or the moment my mom reconnected with me, she'd know everything. I might be a natural at lying to other people, but I was total shit at lying to myself.

Over the next few hours, Lon and I talked circles around the problem. We talked until he refused to say another word about it. He poked around the internet looking for information on Wildeye. Made us breakfast. Cleaned up. And as I waited for sunrise, staring at the TV, a golden glow fell over my arm. I glanced up to find Lon standing in front of me. That I hadn't noticed him transmutating probably said a lot about where my thoughts were.

"You haven't changed your mind," he said.

I shook my head.

He reached down, and I placed my hand in his. Flaming light danced around his spiraled horns as he sighed.

"Let's do it now," he said in a weary voice. "Before I lose my nerve."

7

My head pounded something fierce.
I squinted into warm, strong sunlight and blinked
until my eyes adjusted. Living room. Stack-stone
fireplace, leather sectional sofa, glossy wood floors,
black-and-white photographs of a curly-haired toddler.

Lon Butler's home.

What the hell was I doing here?

I groaned, struggling to remember as I pushed a
fuzzy gray blanket away and stood. It was quiet. All
I could hear was the muffled tick of a clock on the
mantel telling me it was two in the afternoon and the
distant sound of the surf pounding against the rocks
below the cliffs. Was no one home?

Jupe would be in school or on his way home
with the Holidays. Lon would be . . . ?

A sharp feeling akin to déjà vu hit me. I knew this
house well. I'd been staying here, but I couldn't remember why. A flood of fuzzy memories floated in and
out of my aching head. Father Carrow introducing me

to Lon. Lon saving me from my parents in San Diego. Lon introducing me to Ambrose Dare. Me killing Dare. Waking up in the hospital. Waking a month later in Lon's bed with the sigil painted on the ceiling. Talking to Arturo about the PI in L.A.

All these solid memories, but everything else around them was as soft and weightless as packing peanuts. Just like this house. So familiar but foreign. It felt as if I'd spent a lot of time here, but I couldn't remember all the details.

Wait. I was here because of my mother. Yes. I definitely remembered her tapping into my dreams and Priya warning me to undo the Moonchild spell. I also remembered Priya appearing in the alley by Arturo's wine bar last night. I got upset about . . . something. Lon brought me back here afterward. Wait. Wine bar. Did we get drunk? Because that would explain a lot.

My face heated as embarrassment blazed through me. Drunk with Lon. That wasn't a good idea. All my clothes seemed to be on except my shoes. What a freaking relief. I don't think I could face him if I'd done something stupid like hit on him.

Or maybe I had, and that's why I was on the couch.

Maybe he just wanted his bed back. Why had he put me up in his own bedroom? I felt as if there were a good reason, but I couldn't remember why, other than the sigils painted on the ceiling. Must be something to do with that, because I couldn't fathom him trying to seduce me. He was too . . . well, not a gentleman, exactly. And not law-abiding, either—he had, after all, stolen a bunch of old occult books from the Vatican, and he owned a few illegally modified guns. But all in all, he was a decent, stand-up man with a strong sense of right and wrong. Dependable. Besides, I was almost twenty years younger than him. Too young, I faintly remembered Jupe telling me months ago.

And probably stupid enough to throw myself at him given the right amount of alcohol. My mind pulled up some fuzzy images of me cuddling up to him outside on the patio. Me begging for something. Like, *really* trying to persuade him to do something to me.

Ugh.

I should probably find my shoes and slip out now. Do the walk of shame to my car and drive back—

Home.

But I hadn't been to my house in months.

That couldn't be right.

Oh, that's right—Duke Chora broke my house wards. Lon said it wasn't safe to stay there until we could fix them. Had I been living here since then? Jesus. I *had*. What was the matter with me? I shouldn't be here, mooching off him. Surely I'd over-stayed my welcome by now. Once I found a way to sever the ties with my mother or get rid of the Moon-child spell, I needed to reconstruct the house wards and move back into my own place.

But right now, I needed aspirin. Rubbing my temples, I made my way to the kitchen and nearly had a heart attack when I looked up.

Lon was standing in the archway to the dining room, horns spiraling back into his head, halo subsiding. That was unexpected but not startling. I'd seen him like that tons of times. He was dressed in worn jeans and a faded T-shirt. His light brown hair kissed the tops of his shoulders, and—

He was *clean-shaven*.

No pirate mustache.

Oh, God. I was so confused, and he was ridiculously good-looking. And there went my face again. Since when did I blush? I did my best to play it cool.

"Hey," I said.

Had he been listening to my thoughts? And why wasn't he saying anything? He looked just as confused as I felt.

I blew out a long breath. "Look, I can't remember anything about last night after Priya appeared outside the wine bar. So if I made a fool out of myself . . . uh, I mean, if I was coming on to you, I'm really sorry."

"Jesus fucking Christ," he murmured in a low voice. "I knew this was a bad idea."

"I said I'm sorry!" I couldn't be any more embarrassed. I thought I'd seen enough idiotic behavior in Tambuku to swear off drinking, but now I definitely would never touch a drop again. Ever. "Look, if you don't want to go look for this detective with me, that's fine. Let me just go pack a few things, and

I'll drive"—I began backing up as he strode toward me—"myself, and . . . no, no. Please don't transmutate again. Don't read my thoughts. Because my, uh, head hurts, so if you'll just give me some aspirin—"

My ass hit the back of the sofa. He grabbed my upper arms and squinted down at me, face tight and unreadable. "What do you remember about last night?"

"Whatever I did, I said I was sorry. Jeez, give me a fucking break! I'm going through a lot right now."

"What are you going through? Tell me."

"What am I *not* going through? I killed the most powerful man in town, just got out of the hospital after being in a coma for a month, and my crazy mom wants to bodysnatch me." I wiggled out of his grasp, thoroughly irritated. "Look, whatever I did or said, I'm sure you'll get over it. Why the hell did you let me drink, anyway? My mom could've tapped into me. You know I'm not supposed to let my guard down at night."

"Oh, God," he whispered.

Damn right. I wasn't taking the blame for this, whatever "this" was. Surely we hadn't actually had sex. I hadn't had sex in forever. Not since . . . a year or something. Holy Harlot, I was pathetic. Lon probably had his pick of beautiful models when he was on photo shoots. Or maybe he had some girlfriend I didn't know about. I mean, he wasn't exactly forthcoming about his personal life. God, please don't let him have a girlfriend. Especially not if I made a fool of myself last night . . .

He made a small noise.

Crap. "Get out of my head! Those thoughts are private," I said, punching him on the arm.

He absently rubbed the spot where I'd hit him, staring at me as if I was certifiable. "This can't be happening," he murmured.

"Nothing's happening. Zero. Nada. It's exactly the same as it was before between us. Christ, I'm not some virgin girl who draws hearts around your name on the cover of my notebook. Get over yourself." His eyes widened, but I finished my thought. "I'm sure I would've done the same to any man who'd been around."

One brow arched oh-so-slowly. And the way he looked at me, unblinking, as if his head might rotate and explode, almost made me want to cower. Almost.

"Excuse me," I murmured, pushing past him and making a beeline for the nearest bathroom. I did a quick examination of myself—whoa, I needed to make a waxing appointment, and pronto—but even if no signs pointed to a night of drunken sexcapades, I couldn't be sure. Maybe nothing happened. Or maybe it was bad sex—so bad my body had already forgotten it.

A loud crash came from somewhere in the house. I left the bathroom and traced the source to Lon's photography room, where a tableful of equipment was now scattered across the floor. Lon was hunched over the efforts of his rampage.

I thought about backing out of the room, but if he was listening with his knack, he probably already knew I was there. "Please don't be mad."

"It's not you," he answered after a long moment.

"Do you want me to go?"

He shook his head. When he turned around, his eyes met mine. The anger melted away. "Let me make a couple of phone calls, then we can get on the road."

"Okay. I could use a shower, if you don't mind." Where was he showering? He must have moved into the guest room. That didn't seem right.

Lon's head jerked up, as if he'd remembered something important. "Wait. I need to . . ." He sighed heavily. "Let me grab a few things upstairs." He grumbled to himself and sidled around me warily. "Just . . ." He held up his hands and made a few awkward gestures, as if we didn't speak the same language and he couldn't decide how to get his point across. "Just stay in the living room until I come get you."

I felt a little sorry for him when he walked away. He seemed so defeated.

I knew one thing. If it *was* bad sex, it damn sure wasn't my fault. Maybe he was too old to get it up. I'd remember that the next time he wanted to drink.

Lon was determined to leave before Jupe got home, and he only relaxed somewhat when he found out that the kid was going to a friend's house to study for a test. We each packed a change of clothes, and after

Lon made arrangements with the Holidays, we finally headed out in his SUV late in the afternoon.

Golden Peak was a straight shot down Pacific Coast Highway. Fog and clouds ringed the mountains and hills, and the gray sky occasionally threw a spatter of rain droplets on the windshield, but it never actually rained. The GPS put us arriving at eight, but Lon figured he'd shave off a half hour by driving like a maniac once we got out of the city limits. The road hugged the coastline, straightaways broken up by a million hairpin and switchback curves, and all of it dotted with RVs chugging in and out of scenic pull-offs.

Neither of us said anything until we crossed Bixby Bridge. Lon was never one for small talk, but I could tell the difference between comfortable and uncomfortable silence. "Can we put last night behind us?" I finally said. "I still don't remember what happened, but whatever I did, I wasn't in my right mind."

"Don't worry about it."

"How can I not? You're being all weird."

It took him several moments to respond. "Nothing happened between us last night, so stop worrying about it. I'm just . . . sad. It's not your fault."

"Do you want to talk about it?"

"Yes, but I can't."

"Sure you can. We're friends, aren't we? You can tell me anything."

"Yes, we're friends," he said softly.

"But . . . ?"

"We've got enough on our plate right now. Don't need to complicate matters. What's done is done." I didn't know what he meant by that, but before I could ask, he said, "When did we meet?"

"Umm, what?"

"Just answer the question."

"The end of last summer, the day after my parents first showed up on the news."

"Tell me exactly what you remember."

"Why?"

"Because." He exhaled a long, slow breath through flared nostrils. "I need to test your memory."

"Again, why?"

"Do you feel like you're having memory problems?"

"I feel like someone beat me over the head with a baseball bat." I gave him a sidelong glance. "You didn't drug me like you did when we first met, did you?"

A brow lifted. "You remember that?"

"Distinctly."

He nodded, a little happier for some reason. "I want you to go back over everything you remember about our interactions together from the first day we met. Tell me everything."

"Has something happened? Do I have brain damage from the coma?"

He blinked rapidly, eyes on the road, hand slung over the top of the steering wheel. "I'm sure it's nothing that can't be repaired." It almost sounded like he muttered "I hope" after that. "Let's see what you remember. It's a long drive."

And it was. Long and troublesome, because when I went back through all the minutiae of time spent with Lon, I began feeling the same way I felt when I woke up, as if my memories had jagged edges and didn't quite fit together. Some were like pieces of old furniture covered by sheets: I could make out their general shape, but it was hard to tell what was underneath. But this didn't seem to bother Lon. He asked a lot of questions, and whenever I struggled for a missing piece of information, it eventually came to me if I tried hard enough to picture it in my mind.

Struggling for memories was a lot of work. And between that, the road's hidden hairpin curves, and two restroom pit stops (probably all the drinking I did the night before), I was grumpy by the time we rolled into Golden Peak. Grumpy, famished, and tired.

Maybe the PI's office would be located over a pancake restaurant.

Just off the coast, the resort town was a cozy outpost nestled among redwoods and oaks. I couldn't see much more than a couple of gas stations near the highway, a handful of restaurants—all closed, and it was only nine o'clock at night—a post office, and a few shops scattered on either side of a block-long Main Street.

"Population: 101 cats and 329 people," said the road sign when Lon slowed the SUV to a crawl. "Oh, boy. You know how much I love cats."

"There goes your Valentine's gift."

I chuckled, happy that he was in a better mood. Maybe things were normal between us again.

"Just keep an eye out for a private investigator sign," he said in an even-handed, classic Lon voice, flicking a squinty glance in my direction.

Definitely better.

I ticked off a list of what I saw on Main Street. "Souvenirs, camping supplies, rafting supplies, camping and rafting supplies . . . a skeevy-looking medical clinic—oh, look. They care for people *and* animals. That's charming. And weird. You and your cat can get rabies shots together. Like a couple's massage for bestiality fans."

Lon quietly snorted. "This whole community's a little kooky. I took Jupe camping out here when he was younger."

"Lordy. I can't imagine Jupe camping."

"I think his exact words were 'Sleeping on the ground is God's way of saying he hates you.' We haven't been back." He smiled to himself for a moment but didn't elaborate. "The state park entrance is a mile or so away. In the summer, this whole place is packed with tourists."

"How? There's not even a grocery store."

"There is . . . somewhere. Let's ride around and see what we can see."

Which was exactly nothing. Twisty mountain roads led to dead ends and a handful of houses, most of them tucked away in the woods. We spent a half hour combing the area for any sign of a PI and found jack-diddly-squat.

"Maybe we should call the number listed on his website," I finally said.

"Not from our phones. I don't want him tracing us."

"Then we have two choices. That motel or the gas station off the highway."

Lon drove back to the gas station. No one was filling up, and a single beater was parked at the side of the convenience store. We made our way inside, past shelves of beef jerky and Funyuns, and over to the lone employee, who sat on a stool behind the checkout counter. A secondary room filled with camping supplies was beyond an open doorway. I'd never been camping, but I had a feeling Jupe and I would agree on the subject.

The gas-station employee, a teenager with greasy hair, looked up from his magazine. His eyes flicked from Lon's face to my face to my breasts. Lovely. "Can I help you?"

"You have a pay phone?" Lon asked. He sounded pretty irritated. It almost made me think he might be pissed that the boy was ogling me. See? Decent, stand-up guy—just like I said.

"By the restrooms." The boy lifted his chin, pointing us there with minimal effort.

I pasted on a smile. If greasy-headed delinquent here was interested in the modest amount of goods I had up top, he shouldn't be hard to manipulate. "You wouldn't happen to know where we could find Robert Wildeye's office, would you?"

"Who?"

"A private investigator," Lon filled in. "Here in Golden Peak."

"PI?" The boy's face twisted up. He clearly thought we were idiots. "You sure you got the right town?"

"Positive." Lon was clearly wishing he could take a belt to the kid's ass, but he needed to pull back on the grumble.

"We just don't know the street address," I added. "Sure it doesn't ring a bell?"

"Uh, I doubt there's much cause for any business like that here in the winter," the boy said. "We got a lot of rich people with summer homes. They come up from L.A. in June. Maybe he's one of those." He shrugged.

"No one named Wildeye at all? Not even a retired cop or anything?"

"Sorry. Never heard it. I spend the summers with my mom in Sacramento, so I'm not the best person to ask."

"Anyone else who might be able to help us out?" I said. "Town gossip or something?"

"You might ask around at the Redwood Diner. A waitress there, June, knows everyone in town. She's lived here, like, forever."

Well, that was something, at least, and I was damn sure starving. But the diners I'd seen were all closed. "When does it open?"

"Five a.m."

Crap. "Is there anything open right now?"

"Sierra Woodland. That's the motel on Main, between downtown and the park. If you want nightlife,
you came to the wrong place, believe me."

"Not even a dive bar?" Lon asked.

"Are you kidding? You can't even buy beer," he
said, gesturing to the refrigerated cases at the side of
the shop. "Only thing here is a feral cat colony and
a bunch of hippies who like to backpack and paint
pictures of the waterfall."

I hear ya, kid. Godspeed getting yourself to a bigger town, where you can use that apathetic attitude
to charm someone just as depressed and misunder-
stood.

We thanked him and headed to the restrooms.
Lon volunteered to call. I kept an eye on the kid to
make sure he wasn't listening in on us. But there was
no need; he couldn't have given less of a shit. Soon
after inserting a few coins, Lon hung up and reported
that all he got was a voice-mail greeting. "It said he
was currently in the office and taking cases," Lon reported. "But otherwise just directed the caller to leave
a name and number and said he'd return the call
within twenty-four hours."

I groaned. I really didn't want to spend an entire
night here. "It's only ten. We have seven hours before
the diner opens. What do we do now? Can't drive back
home. We'd just have to turn around and come right
back. Maybe this whole thing was a lousy idea."

His eyes sparkled with something close to humor. "Patience, witch."

Since when did I get a nickname? Or had he called me that before? Either way, I was amused, and sort of happy that he wasn't feeling as hopeless about all this as I was.

He glanced at the kid behind the counter before squinting down at me. "Maybe I've been thinking about this all wrong."

8

Jupe nearly fell off his bed when the voice spoke.

May I show myself?

"No," he answered. "Go. Away."

For the love of God, couldn't a guy have some peace and quiet? It was after ten. Not that he was sleeping; his official school-night bedtime was midnight, not that Mr. and Mrs. Holiday were awake to enforce it. He was, however, busy trying to crack the new password for the parental controls on their internet connection.

Important shit.

His dad used to use a brand of film for all his passwords. Like that was smart. Everyone knew his father was a famous photographer. Might as well have just used his own birthday. For that matter, might as well have just used "PASSWORD."

When the telltale ball of light appeared at the foot of his bed, he barely had time to slam down the screen of his laptop before Priya's gigantic wings materialized.

"Don't you understand the meaning of 'go away'? Hey, watch it!"

The creature's wings created a brief vortex of wind that scattered loose pages of his math homework and fluttered his hair.

"You almost knocked over my Frankenstein's Laboratory model," Jupe complained as Priya's wings folded behind his back. "It took me an entire week to paint that. And while we're at it, you owe me for ripping the corner off my *Foxy Brown* poster last time you showed up. Dad got that signed for me by Pam Grier. Which means it's one of a kind. Unreplaceable." That didn't sound quite right. He quickly corrected himself. "Irreplaceable. Whatever. It's priceless."

"I don't have time for your nonsense, Kerub. This is important."

So was free porn, but Jupe didn't feel like explaining this to a being who didn't understand the meaning of privacy. "What is it now?"

"Did you know our mistress carries your father's offspring in her belly?"

"What the hell are you talking about now, birdbrain? Are—" Jupe stopped in mid-sentence. He stared at the gray-skinned creature as realization dawned. "Cady's pregnant? You're a big fat liar." Had to be. She didn't look pregnant. And she'd tell him and his dad before she told some stupid servant creature from another plane.

"I saw the threads with my own eyes a day ago. The Kerub's seed is growing within her."

Seed? Gross. He did *not* want to think about that. And what was more, if Cady was pregnant, how was she going to do her job? He'd never seen a pregnant bartender. And if she was pregnant, that meant—

"I'm going to have a brother? Or a sister?"

"Not if Enola finds out. Our mistress's mother is a murderer. She will slaughter the child or take it from her if our mistress does not find the Moonchild spell and reverse it. Do you understand?"

Jupe barely heard him. He was too busy freaking out. If Cady was pregnant, it was either the best thing, like, *ever* or his worst nightmare. He couldn't wrap his head around it. And why hadn't she told him? For that matter, why hadn't Dad told him? He felt sort of betrayed.

"She did not know," Priya said, as if he could read his mind.

Jupe hated when he did that. It was worse than his dad's knack. He crawled across his bed to reach for the bedside table. "I'm texting her right now to see if you're lying."

"Are you a boy or a man?"

Jupe's hand stilled on his bedside table. "What?"

"I said, are you a boy or a man? Because if you're a man, you will understand that our mistress is in grave danger, and you must protect her at any cost. But if you are only a boy, I will seek someone else who cares more for her life and will take steps to keep it safe."

Oh, hell, no. Bird boy was insulting him? Heat

rose in Jupe's chest. "I'm more of a man that you'll ever be."

"Prove it."

"You wanna fight? I'll pound your feathered ass into the floorboards." The guardian wasn't much taller than him, and Dad said that nine times out of ten, people who wanted to pick fights were all talk. Dad had also been showing him where to punch someone in the face, because the antibullying campaign at school was a load of shit. Okay, not all of it, but the tattletale part. Mrs. Henry said to run away and tell a teacher if someone was acting like an ass; Dad said that advice was for savages—humans who didn't believe Earthbounds existed—and that Jupe should learn to hit back if someone hit him.

Hit first, *then* tell a teacher. Basically. At least, that was how Jupe interpreted it.

"I am not challenging you to fight me," Priya said. "I am challenging you to fight for your mistress. She is confused and not caring for her own safety. If your father will not heed my warnings, then you must take up the charge. It is your responsibility to protect her."

Jupe started to argue that, actually, Cady had promised to protect Jupe, not the other way around. But he realized it made him sound kind of pathetic, so he kept that to himself. "What are you suggesting?"

"If she will not heed my warning to find the Moonchild spell, then you must find it for her. If you are a man, you are honor-bound to do so." Priya held his chin high. "I once gave up my life to protect her. Are you willing to do the same, or are you going to cower like a small child and allow her to be killed?"

"How am I supposed to find a spell no one else has been able to find?"

"You possess the voice of persuasion, do you not?"

"My knack?"

"Use it to interrogate members of her occult order. Trace her history, and find the spell."

"But her order is in Florida. That's a long way away. There's no way in hell Dad will let me go alone."

"Then do not tell him. Be your own man." Priya's gray skin crackled with energy; he was fading. "Summon me if you need help. I will assist you however I can."

And with that, the creature disappeared.

"Goddammit!" Jupe shouted, hurling an empty video-game case at the place where Priya once stood. It hit a shoe on top of a stack of books, which all fell off his dresser with a loud thump.

He immediately heard a muffled call from the guest room.

"Sorry," he called back to Mrs. Holiday. "It was an accident. Everything's fine."

After hearing whining and scratching outside his door, he pushed himself off the bed and let Foxglove inside. The Lab sniffed around the area where Priya had materialized. Good thing she wasn't there for the visit, or she would have barked her face off, because

Foxglove didn't like Priya any more than Jupe did. Smart dog. He gave her a quick scratch behind her ears and watched her trot over to the hedgehog crate to inspect Mr. Piggy's well-being—who, unlike Foxglove, couldn't care less about anything but snacking on fruit and projectile pooping.

Had to admire that kind of simple life.

So Cady was pregnant. He blew out a long breath. Before everything happened—before Mr. Dare, the biggest asshole in the world, may he rot forever and ever, put Cady in the hospital—Dad sat down with Jupe and told him all his plans. About buying Cady an engagement ring. Asking her to marry him. Everything was so much better then. Cady would say yes to Dad's proposal, of course— why wouldn't she?—and they'd all be a real family.

But his real mom showed up and caused major drama, and then Mr. Dare did what he did.

And now all this junk.

Cady had told Jupe all about her real identity. When she was in the hospital, he'd tracked down all the books about her parents and the Black Lodge slayings. He read one from cover to cover and skimmed the rest. They all basically said the same thing: her parents were crazy serial killers who went around murdering the heads of other occult orders. Dad told him about how they'd tried to kill Cady, too. That her mom gave birth to her already planning to kill her and take her power after Cady had reached some sort of age of magical maturity.

That was fucked up. Jupe's mom was a piece of work, but she'd never tried to kill him.

He thought about Yvonne—that's what he called her in his mind, just to remind himself that she wasn't his mom in spirit, not really, and so he shouldn't get his hopes too high. She was staying with Gramma Rose in Portland. Had been there since the Incident at Christmas. Auntie Adella e-mailed him updates every few days. She said Yvonne was doing better. Still sober. He wondered what they'd all think about Cady being pregnant. He considered calling them to ask their opinion. But Auntie had lost a baby a long time ago after her husband killed himself. He didn't want to upset her.

He glanced at his alarm clock. Dad had called to say he and Cady were staying in Golden Peak for the night. Should he call them? And say what, exactly— I'm afraid you're going to love the baby and forget all about me, and by the way, Priya called me a pussy?

No, that didn't sound needy. Not at all.

He fell onto his bed and stared at the ceiling, listening to Mr. Piggy make his little hedgie noises at Foxglove. Putting his needy feelings aside, he wondered if Cady was in real danger. And the more he thought about everything he'd read about her parents, the more he began to worry.

What if he *could* really fix this for her? He wasn't allowed to use his knack without permission, but surely Dad would want him to use it if he could save Cady's life. And if he saved the baby's life, he'd be the kid's hero. No one forgot about heroes.

He cracked open his laptop again. The name of Cady's order was Ekklesia Eleusia, otherwise known as the E∴E∴. He did a search for their website. Their main headquarters—the Grand Temple—was located outside of Miami. It was only open to the public once a month.

He was too young to get on a plane without his dad's permission, so flying was out of the question. If only his GTO was ready to drive, but it was months away from being finished, and he didn't have a license.

Okay, so he might not be able to rush off to Florida and save the day, but he remembered a place that might be within his reach. The E∴E∴ had a local branch, a half-hour bus ride into Morella. It just might require a few white lies to Mr. and Mrs. Holiday and a little bit of stealth. So for maybe the first time in his life, he decided to follow his father's advice and keep his mouth shut.

9

Lon scanned the gas-station shelves. I could tell by the glint in his eye that he was brewing up some kind of devious plan, but I was suddenly dead tired and angry-hungry. Whatever he was planning, it was all just going to have to wait.

"Screw Wildeye and my mother right now. There's got to be an In-N-Out somewhere up the road." I was having Donner Party fantasies—blame it on the mountain atmosphere and talk of sleeping on the hard ground. On top of feeling ravenous, I had to pee. Again. It was getting a little ridiculous.

Lon saw me eyeing the restroom. "Go on," he said. "I'll just have a look around and see if I can find a couple of things."

"Food."

"Food, too. Then we can head to the motel. If we're stuck here, let's make the most of it and get a little research done."

After emptying my bladder and using a criminal amount of paper hand towels to shut off the dirty faucet, I discovered that whatever Lon had in mind involved a tarp—the kind you use to cover a tent when it's raining—and some spray paint. I started to ask him what it was for, but he shut me up with a packet of smoked almonds. I downed them in the two minutes it took us to drive to the motel.

"Wait in the car," was all he said, handing me some orange juice. Leave it to him to find the only halfway healthy things in the gas station. Before I could see what else was in the bag of goodies he'd bought, he strode out from beneath the orange neon of the Sierra Woodland lobby and jumped back into the driver's seat.

"What's going on? Did anyone know Wildeye?"

"No luck." He handed me a chunky blue motel key fob with a room key attached.

"Cottage thirteen?" I read from the diamond-shaped plastic.

"They're all individual cabins. Ours is down this hill."

A funny sort of panic washed over me as we drove past tiny log cabins to a parking space in front of the one marked thirteen. Thirteen? Really? Not that I was superstitious about numbers, because most of numerology was total bullshit. What concerned me more was the single cabin. And the sharing. I guess I just figured we'd have adjoining rooms or something. But hey, it wasn't as if we were here to sleep, so what I was so worried about?

I grabbed my overnight bag out of the back of the

SUV and opened the cabin door. Lon carted the stuff he'd bought at the gas station inside as I flipped on the light. Sort of musty. All the furniture was the bad end of retro, and the bear-print curtains burned my eyes. At least it seemed fairly clean, and the bathroom had soap and towels. And there were two twin beds—a small relief. "God, I hope this isn't bedbug country," I said, setting my bag down on a luggage rack.

"Probably more likely to find those at one of the four-star hotels in Morella. The problem has more to do with the lack of tech."

"No TV," I said, realizing. "Wait, no phone, either?"

"According to the German lady at the desk, it's so you can leave the real world behind and relax," he said, tossing a motel pamphlet onto one of the beds. "Let's hope we get a mobile broadband signal."

"What are we going to do if we don't?" I said, digging out my phone. "Are there even electrical outlets? I need to charge this thing."

"I have a signal," he said. "Barely.

"I don't."

"Doesn't matter." He shrugged out of his thin leather jacket, revealing tightly muscled golden arms. Never in my life had I been around a man whose body wound me up the way Lon's did. Not even salacious parts of him, either. Just everyday parts. His arms and hands. His feet, even—how absurd was that? And I couldn't even bring myself to think about his bare chest without having a hot flash. I'd seen that chest, in my backyard, when we'd built my house ward. I had the strangest feeling I'd seen it other times, but the exact when, why, and how were a little fuzzy.

Why was I even thinking about this? Empath, hello! He could hear what I was feeling, so I might as well be whistling and catcalling as if he were some stripper for my own personal amusement. They were just arms, for the love of Pete. Every man had them.

"I brought some research material."

"Oh?" I said, trying to sound terribly interested. Focus, Bell. Focus.

He opened his bag and rummaged around for two cloth-wrapped books. Both of them were moldering Goetic tomes, illustrated encyclopedias of demons, written by medieval magicians who painstakingly cataloged each demon's attributes, seal, class, innate powers, bargaining favorability, and so forth.

"That's one of the books you stole from the Vatican when you were in the seminary," I said, walking over to the small writing desk where he had laid them both out. "You found the name of the albino demon in that. It's . . ."

"A Goetia of female demons," he said in a low voice, eyes flicking to mine.

"But—" Oh. Yes, I understood now. He was looking for me. Or the essence of whatever was inside me. The building block my parents had used in their conception spell. "Have you looked through it? Is there an entry for something called Mother of Ahriman?"

"I've run across plenty of demon classes with serpentine attributes but haven't read the entire book. I was too busy worrying you wouldn't wake up from your coma."

"Oh." I busily scratched my arm, feeling overwhelmingly grateful. "Thanks. You know, for everything. For looking out for me. No one's ever done that before."

A strange look passed over his face, fading as quickly as it began. He gave me a curt nod before turning away. "Don't thank me yet," he said, pulling out the tent tarp and spray paint. "I need you to help me re-create the sigils I painted on the ceiling in the bedroom."

I cocked my head. "Not getting it. What do the Goetias have to do with warding magick?"

He slowly shook the paint can and squinted at me. "I think it's time we did a little experiment to see the real you, and those sigils are going to be your safety net."

"Hold on. You want me to—"

"You can't hide from her forever," he argued evenly. "If she wants you so badly, and she's powerful enough to murder an Æthyric demon like Chora, she's going to find a way to get what she wants. Either you stand by and let it happen, or we find out what weapons you have against her. If you transmutate—"

"I can't transmutate without getting her attention."

"So says Priya. And he's only basing that on what he's seen in the Æthyr when you've done it in the past. He doesn't have all the answers, Cady. I know you're fond of him, but I've talked to him several times while you were in the hospital. And he's trustworthy—I've got no doubts about that—but he's . . ."

"What?"

"There's an innocence in him. A . . . youthfulness. And his instincts lean toward passive. He'd encourage you to hide rather than fight, because that's all he knows."

"Not everyone can be a fighter, Lon. He's a messenger. An adviser."

"And you aren't," he said firmly, offering the can of spray paint.

"You're suggesting . . . what, exactly?" I asked.

"Transmutate inside a protective ward."

"So you basically want me to put up a flashing sign in the Æthyr to let her know I'm awake, so she can start hijacking my dreams."

"No, I want you to see if you can tap into your power quietly, without getting her attention. And if she notices, then she does. We know she uses moon energy to connect to you, and you're sleeping in the day, so she can't get inside your dreams. If she's found a way to cross the planes, she'd have already done it."

True.

"You can't learn something without practicing," he said. "Better you master it while you can. And maybe you'll find that you don't have to light up the Æthyr when you shift. Just because I transmutate, that doesn't mean I instantly turn on my knack."

This surprised me. "You mean, you can shift and not hear my thoughts?"

"It's like a radio. I can choose to turn it on or off. Turn it on just loud enough to hear, or crank it up to full blast. Maybe it's the same for you, too. Maybe you can shift and refrain from—"

"Burning you to a crisp?"

He pointed a finger at me and winked. "That, for a start. If it's possible, then it would allow me to get a look at your shifted form."

He'd only seen it once, from a distance, outside his house while I was tearing the transmutation spell out of his ex-wife.

"You might have markings that would help me better identify what your parents were trying to create when they conceived you. I wouldn't suggest this if I wasn't confident that it was safe."

I thought about the ward on the ceiling of his bedroom. I knew that magick well, and he was probably right.

"Look," he said. "Afterward, you can call Priya and see if he 'felt' you connecting to your demon side in the Æthyr, just to be sure."

"I'm not a demon."

Lon pressed the paint can into my palm. "You damn sure aren't human. Might as well face that fact and make the best of it. We aren't all bad."

True. In fact, I'd say when it came to good and bad, humans and demons were pretty evenly matched.

Lon unfolded the tent tarp and spread it over the carpet. It looked as if we were psychotic serial killers, readying the room for bloodshed. Seemed somehow appropriate when dealing with matters related to my mother.

"Well, what do you say?" he asked when he was finished.

I tossed the can onto the bed. "Plastic paint isn't going to hold a charge for shit. I have some red ochre chalk in my purse."

I spent the next half hour or so carefully constructing a ward on the tarp with the heavily pigmented chalk, then blowing off the excess dust to prevent me from smudging it when I stepped on it. Pig's blood would have been better, but a town that didn't sell beer certainly didn't have a late-night butcher. When I was done, I had a ward with a nine-foot radius, give or take. Now for charging it. I dug my portable caduceus out of my overnight bag.

"No," Lon said. "Let me do it."

"You barely have any Heka stores."

"I don't like you pulling a lot of electricity if you don't have to. It's dangerous."

What in the living hell was he talking about? "It's only dangerous without something to even out the release." I held up the caduceus. "I'm prepared."

He hung his head and muttered a string of obscenities. "Just don't use any more than you need to, please. It might have a negative effect on . . . your memories."

"Why would you think—"

"Christ, Cady," he barked. "Can't you please trust me, just this once?"

"All right, jeez. No need to shout." I grumbled silently as I knelt by the tarp.

"Please be careful," Lon mumbled.

"Hush. I don't need much Heka for this." I reached for the nearest current and gave it a delicate tug. Electricity flooded into me, nice and easy. It kindled my Heka reserves and created the more powerful energy I needed to charge the symbols. After setting the tip of my caduceus staff on the outer ring of the ward, I exhaled and pushed Heka into it. Like a lit fuse, white light sped along the sigils, giving life to the magical equation.

"There," I said. "Easy-peasy."

Lon looked me over and sighed. "If you feel any unusual pains, tell me immediately."

"Are you sure *you're* not feeling any pains? Because you're being awfully weird."

He didn't respond. Just muttered to himself and brooded while he closed the curtains on the windows and checked the door lock. When he was satisfied, he crossed the room and pulled something out of his luggage, a black leather bag. Out came a camera.

"What are you doing?" I asked.

"Making a record that I can refer to," he said without emotion as he changed out the lens on his camera. "Take off your clothes."

My jaw unhinged.

"How else am I going to see if you have any special markings?" he asked without turning around. I hated when he did that. Made me feel as if he had eyes in the back of his head. "The times you transmutated wearing jeans, your tail ripped right through them. So unless you want to shop for hiker's shorts tomorrow, you're going to want to take off your pants."

Oh, he'd like that, wouldn't he? I might have been fuzzy on a few details about Lon, but I definitely remembered standing in the doorway in my underwear the first time he came to my house and his "nice ass" comment.

"Do you know how many bodies I've seen?" he said, still not turning around. "Models aren't shy, believe me."

Anger warmed my chest. "And this is supposed to make me feel better how, exactly?"

"Everyone's imperfect. I'm the one who has to Photoshop out the blemishes and knobby knees." He switched on the camera and fiddled with the settings. "Let's just get this over with so we can eat."

Had he heard my stomach growling? What a cheap ploy. I supposed when I really thought about it, he was right about needing to see all of me. Hell, I didn't exactly have a clear idea of what I looked like in that form, other than from a quick glance or two at my reflection.

Fine. Starting with my shoes, I systematically stripped down. At least he was polite enough not to watch. The entire time, I reminded myself I could trust Lon. He wasn't going to be looking at me as if I were a three-layer cake, which was pretty much how I'd been looking at him.

"You can leave your bra and panties on if it makes you feel better," he said.

Oh.

I glanced at said items on the floor. Too late now. And with my luck, he'd catch me trying to put them back on. I licked dry lips and quietly shuffled onto the tarp. At least the magick was solid; I could definitely feel a soft prickling sensation when I stood inside the ward, much in the same way I felt electricity.

If that were all I felt, it would have been fine. But my mind had emptied itself to make room for all the blind panic it was brewing up. It was as if the rational part of my brain had woken up and realized that it had fallen asleep and left the stupid, foolish part of my brain in charge, and now the house was on fire.

"I want to see you shift," he said. "Might learn something we didn't know."

"All right," I said, voice cracking. "I'm ready."

Lon turned around. When his head tilted up, his lips parted.

Just for a moment, my shield of panic dropped, and I could have sworn no one had ever looked at me like that in my entire life. But maybe I just wanted to believe I'd seen something more than I had. Because when I blinked, all I saw was his usual poker face.

He stopped in front of the tarp, expectant, not

saying a word. I wasn't sure what freaked me out more: standing in front of him naked or standing in front of that camera. "This better not end up on the internet," I mumbled. Then I shut my eyes to concentrate.

Most times I'd called up the Moonchild power, I'd done it in a panic and under duress. But now I reached for it gingerly. The same instincts I used to sniff out electricity kicked in, and it took some effort to push past that and aim for the bigger source of power. It came rushing at me, fierce and chaotic. I did my best to slow it down. A little like trying to reel in a shark instead of a trout. Hard to do that delicately, but I managed.

The power streamed into me. I opened my eyes.

A silver light tinted my vision, lit by the fog of my expanding halo. Everything was now bathed in an eerie quicksilver glow, including Lon, whose eyes followed the chain of sensations I'd experienced only a few times: a strange coolness spreading across my skin, the pressure of horns springing from my head, and the disconcerting slither of a long reptilian tail as it tickled the back of my legs.

"Don't panic," Lon said. His voice sounded muffled and distant. "And don't try to will any magick into action."

"Oh . . . God," I whispered, suddenly feeling as if I wouldn't be able to stop myself.

"You're safe. I'm here. Just breathe. Long breaths in through your nose, slow exhalations through your mouth."

It was easier to be calm when he was. And before I knew it, I was following his advice. Long breaths in, slow breaths out. His camera hid his face as he started snapping photos. And once I felt I had a handle on myself, I glanced down.

My skin was covered in iridescent scales. Dark ones. The first time I'd seen them in the mirror, I decided they looked black, but it was hard to tell with the quicksilver tint covering everything. A striking white-and-gray reticulated pattern broke up the black scales over my neck and shoulders.

"Breathe."

Yes. I'd forgotten.

I lifted a hand to my head, to feel what I couldn't see. Ridges came to a point on my forehead, like a widow's peak, just above my eyes. The ridges flared to make a V shape, and above my hairline, they changed to horns, gently curving backward like crests on a dragon: one, two, three horns lined up in a neat row on either side of my head.

So different from Lon's spiraling ram's horns. His were textured like a fingernail; mine were glossy and smooth.

He snapped a million pictures, circling me. I looked over my shoulder as he did, seeing what the camera's eye captured: black and white stripes lining my back. Flowing into my tail.

It jutted out from my lower back and was a couple of inches in diameter and the same length as my legs. Black and white rings, all the way to the tip.

Sort of attractive, in a strange way. I tested it, willing it to move. It swished around my ankles. I could *feel* my ankles with my tail. It was just another append-age, swaying back and forth like a pendulum over my ass cheeks.

Lon was taking an awful lot of pictures. Then again, my backside was my best side. While he cir-cled me, I ran my fingers over the scales between my breasts. They were so smooth. Tougher than human skin but still soft and flexible. The camera stopped clicking. Warm fingers joined mine. I tried not to flinch, and I didn't pull my hand away. He was inside the ward now, only a couple of feet away. And the tips of his fingers moved between mine, touching the scales that I touched. Marveling with me.

My heart fluttered. Chills ran down my arms as a familiar heat spread between my legs. Wow. A couple of seconds of innocent touching, and my body was eager to climb his. My overenthusiastic reaction wasn't as much of a surprise as what I saw when I glanced between us. No mistaking the tented fly of his jeans.

I mean, good God.

His fingers stilled on my scales.

He knew that I knew, which freaked me out. My conscience—surprise, I had one—backhanded my sex-starved body, and I lost my grip on the trans-mutation. The silver light faded. Sound returned to normal. And everything seemed to just draw up inside me. Horns, scales, tail—all of it receded, then disappeared. It was almost painful and very uncomfortable.

I stood in front of Lon, self-conscious and freezing and gasping for breath.

He made a low, frustrated noise as his face tightened into a scowl. Then he spun around and stomped away to the door. "Don't summon Priya yourself," he barked as he struggled to unlock the door with shaking hands. "If that got your mother's attention, you don't want her finding out Priya's alive. Call Jupe, and get him to question Priya while he's on the phone with you."

And with that, he rushed out the door and slammed it hard behind him.

10

The awkwardness between us faded as the night bled into morning, but it was pretty easy to ignore something when you didn't discuss it. And we didn't. Not a single word. Which was fine by me. Because after hours of flipping through brittle pages of medieval woodcuts, I realized the likely cause of Lon's brief carnal interest in me: my transmutated form must have brought back memories of Yvonne.

I'd seen her in her shifted state, right before I ripped out the spell that fueled it. She was easily the most beautiful woman I'd ever laid eyes on. God only knew how many times Lon had lusted over her when she was sporting horns. Plus, she was the mother of his child, so it was only natural that he still wanted her—and only natural that my serpentine form stirred up old feelings.

Maybe my supremely good ass helped. I liked to think so. But it was over and done, and as I sat across from him in a booth in the Redwood Diner at six a.m., belly filled with griddled breakfast, I was thankful it hadn't created anything too weird between us. If I was going to struggle with it, better to do so alone, when he was well out of empathic earshot.

Besides, I had other things to worry about. Like how my pupils hadn't returned to normal since I shifted last night. They were elliptical, slitlike snake eyes, and my blue irises were shot through with silver. My halo was also brighter than normal. A couple of hours ago, both of these problems were worse, so at least it was fading.

But still. Not good. I thought of Priya's warning that the Moonchild would overpower the human part of me, which could strengthen my mother's choke hold.

Lon wasn't convinced. He thought maybe this was just a temporary side effect—that because my transmutation wasn't aided by an artificial spell, as his was, maybe shifting back down just wasn't ever going to be as clean as it was for him. We were both hopeful that the side effects would continue to fade, but for now, I was forced to hide my silvery irises by wearing sunglasses indoors, like a complete jackass.

"I don't think I've ever put away that many pancakes before," I said, slumping in my seat.

"I'm impressed," he said, giving me a soft smile as he slid his empty plate over the scratched Formica tabletop. "Vitamins." He nodded toward the three pills he'd foisted on me like some nagging parent—to aid in my continued recovery from the hospital stay, he insisted.

I took them with the pulpy dregs of my orange juice, then ran my finger through the puddle of cooling syrup on my plate and licked it. "If our waitress doesn't show up soon, I might eat a few more."

She was running late, apparently. And neither the cook nor the other waitress had heard the name Robert Wildeye. If our luck didn't change soon, I didn't know what we'd do. Walk around town holding up a sign like chauffeurs in airports?

I'd called Jupe after the whole naked, scaly modeling session. The kid sounded a little weird—I think he said "uh" a dozen times during the phone call—but he did what I asked and summoned my guardian. Upon being questioned, Priya informed us he hadn't noticed my transmutation in the Æthyr. The tarp ward had worked. Whether my mother had noticed, though, Priya didn't know. All he could tell was that she was still in the Æthyr, she was still on the run, and he was still tracking her.

Better there than here, I supposed.

The diner's front door squeaked open. Lon and I both glanced at the woman striding into the restaurant. Middle-aged. Curly brown hair streaked with gray. A little plump and a whole lot in a rush. "Sorry I'm late, Carol," she said, disappearing behind swinging doors for a couple of minutes before reappearing without her coat. Like the other waitress's, her dress matched the avocado tile floor. She was still tying an apron around her waist when she approached our table with a pencil clamped between her teeth.

Her nametag read "June." That was our gal. I guessed I hadn't realized just how enthusiastic I was to finally see her, because I heard a loud crack and looked down to find that my fork had snapped in two, right in my hand. The tine side clanged against my plate as it fell.

"Oh, Jesus," I said. "I'm sorry."

June stuffed the pencil in her apron pocket and smiled. "Don't be. Those things break in the dishwasher all the time. Customers complain that they can't cut into a steak without bending the knives. The owner is too cheap to buy anything better." She whisked up the broken fork pieces along with our plates, deftly cleaning up the table as she talked. "Carol said you two were asking for me?"

"Kid at the gas station said you might be able to help us," Lon said.

"Joey or Henry?"

"Joey," I lied smoothly. As good a name as any. I didn't want to get into a Who's Who of Golden Peak; the sun had risen, so it was now officially my bedtime, and the fake maple syrup was giving me heartburn. "We're looking for a man named Robert Wildeye. He's a private detective. Supposed to have an office in town, but we can't find it."

"Robert Wildeye?" The waitress scrunched up her nose. "You don't mean old Bobby Wilde, do you? Not a detective—at least, not to my knowledge. A retired pilot."

I glanced at Lon and read what I was thinking on

his face. Never discount coincidence, and that name was too close to the one we sought. Someone who kept his address secret—and someone who was able to uncover things about my family that an entire army of journalists and cops failed to find—well, someone like that could very well be using another name. Magicians did it all the time to keep their private lives private. Hell, I was doing it right that second.

"He's a retired pilot?" Lon asked. "Does he have a son, maybe?"

The waitress shook her head. "Never married, no son. And he *was* a retired pilot—as in, he's passed on."

Dammit. I discreetly kicked the table leg. Metal creaked. Loudly. For a second, I thought I'd kicked the leg away from where it was bolted to the floor. This diner was a freaking shambles.

"Maybe this isn't the guy we're looking for," Lon said. "I think he would've had an office downtown—"

"Definitely not," the waitress said. "Bobby hated coming into town. Never was much of a social creature. He moved out here about ten years ago now, I guess. Mostly kept to himself. Had a cabin near the state park. That's where they found the body in early January. First murder in this area since the late eighties."

"Murder?"

"Shot," she said in a low, salacious tone. "One of the park rangers found him in his backyard. He'd been dead for two weeks, and no one knew. At first, they thought maybe a hunter had shot him, but the bullet was from a handgun at close range. Terrible. Scared the whole town to bits. Sheriff said we weren't in danger, though. Bobby had likely just made the wrong person mad. He had dealings with a lot of the rich folks who build on the mountain."

"Is that so?" Lon murmured.

"People from L.A. were always heading up to see him," she said. "My bet is that it was something to do with a debt or money."

"Usually is," Lon said.

June smiled, happy to have Lon's validation. "Anyway, his only family is a brother from Vancouver. He came down for the funeral. Nice man. Little harried and overwhelmed. Said he'd be back in a few weeks to clear out Bobby's things and sell the cabin. I had to do that when my mother died—estate taxes and paperwork. What a nightmare."

"I can imagine."

"Still, the brother will make a pretty penny off that property. Everything on Diamond Trail is selling these days, and Bobby's land butts up against the old state park entrance. Once the park gets its funding approved, they're building a nice restaurant and gift shop up there. Oh, the Deacons are here."

The waitress excused herself as an elderly couple entered the diner.

Lon watched her saunter off before pulling out a couple of bills and sliding them under his water glass. We raised our hands to thank June on our way out.

It was all I could do to keep my mouth shut until we got into the SUV.

"Are you thinking what I'm thinking?" I said.

"They found him in early January, and he was killed two weeks earlier. That would be right before—"

"Dare."

"Wouldn't be the first person he killed to keep quiet," Lon agreed. "And if the PI had all that information on you, maybe Dare didn't want others finding out."

"But if this is our guy, and Dare killed him, what are the chances Dare left any information behind?"

"I doubt he did the deed himself. Probably hired a gun," Lon said. "But you're right. They wouldn't have been sloppy. And the cops have probably gone over every inch of the house."

We sat there for a moment. "But we're still going to break in, aren't we?"

A slow smile lifted the corners of Lon's mouth as he turned the car's ignition. "Damn straight."

It took us a few minutes to find Diamond Trail on the GPS and another half hour to drive the length of it, but the two-story house was exactly where the waitress said it would be, half hidden by oak trees in a secluded area. It must have cost a few hundred thousand dollars to build, which made it less like a cabin and more like a house that had gotten lost in the woods and given up.

Lon drove up the steep driveway and parked

on the side of the house, where we couldn't be seen from the road. Leaves crunched underfoot as we trekked to the side door. It was sort of pretty here, with the craggy mountain rising in the backyard. Lon knocked, just in case, but no one answered. Shades covered all the windows.

"Can you hear anything inside?" I asked.

Lon glanced around, peering off into the woods and up the mountain. We hadn't seen a single car once we turned off of Main Street. Guess he was thinking that, too, because a moment later, the horns were spiraling out. Super. Now I had to guard my thoughts.

"It's good practice," he said. "You're supposed to be learning to guard yourself against your mother if she ever tries to tap into your head again."

I glared at him. "Just tell me what you hear."

"Nope," he said, fishing around in his pockets for leather gloves. "Empty."

"What if there's an alarm on the door?"

"You feel any electricity?"

Oh. I reached out for current, and apart from some weak sources in the house and the SUV—all batteries, most likely—the nearest substantial cache of it felt far enough away to be in the lines at the road.

"Wouldn't be surprised if got shut off for nonpayment," Lon said, reading my thoughts. "The backup for alarm systems usually only lasts a day or two."

Assessing our options, we hiked around the house and stopped in front of sliding glass doors, where Lon shielded his eyes to peer into shadows.

"How're we going to get inside, anyway? Break the glass?" I pulled the handle to make sure it was locked and felt something give way. The door cracked, jerked, and slid open. Didn't expect that. I stumbled, and when I looked to see what had happened, I saw the damage. "Shit."

"Christ, Cady."

The metal framing was bent. I'd torn the whole damn lock off.

"I didn't do it on purpose!" For a moment, I remembered the table leg in the diner and panicked. "Maybe whoever killed him tried to break in here and damaged it already."

"Maybe," he said as he shifted down from his transmuted form.

"Let's just get this over with." Taking off my sunglasses, I led the way inside and whistled. "Nice pad. Being a PI pays well." The whole rustic-cabin thing was a false front. Inside, it was all modern and sleek, straight out of an architecture magazine.

"God only knows what Dare was paying him."

A large open living area with high ceilings spilled into a kitchen almost as nice as Lon's but with much less personality. From there, we quickly went from room to room on the bottom floor, then headed upstairs when we found nothing of interest.

"Bingo," Lon said when we strode into a home office. An oversized world map hung next to a calendar over an L-shaped desk that looked as if it had been stripped.

Lon ran his fingers over a bundle of limp cable cords sticking out of a hole in the desktop. "All his equipment's gone. Either the guy who killed him took it for safekeeping, or the police seized it for evidence."

We opened up all the drawers in the desk and two freestanding filing cabinets. Apart from some loose change, gum, and a few pens, nothing was left. "It had to be Dare," I said. "We'd probably have more luck knocking on his widow's door and asking her for help."

"Already tried while you were in the hospital. She didn't know anything. I went through two warehouses looking for anything he had on you. Didn't find a thing."

I closed an empty file-cabinet drawer and glanced at Lon's face, feeling self-conscious and . . . odd. Why did he go to so much trouble to help me? I wasn't sure I deserved it. When his gaze rose to meet mine, I quickly looked away. "Seems crazy that a man like Wildeye—or Wilde, whatever—could be so good at gathering information even the feds couldn't find on my parents, but all it took was him dying for everyone and their brother to walk in and steal it."

Lon grunted, surveying the empty room. "He would've had a backup. Somewhere safer."

"Another house or a warehouse?"

"Maybe."

"I kept all my medicinals locked up in my bedroom closet . . ."

"They're all in a safe in my closet now."

We looked at each other before making a beeline to Wildeye's bedroom. It was too dark with the power out, so I raised the shades on a wall of windows. Sunlight spilled in over the quiet room, giving us a stunning view of the mountain rising in the backyard. A nice little retreat. Neat. Tidy. But when we pulled open his dresser drawers, it looked as if someone else had already searched through their contents.

We checked the walk-in closet next. Nothing but clothes and shoes, I thought, peering into the dark space. It was hard to see without electricity, and I was about to ask Lon if he had a flashlight. Glad I didn't, or I might not have noticed the faint white glow behind a row of hanging shirts.

I parted the shirts, sliding the coat hangers along the rail. "Hello, secret door."

It was hiding magick, a nice two-by-three-foot ward. Same thing we'd seen on the yacht in November. An old spell that grizzled old magicians had used over the centuries to hide treasure and grimoires and secret sex chambers. Other humans wouldn't see the telltale white Heka that kept the ward charged; other humans didn't have the same supernatural sight that Earthbounds had. That I had.

My heart raced with excitement. Please let this be worth it.

"Haven't seen an Earthbound since we got into town," Lon said as he pressed around the wood paneling, looking for a way inside. "Maybe the murderer was human, too. Here we go."

He pulled his hand away, and a hidden door in the paneling popped open. Shelves lined the dark space. Lon flicked on a penlight and moved the beam of light over the contents. Two guns. Bullets. A long metal box filled with cash, IDs, and passports. A few fat black organizer cases filled with USB drives. A box of files, which Lon hefted from the closet to the bed, and a skinny pocket notebook, which I grabbed.

I strolled to the wall of windows for light. The guy had terrible handwriting and some sort of short-hand I could barely decipher. Dates. Times. Names all seemed to be condensed to three capital letters. I flipped to the middle of the notebook, where the writing stopped: dates in December.

At first look, nothing seemed to pertain to me. A few of his scribbles looked to be street addresses—no cities. One block of text from late September caught my attention. The initials here were "DUV/BEL." My real surname, Duval, and Bell? Had to be. Below it, he'd crossed out several words, variations on spellings. The last variation was ringed several times in looping inky circles: "NAOI NAAS."

Odd. Sounded vaguely occult, but I couldn't place the name.

The pages shook.

I stilled.

The fringe at the edge of the rug jumped. Earthquake? But it wasn't steady. It stopped and started again.

Something rumbled in the distance, like a cosmic bear waking from a long winter nap.

I lifted my gaze to the wall of windows and the mountainside beyond.

Not an earthquake. Landslide.

"Lon!" I shouted, turning to run. But there wasn't time. The sunlight behind me was eclipsed by a growing shadow that increased in size until it blotted out all the light in the room.

Then it exploded.

11

Splintered wood and dry earth.

I caught the scent of both as the massive boulder smashed through the wall of windows and turned Wildeye's bed into kindling before ripping through the floor in front of us as if it was made of butter.

"Cady!"

Lon rammed into me. Boards cracked. The room tilted. For a moment, I thought we were going to slide into the hole. Then a joist snapped in two, and the entire floor collapsed, along with my stomach. One second I was upstairs, and the next I was rocketing downward with Lon through a cloud of dust.

A sofa broke Lon's fall. Lon broke mine. For a moment, I couldn't breathe. Everything seemed to be vibrating inside—my nerves, bones, teeth. Wood and plaster and glass rained over my back as he covered my head with his arm. When it stopped, we both gasped for air at the same time.

My ears rang. I coughed up plaster dust while attempting to stand, but Lon was holding on to me like grim death. I was terrified he'd broken his back or neck. "Lon—"

"I'm okay," he said through a cough.

I barely had a chance to feel relief as another rumble shook the house. It sounded like the whole damn mountain was coming down. Adrenaline fired through my limbs. We pushed off the couch and stumbled over broken boards into the kitchen.

Another rock roared through the living-room wall.

"Out!" Lon shouted, grabbing my arm to shove me toward a door.

I didn't even think. Just shouldered into it like a human battering ram and broke the whole damn thing down. Believe me, I couldn't have been more surprised when it exploded off its hinges, but I didn't have a chance to wonder how.

Morning sun blinded me as we burst from the rubble into open air. It took me a second to get my bearings. We'd exited through the cabin's side door, where Lon's SUV was parked—I almost ran into it. And by some miracle, it was unharmed. But not for long.

The driveway quaked. I glanced past the car toward the mountain. Nothing but dust and cascading rocks. A wave of destruction tumbling from the heavens and blanketing Wildeye's backyard in stone.

The driver's door swung open, and a hard hand shoved me into the SUV. I half sailed, half scrambled over the center armrest, banging my head in the

BANISHING THE DARK 109

process. I'd never seen anyone start an engine so fast. Dirt flew from the wheels as Lon threw it into reverse and swung the car around. Metal crunched. I yelped as my head bounced against the headrest.

"Shit!"

He'd hit a boulder. Or a boulder had hit the SUV. Either way, it was in back of us—not in front—and the back window was still intact. Teeth rattling, I twisted in my seat in time to see a giant oak crack and sway toward the back of the house. It crashed into the roof with a massive *boom!*

"Go, go, go!" I shouted.

Lon slammed the SUV into gear and tore down the driveway like a bat out of hell. In seconds, we were speeding onto Diamond Trail, away from Armageddon.

"Jesus fucking Christ," Lon repeated several times, staring wide-eyed at the road ahead. After sobering up a little, he asked, "Are you okay?"

"Considering? Yes, I think so. What just happened?"

"Hell if I know. Did we set off a ward?"

I knew what he was thinking: the putt-putt golf course last fall. But that was strange Æthyric magick etched in pink light, not earthly white Heka. I would have definitely noticed something like that in Wildeye's house. The warding magic he'd used in the closet was an oldie-but-goodie spell, nothing all that special. A kindergartner could cast it—at least, I could when I was that age.

"I didn't see anything. And no warning whatso-ever," I said. "Are there a lot of landslides out here? Could it have been a coincidence?"

"You don't believe in coincidences."

"I'm willing to start now. Slow down. I see a car over that next hill. I don't want it to look like we're fleeing a crime scene."

"We are."

"But we didn't do *that*!"

He grumbled and slowed to a speed barely under a reckless-driving violation. The car I'd spotted was now cresting the hill and turned out to be a truck. The truck belonged to a park ranger. Orange warning lights flashed as it sped toward us, sending a fresh flood of panic into my brain. It took me a couple of seconds to realize the ranger had zero interest in us. He passed us and continued on his way. Headed to the landslide, I supposed.

Lon banged the heel of his palm against the steer-ing wheel. "All of that for nothing."

"You didn't see anything in the files?"

"They were all several years old." He flashed me a glance. "How did you knock down that door?"

"Adrenaline?"

"You snapped a fork in two, and you ripped the lock off the patio door."

And nearly knocked the leg off the table in the diner, but I didn't say this. "You think it might be part of the moon magick, some kind of Superman strength?"

"You aren't experiencing other demonic abilities, are you?"

"Not that I know of." Just to ease my mind, I tried to manage the most common of knacks—telekinesis—by willing something to rise into the air, a pen rolling around an open compartment in the console. Nope. Nothing.

"Are my eyes . . . ?" I pulled down the visor mirror. Still had the elliptical pupils. Great.

Lon gestured at me. "What's that you're holding?"

I glanced down and was surprised to see my hand balled into a fist. My fingers were stiff, locked around a couple of scraps of paper. I loosened my grip and flattened out the wrinkles against my knee. "It's from Wildeye's notebook." I must have lost the notebook itself in the landslide, but by some miracle, I'd managed to hang on to three pages. The tops were torn off, and the bottom two pages were empty. But I'd snagged the one I'd been looking at when the mountain smote us.

"Looks like coded notes from September," I explained to Lon. "But I think these could be my initials."

"He was investigating you back in September?"

Not long after I'd met Lon and before Dare had revealed that he knew my real name. "Guess so, but don't get your hopes up too high. Only three things are listed. One is a street address with no city. The second thing is just a note that says '3AC 1988.'"

"Not the year you were born."

"No. But it's my fake identity's birth year. And I have no idea what '3AC' would have to do with that."

He grunted. "What's the third thing?"

"Variations on spelling for 'Naos Ophis.'" I spelled it out for him.

"*Naos* means shrine, or an inner temple."

"A cella."

Lon nodded. "That's Latin, but yes. *Naos* comes from a Greek word. I don't know what *Ophis* is, though."

I stared at the paper for a couple of moments, but my brain was in no mood for solving riddles. The clock on the dash said it was half past seven. And whether it was the power of suggestion or my adrenaline running out, exhaustion hit me like a brick.

"We'll research all that later," Lon said as Golden Peak came into view in the distance. "Right now, we need to rest. If you don't sleep, you'll be nodding off when night falls. Or I will. And I need to watch out for you."

My stomach tightened when I thought about being alone with him in a hotel room again. I hoped I'd manage to keep my clothes on this time. "I'm not sure if it's the best idea to crash at the Redwood Motel. What if that waitress tells people she sent us up to Wildeye's house?"

"They won't be looking for two people who triggered a landslide," he said. "But on the other hand, I don't want nosy people knocking on the door or logging my tag number while we're sleeping."

I certainly didn't disagree. So while he made a quick stop to pick up the things we'd left in the motel room, I futzed around with the search function on the GPS until it brought up the closest motel off the highway, about ten miles south of Golden Peak. It took us a half hour to get there.

Tucked into grass-covered cliffs facing the ocean, the Lucia Inn was all beachy clapboard and white picket fence, geared toward retirees taking leisurely excursions up the coast of California. We got the last room with double queen beds available and dumped our bags onto the creaking wood floor.

While Lon showered in the pale pink bathroom, I managed to get a broadband signal on his tablet and unfolded the scrap of paper from Wildeye's notebook. I tried looking up "Naos Ophis" in quotes. Nothing. Not one single hit. How was that possible? Maybe Wildeye had the spelling wrong, after all. But searching for variations proved just as futile. Maybe Lon would have other ideas. He was the linguaphile.

Changing tactics, I typed Wildeye's mystery address into a map search, which located it in fifteen cities. Better than hundreds of hits, I supposed, and most of them were in the West. But we couldn't exactly traipse around the country searching for the right one. And what was I even looking for, exactly? Most of the locations looked to be houses in residential neighborhoods. One convenience store. And—

Rooke Gardens. Pasadena, California.

Long-forgotten memories bloomed inside my head.

I raced to the bathroom and knocked, shouting against the peeling pink paint. "Lon! I know the address in the notebook. It's in Pasadena."

The door swung open. I saw half a second of glistening naked male flesh. Mostly chest—holy crap, better than I remembered—and the vague promise of other alluring body parts in my peripheral vision.

For the love of God. Didn't this place have towels?

Just because I'd gotten naked for research didn't mean all bets were off. Rattled, I held out Wildeye's torn notebook page in front of me to block the view.

He cleared his throat. "Repeat what you just said."

I tapped the paper with my index finger. "This is in Pasadena. Rooke Gardens. It's a private botanical garden owned by Karlan Rooke."

"And I should recognize that name because . . . ?"

"He used to be a high-ranking member of the E∴E∴, but he quit when . . . well, I was about Jupe's age, I guess. Caused a big hubbub at a national occult convention in Florida. He hated my parents. *Hated.*"

Lon made a small noise. "Interesting."

"He was grandmaster of the Pasadena lodge, but when he quit the order, the lodge fell apart and eventually shut down altogether." A droplet of water fell from Lon's wet hair and plopped on his shoulder. Very distracting. I forced myself to look away and refocus on Wildeye's notes. "Those words, 'Naos Ophis,' were scribbled below the address. Can't find anything at all on that exact phrase—"

"I remembered in the shower," Lon said. "*Ophis* is Greek for 'serpent.'"

A dreadful chill ran through me. The hand holding up the torn paper fell to my side. "Temple of the Serpent."

"Was that the name of the Pasadena lodge that disbanded?" Lon asked.

Each E∴E∴ lodge had a different name. Seventeen lodges in total, but the Pasadena lodge had been named Astera, and none of the other lodges was named after snakes or serpents. No dragons or lizards, either. "Naos Ophis definitely isn't an E∴E∴ lodge."

"A rival order's lodge? The Luxe, maybe?"

I thought for a second, just to be sure. "No. Not Luxe. Not any of the other orders. I would remember." Hard to forget when your parents made a habit of murdering other orders' leaders.

"Maybe this Karlan Rooke started his own order."

"It's possible. Oh! And there's something else—his father was one of Aleister Crowley's secret bastards."

Lon's eyes narrowed. "Very interesting."

"No proof, of course. But everyone in my order seemed to think it was true. I remember my parents talking trash about him, saying that he was no better than a commoner with no magical skills. Calling him slurs like 'half-breed,' that sort of thing."

Lon grunted. "Wish we had a better idea of what we'd be walking into."

"I could contact the E∴E∴, see if someone will talk to me about Rooke."

"I don't know if that's a good idea. The fewer people who know where you are, the better. Your order may rise to the occasion and help you—"

"But with the caliph gone . . ."

"Let's not sound an alarm just yet. I say we follow this independently until we're forced to ask for help."

He was probably right. I just wished I knew whether Rooke would see me as friend or foe now that I knew the truth about my parents. He had to be in his seventies by now, which meant he knew a hell of a lot more about E∴E∴ politics than I did. And that made me both nervous and curious. Mostly nervous.

Lon's fingers curved around the back of my neck, as though I were a wilting tomato bush needing a support stake. "Let me call Jupe," he said in a soft voice. "I'll tell him we'll be driving to Pasadena later tonight."

12

Jupe stepped off the Morella city bus and squinted into the morning sun, trying to get his bearings. This wasn't the nicest neighborhood. Lots of warehouses and trashy cars lining the curbs and a bunch of old, ratty houses at the bottom of the hill. Not exactly the kind of place he'd imagined when he pictured Cady's occult order. Then again, she never really talked about it. Guess it brought back a lot of bad memories.

He checked his phone. Crap. It was already eleven. It took him half an hour to walk from his junior high to the Village, then another two hours on the bus. Ditching school was a lot of work, and things only got harder once he made it to the city. Mission Station—where the La Sirena bus dropped him off in Morella—was crowded with weirdos and smelled like sweaty balls. And deciphering the Metro schedule was beyond ridiculous. If it weren't for the lady at the information kiosk, he might be in Reno by now.

Kar Yee was right: public transportation sucked, big-time.

On top of all that, his dad had called in the middle of all this, forcing Jupe to lie: no, that wasn't a car engine, it was, uh, the school janitor polishing the floors. So lame, but it was all he could think of in the moment. At least his dad's knack didn't work over the telephone.

He surveyed nearby warehouses for a street address while he waited for the GPS on his phone to show him which way to walk. Looked like he was three blocks away—not too far, thank God. His feet hurt, and it was chilly. He flipped up the collar of his jacket and followed the arrow on his phone.

The GPS pointed him to a run-down building next to a pest-control company. Two straggly palm trees flanked the main door, where a silver hexagram was painted. Surely this wasn't the Bull and Scorpion Lodge—the name listed on the website for the local chapter. Jupe had envisioned a spooky-looking temple. Maybe some flashy occult artwork of a bull fighting a giant magical scorpion, *Clash of the Titans* style. But this place looked like it existed just to provide homeless people with shelter from the wind.

The front door opened, and a Hispanic girl about his age stepped onto the covered stoop. She was dressed in jeans and a pink hoodie, and her dark brown hair was twisted into two messy buns on either side of her head. When she saw him, she stilled. Big brown eyes blinked at him over the apple she was eating.

"Hi," Jupe said.

She disengaged her teeth from the apple and wiped her mouth on her hoodie sleeve. "Hi."

"Is this the Bull and Scorpion?"

She blinked again and gave a suspicious glance up and down the sidewalk. "Yeah."

"You should have a sign."

"We don't need one. This isn't a grocery store. We don't need to attract customers."

Kind of snotty, jeez. Jupe was ready to fire back with something just as smart-ass, but his gaze dropped to her boobs, and he got a little discombobulated. Half the girls in his class were flat-chested. This girl . . . was not. She was a little bit round everywhere, now that he was looking closer. Not fat, exactly. Just sort of cushiony. Folded arms suddenly blocked his view. He glanced back up at her face. Uh-oh. She wasn't happy.

"What do you want?"

At that moment, Jupe had no freaking idea. It felt like someone had scooped out his brain and replaced it with marshmallows. He tried to smile. A lot of girls at school would get all weird and spacey when he smiled at them. Unfortunately, this girl did not. He cleared his throat. "I'm Jupiter—Jupe. Uh, you can call me Jupe, I mean. My last name's Butler."

"Do you go to St. Pius?"

"Church?"

"Private school."

"I go to La Sirena Junior High."

One dark brow arched. "What are you doing out here in Morella, then? Shouldn't you be in school?"

"I could say the same about you."

"I *am* in school. My mom brought me here during lunch to help with some stuff." She gestured with the apple toward some unspecific place down the street. "I go to Pacific Bay."

Jupe shook his head in confusion. "I don't know what that is."

"It's a middle school two blocks from here. My mom teaches drama."

"I'm in eighth grade," Jupe said stupidly.

She blinked a few more times and uncrossed her arms. "Me, too."

"What's your name?"

She opened her mouth to answer but seemed to change her mind. "Why do you want to know?"

"Because it's polite to ask?" God. What was her problem? "Or don't tell me. I don't care. I didn't ditch school to shoot the shit. I'm here to get some information."

"You ditched school to come here?"

"That's none of your business." Ugh. Now she was making him cranky. He waved her to the side. "If you'll please move, Miss No-Name. I have important business."

She didn't budge. "It's not open."

"But you just came out of there," he protested.

"My mom's the grandmaster, which means I can

come here whenever I please. It's not open to the public today."

"Grandmaster? What's that? Is that like a caliph?"

There went that brow again, sliding halfway up her forehead. "How do you know about the caliph?" she asked.

Oh, *now* he had her attention. Best to play it cool. He leaned back against one of the palm trees. "I know a lot of stuff. My dad's girlfriend is a magician."

She didn't seem as impressed as she should have been. "Is she a member?"

"Just of the main lodge in Florida."

"*Hmph*. My mom's the head of the Bull and Scorpion. That's what grandmaster means, since you didn't seem to know."

"I thought you said your mom taught drama class."

"She does."

"Both?"

"Why is that so strange?"

He shrugged. Cady had a normal job, too. So he guessed it wasn't. If his weirdo drama teacher back in La Sirena was a magician, it might actually make monologues from *Macbeth* more interesting. "Look, I just need to talk to someone about helping me out with a project."

She took another bite of her apple. "What kind of project are you talking about?"

"I need some information."

"What kind of information?" she asked

"Lodge secrets."

"You're going to have to be more specific."

"How do I know I can trust you?" he asked. "I don't even know your name."

A muffled voice called out from the other side of the door. "Coming, Mama," the girl shouted over her shoulder before turning back to Jupe. "Sorry. Lunch break's over, and I've gotta walk back to school before the bell rings."

"Wait!" Jupe detached himself from the tree. "I'm being serious about needing help. It took me two hours to get out here."

She hesitated. "You'll have to come back when the lodge is open to the public."

"Which is when?"

"Sophic Mass is tomorrow at seven p.m. And that's seven p.m. sharp—if you're even ten seconds late, they won't let you in. They lock the doors. So don't be late." She tossed her half-eaten apple into a trash can and opened the door.

"Mass? What the hell is that? Do I have to dress up?"

"It's a public ritual to raise energy. Bring ten dollars for a donation. We have dinner afterward. It'll be good. My dad grills out back. And it's casual dress. I just wear whatever I had on at school that day."

"Seven tomorrow," he said, more to himself than to her. How the hell was he going to catch another bus out here? He'd have to think of a good story to tell the Holidays, which made his stomach hurt a little, because he didn't really like lying to them.

The girl slipped inside the door and turned around to look at him one last time. "I like your jacket," she said in a softer voice, gesturing toward the monster patches on his sleeves. "A lot of old movies are better than new ones, but I usually like books the best."

Oh.

Wow.

Jupe had a lot to say about that, but he couldn't seem to get the words out. His mouth went all dry, and his heart was beating like he'd been running.

"By the way, my name is Leticia Vega," she said from the shrinking darkness of the closing door, pronouncing her name with a rich, rolling accent. Le-*ti*-ci-a. "And if you *ever* call me 'Letty,' I'll lay a hex on you that'll make all your teeth fall out."

13

If Lon intended to give me another chance to see him naked, I missed it. He called Jupe and the Holidays to report in, and I fell asleep before he'd even finished his phone call. When I woke to the sound of our dueling cell-phone alarms, he was in the other bed, and it was half an hour before sunset. We quickly packed up and began the five-hour drive to Pasadena, trading barren wild coast for the sprawl of Southern California.

And the landscape wasn't the only thing changing: my unexplained strength had abandoned me. Whether it was time or sleep that erased it, I didn't know. But when I tested it on a metal letter opener I found in the motel desk drawer, all I got was a hand cramp.

"Had to be a side effect of your transmutation that first night," Lon said as night settled across the Pacific Coast Highway.

"Almost makes me want to try shifting again if that's the freebie I get for the effort."

"Nothing's ever free."

True. And my eyes were still a little silvery. Not noticeable enough to have to wear sunglasses, so that was something. But deep down, I was still worried the whole thing was a bad omen.

I spent the first couple of hours of our trip chasing broadband signals as I searched for any information I could find on Karlan Rooke. He was in his early seventies, a wealthy man who'd traveled around the world collecting plants for a twelve-acre private estate, which he opened up to the public in the 1980s. It was one of several botanical gardens in the City of Roses, and although it was not as vast as the gardens at the Huntington Library, it was successful because of its niche collection of unusual plants and had earned a quirky nickname.

The Witches' Garden.

Seemed Rooke displayed plants prized for their medicinal value to occultists and magick workers. Some of them were run-of-the-mill herbs. Sage, pennyroyal, mandrake root, and belladonna. But there were also unusual things, such as bloodvine and valrivia—prized by Earthbounds but not typically featured in a botanical garden.

Magus Rooke had been busy.

And although I was able to find the occasional reference to both his time spent in the E∴E∴ and his alleged Crowley lineage, it was only speculation; one of the articles pointed out that although these salacious tidbits often popped up in his Wikipedia entry, they were almost immediately removed.

For all appearances, he was just an eccentric old rich guy, one who was inaccessible to the general public. He was said to live in a private house on the estate and only occasionally spoke at fund-raisers or lectured at local universities on the history of magical herbs. But I didn't have time to contact the Rooke Foundation and formally request a meeting with the man. And after Lon and I discussed the pros and cons, I decided to do something I hadn't done in years. I decided to use my magical pedigree.

As I've said, only a few people in the E∴E∴ knew I was still alive. It was risky to expose myself outside of that circle, especially to someone who'd publicly declared himself an enemy of my parents. But because it was starting to look as if it might be easier to contact the spirit of Howard Hughes than to get an appointment with Karlan Rooke, I figured a spectacle might get his attention.

Lon was still adamant that it wasn't wise to open up a direct channel to the Æthyr with my Heka signature all over it—my mother might pick up on it—so instead of calling Priya directly, I had Jupe send my guardian out to greet Rooke.

Hermeneus spirits had been used as messengers for centuries. In fact, it was the preferred method of long-distance communication between magicians before there were telegrams or telephones or e-mails or texts. Not every magician had a Hermeneus at his or her beck and call, and the ones who did merely *heard* their Æthyric carrier pigeon, because they couldn't see supernatural things such as halos and Heka lines and guardian-spirit projections.

But Priya was no projection; he was solid flesh.

And his appearance in Rooke's bedroom proved to be the attention grabber I'd hoped. Priya reported back that the man was, indeed, shocked to see my guardian, but when Priya pointed out that he hadn't set off the man's house wards and therefore was not hostile, the elderly magician listened to Priya's message and agreed to meet with me.

We arrived at the entrance to Rooke Gardens just before midnight. Down a gated road to our right, lights shone in the windows of a grand mansion that overlooked the grounds from a sloping hill separating the private part of the property from the public gardens. It probably said something about Rooke's trust in our intentions that he didn't welcome us into his home with open arms, but I didn't care.

An old Victorian carriage house served as the public gateway to the gardens. Its Green Man drinking fountain and gargoyle-tipped gutters were pretty charming. Seemed silly to knock, so I ignored both the OPEN EVERY DAY 8 AM TO DUSK sign and the white Heka glow of the low-key protective ward and pushed open the main door into the lobby.

A large mosaic pentagram sparkled over the granite floor. To one side of it sat a quaint ticket booth. On the other was a gift shop, where whimsical esoteric souvenirs filled the windows: kitchen witches, gnomes, and wooden garden signs that encouraged visitors to relax for a "spell" and have a "magical" day.

We didn't get a chance to do either.

A buxom beauty with black hair and a golden tan appeared from a dark hallway. She might have been Lon's age, perhaps a little younger, and she gave off a soft-focus centerfold vibe.

"Hello," she said coolly, heels clicking on the pentagram as she swayed toward us in black slacks and a tomato-red top that showed enough cleavage to make *me* stare. "I'm Karlan's daughter, Evie Rooke. You are Sélène Duval?"

Always weird to hear my real name on a stranger's lips. And she was just that, a stranger. I couldn't remember ever meeting her or her boobs when I knew her father.

But I extended my hand and said, "Thank you for meeting me on such short notice."

She nodded curtly and eyed Lon. If she was reserved with me, she thawed for him, projecting a little extra warmth in her smile. This made the muscles in my neck tighten uncomfortably. "I apologize for the urgency of my request," I said when she'd finished looking him over. "But I'm hoping your father can help me."

"I suppose that depends on what you need . . . and why. Forgive me, but how do we even know you're who you claim to be?"

"It's all right, Evie," a deep voice said from across the room. "It's her."

A tall, thin man with silver hair and black-rimmed glasses stepped into the lobby. His quilted smoking jacket made him look a little like Hugh Hefner's less decrepit brother. And as he padded toward me in black leather slippers and silk pajama bottoms, I recognized the square jaw and the dark eyes behind the glasses.

"Hello, Magus Rooke."

"No one calls me Magus anymore. Or Grandmaster, thank the gods. I'm just plain old Mister." He squinted at me. "Heavens, you're all grown up. It's like looking at a living ghost."

"Real girl, I promise."

"I had a feeling you weren't dead when I saw your parents on the news last year. Do I need to worry about them showing up here, too?"

"I banished both of them to the Æthyr months ago," I said. Not a lie. Not the whole truth, either. "They tried to ritually sacrifice me, so I can assure you that any loyalty I once had for them has vanished."

He looked mildly shocked for a moment but recovered quickly. "Enola was always one for high dramatics." He flicked curious eyes toward Lon. "And who might this be?"

"Someone who watches over her," Lon said, slipping his hand around the back of my neck. "We need your word that you'll keep this meeting quiet."

Mr. Rooke gave Lon an amused smile. "I'm not sure who you think I'd tell. I haven't had contact with another E∴E∴ member in years, and I don't plan to change that. Although I must admit, I'm rather interested to hear why you think I can help you."

I lifted my chin. "Perhaps you could start by telling me if a private detective came to see you about me?"

"Ah." Rooke stared at me for a moment before gesturing toward the inner door leading into the gardens. "I knew this would come back to haunt me. Why don't we take a walk outside and discuss it privately?" When I protested, he cut me off and gestured to Lon, saying, "Your watcher here can follow along with Evie, but I can't talk about other Ekklesia Eleusia members with an outsider. I'm still under magical oath."

"You discussed it with Robert Wildeye," Lon said, slanting Rooke a cold look.

Rooke tugged the lapels of his smoking jacket together and shuffled toward the garden door. "And I hope you are smart enough to realize what this tells you about that man."

Wildeye was one of us.

"Come, Miss Duval. I'm an old man with limited stores of energy."

I didn't want to be separated from Lon. And I definitely didn't want to leave him alone with Tits Ahoy, but the magical oath was a real thing—all the lodge leaders had to undergo it. And I needed information he had, so I tamped down my uneasiness and followed him out the door.

The night air was warmer here than on the coast,

and the wide cement path that snaked through the lush grounds was lit by tiny white lights and the occasional gas lamp that stood over benches or the warm spotlights artfully installed at the trunks of trees. I walked side-by-side with Rooke, who didn't speak until we were several paces ahead of Lon and Evie.

"Quite a showstopper, that guardian of yours," he said. "I've seen a lot of odd things in my life, but that was new."

"Puts other Hermeneus projections to shame," I agreed. But I didn't come to swap magical pointers with him, so before he asked how I'd managed to end up with a guardian like Priya, I said, "Wildeye was E∴E∴?"

"Vancouver lodge in the 1980s. His family's there. He apparently never broke with the order officially—"

"Unlike you," I said.

He shrugged casually, a smug smile on his lips. "No, he never caused a stir. I asked an old friend to look into him when he first contacted me last fall. His family had been in the order since the 1930s, but they were quiet and forgettable."

But memorable enough for Dare to want to use him. "Did he tell you who he was working for?"

"He wouldn't give me a name, but he indicated that it was a client with more cash than sense and someone powerful enough to make his life miserable. I felt a little sorry for the man. He was warded to the hilt with charms when I met with him in September."

Rooke's words came easily, and it felt as if he was being honest, but I wished Lon could verify it for me. I briefly glanced over my shoulder to spy him talking with Evie, who was smiling and using sweeping hand gestures to point out things along the path. I supposed if Lon heard something in her emotions to raise his hackles, he'd let me know.

"What exactly did the detective want to know about me?" I asked Rooke.

"If I knew whether you were alive and, if so, where you'd been hiding. As I said, I suspected you might be alive when I saw the Duvals on the news. But it was just a passing curiosity, and I didn't care one way or another, to be perfectly honest. No offense."

"None taken. What else did he want to know?"

"Mostly about your parents. How well I knew them, for how long, whether I believed they were capable of all those killings."

"Believe me, they were."

"You're preaching to the choir, my dear. Enola was one of the reasons I left the order."

"I remember you fighting with my parents. And with the caliph."

Rooke sniffled and glanced at me. "You heard he passed away last month?"

I nodded stiffly.

"Made me sad to hear it, frankly. I don't know how he's fared over the last decade, but when I knew him, the caliph was a decent man."

"Not decent enough to keep you in the order?"

"He wasn't the reason I left, but I'll admit that his lack of action frustrated me. He was blinded by his loyalty to Enola and her New Occult Order malarkey. Anyone could see she had no interest in uniting all the orders. She was a power-hungry manipulator who'd use anything at her disposal to get her way— sex, medicinals, dark magick. Nothing was sacred. The E∴E∴ was her playground, and she used every resource it had for her own personal agendas."

That I could believe.

"Even your father was her dupe. I apologize for being frank, but he worshipped the ground she walked on and would've done anything she asked, no matter how immoral or dangerous. Enola was a tornado ripping through the order, and Alexander was her one-man cleanup crew, sweeping all the evidence beneath the rug."

"Even bodies?"

"Takes a special kind of evil to murder your own child."

"My brother," I murmured, studying Rooke's face. "You're the one who told Wildeye."

He nodded. "I hadn't thought about little Victor Duval in years. When I was grandmaster of the Pasadena lodge, I traveled to Florida twice a year, so I saw Victor a handful of times. Your parents proclaimed him the first Moonchild, but he was a sickly child, physically and mentally. I think they knew fairly early on that their conception ritual was a failure."

"So they killed him?"

The garden path split in front of us. A wrought-iron signpost held two hand-lettered signs, one pointing to a succulent garden, and the other to "Sacred Trees." Rooke headed toward the trees. "I don't know for certain, but a rumor circulated among some of the officers. One of the caliph's magi, Magus Frances—did you ever hear about her?"

"Vaguely. I think she died when I was a toddler."

He nodded. "Back before you were born, she had a vision during a psychotropic ritual and claimed to have seen your father drowning Victor in a bathtub."

"Dear God . . ."

"The caliph dismissed it, was furious at Frances for making accusations. Frances wasn't exactly the most stable of magicians, so the rest of us dismissed it, too. And your parents appeared to be grieving. I didn't know your mother very well at the time, so I just chalked it up to Frances partaking of one-too-many magic mushrooms."

"When did you discover her vision was real?"

He pushed his glasses farther up the bridge of his nose. "No one did, to my knowledge. It was only the word of one crazy old magician against your parents'. But as I came to know your mother, I began to wonder."

"Why? What else did she do?"

"Nothing concrete, really. Just the way she treated people. She was beautiful, and she had this way about her that made you feel as though she were royalty—aloof and bored one moment, ripping you to shreds the next. You never knew what to expect. People secretly called her Queen, comparing her split personality to one of two Lewis Carroll characters. Was she the calculating Red Queen today or the furious Queen of Hearts? We never knew."

This astounded me. Growing up, I never saw her angry. Not really.

Rooke stooped to pick up a slender broken bough and, after snapping off a few dead branches, wielded it like a walking stick, tapping its tip against the path. "People were frightened of her anger, but it was the coolness that bothered me."

As I kept an eye on Lon and Evie, Rooke went on to relate a story about my mother unemotionally slapping a teenage boy in the middle of a ritual for flubbing his Latin and another about a time she calmly stabbed a waitress's arm with a fork after the girl accidentally knocked a glass off the table. When Rooke started a third story, I cut him off.

"You don't have to convince me that she was damaged," I said. "I know it firsthand. I'm more interested in the circumstances of my origins, my conception. What can you tell me about the Moonchild spell?"

He lightly tapped the end of his walking stick against an open-mouthed gargoyle molded into the arm of a cement bench. "Ah, yes. Call down a great spirit into the womb, and give birth to a goddess. A classic ritual. I'm assuming you've researched my grandfather's version."

"We both know she didn't use Crowley's version or the older standard ritual."

"She claimed to have perfected it. Altered it somehow. The order toasted her success when she gave birth to Victor, but after years of watching him catch every virus known to mankind and be shuffled in and out of the hospital, people began to wonder. And when he showed no magical aptitude whatsoever? Well . . ."

"What changed between my brother's ritual and mine?"

"It was modified—no doubt about that. Enola told the caliph she came across the solution during one of her trips home to France. One of her secret magical partners oversaw your conception. Someone from another order—"

"Frater Blue. He showed up with my parents to oversee me being sacrificed last year. I sent him to the Æthyr with my parents."

Rooke raised a brow. "My, someone's been busy. I suppose there's no point in suggesting you track him down and ask him for a copy of the ritual."

"Dead end," I quipped with a tight smile.

We passed an unusual tree from India known as the sleeping almond. A small metal sign identified the bark as having properties "similar to milk of the poppy" during certain years of its growth. I blinked at it for a moment; the geeky magician in me was awed. Powdered and charged with Heka, the bark of this tree was a valuable ingredient in a couple of the medicinals I made. On a few occasions, I'd ordered it from shady overseas vendors, shelling out several hundred dollars a pop for a sliver of bark the size of a fingernail. Crazy that Rooke had it here. And at the tree's base grew a thick shrub of a rare variety of silver jasmine. No wonder this man was rich.

"You know nothing else about the modified ritual?" I said, breathing in the scent of the jasmine as we continued strolling. "How the Moonchild is supposed to manifest? What my mother hoped to accomplish?"

"Oh, she promised to give birth to the greatest magician known to the world. My grandfather would be a mere footnote, she bragged, forgotten under the Moonchild's superior abilities. Magick would become respected across the globe, and we'd no longer be pushed to the fringes of society."

"Yes, I heard that on a regular basis," I said sourly.

"We all did. I'm sure it was humiliating when she realized we all knew you weren't a messiah. Skilled with Heka, yes. But you didn't bring about the 'New Aeon' that Enola promised."

"Which is probably why she eventually snapped and went on a killing spree. Were there no rumors about her documenting the Moonchild ritual somewhere? I can't believe she wrote all those books about magick theory but didn't want to publish her greatest achievement."

"That is a puzzle, isn't it? From my perspective at the time, their Moonchild rituals were a lot of talk without substance, like everything else your parents embarked upon. No offense."

"None taken."

"But it wasn't them alone. One day, I looked up and realized that I was sitting around with a group of men and women, supposedly the most talented magicians in the world, yet half of them were *déclassé* trash with boring middle-class lives. They got cancer, suffered through divorce and depression, lost their savings after making poor investment decisions."

"They were only human."

"Precisely. If they were so prestigious and talented, why couldn't they use magick to better their lives? They should all be successful politicians or great actors, wealthy and healthy. Magical talent was a gift, and they were squandering it. I was surrounded by fools, murderers, and some of the dullest people I'd ever known in my life. So I left before their bad karma brushed off on me and my family."

I couldn't really argue. I hadn't been active in the order since I left home at seventeen. Lon always joked that he wasn't a "joiner," and maybe I wasn't, either.

"So my advice to you would be to stop seeking the Moonchild ritual. Whatever evil intent Enola had when she conceived you doesn't need to define your life. My grandfather was a great magician, but he was also a loathsome human being who didn't give two goddamns about the people in his life unless they helped him reach magical nirvana. So when it comes to my bloodline and his legacy, I try to discard the bad and keep the good. Maybe you should do the same."

If only it were that easy.

We stopped in front of a hedgerow labyrinth. Rooke held out his hand, offering to take me through the maze. He had to be freaking kidding. No way was I going inside something like that at night. A memory surfaced of watching the snowy labyrinth scene in *The Shining* at Lon's house. I remembered holding Jupe's feet hostage and tickling him during the scary bits. I think Lon was tickling me, too, but that seemed . . . odd for him.

At that point, the memory went a little fuzzy. My temples started throbbing, so I stopped trying to force it and turned around to track Lon and Evie. Watching her flirt with him in that low-cut red top of hers made me feel like a snorting bull, ready to charge. But I still needed one last piece of information from her father.

"What is Naos Ophis?"

14

Rooke didn't respond right away. He watched his daughter step off the path to pick a stem of the jasmine we'd passed and hold it up for Lon to smell. After a time, he finally said, "Temple of the Serpent."

"What is it, and what does it have to do with my parents?"

"Are you familiar with Ophites?"

I shook my head.

"It was a heretical Gnostic sect that popped up in the second century or so. They thought the serpent in the Garden of Eden was a hero, because it gave mankind the gift of wisdom, Sophia."

"As in the Sophic Mass?"

All E∴E∴ lodges put on this dog-and-pony show one night every week or month, depending on the size of the lodge. I'd attended mass regularly in Florida until I went on the lam.

"Yes. Only this Gnostic sect took things to the extreme, shall we say, and believed Sophia and the serpent to be as important as Christ himself. For the most part, the sect died out in the third century. But a small group of followers persisted. There's said to be a group of them in both Greece and France."

"France? Is this what my mother found there?"

"I don't know. There's rumored to be a secret sect of them in the States. Your mother mentioned them on occasion when she was visiting the Pasadena lodge in the 1980s."

"What did she say about them?"

"Nothing substantial. She was always interested in other magical orders, so any comment she made went in one ear and out the other . . . that is, until Magus Frances had another vision. She said she saw your mother studying in the serpent temple in secret."

"Studying what?"

"She didn't know, but she said Enola was hell-bent on it. Whatever it might have been, Frances thought it would tear the order apart. Perhaps it was a coincidence that she and your father attempted the Moonchild ritual again and you were born a year later. I don't know." He bent his stick in the middle, snapping it in two, and tossed it into the maze. "But if you're looking for the key to your origins, I'd seek out the Ophites."

My pulse pounded. Okay, this was good, something substantial to follow. Worth the whole trip down here. But just when I was about to ask Rooke about the temple's location, I got a little distracted.

Several yards behind us, Evie sat down on a

bench to scribble something on a business card while Lon remained standing. She handed it up to him, then playfully snatched it back when he reached for it. Laughing, she held it out for him again, and when he took it, she slowly ran her fingers over his.

What the hell did she think she was doing?

Any temporary excitement I'd felt over Rooke's information vanished under the flare of jealousy that twisted my stomach into a knot and made my face overheat. Violent girl-on-girl thoughts filled my head.

Her fingers fell away from his, only to trail down the front of his shirt and rest on the waistband of his jeans, which she gave a gentle tug.

Nuh-uh. No. Hell, no.

I felt the rush of power ripple over my skin but didn't recognize what was happening. Hot anger mixed with an oblique energy that swirled around me and shot toward Evie like an arrow. Branches swayed. Leaves scattered. I hadn't moved an inch, but I felt the bark and leaves and flowers as if I were a stormy wind howling down the garden path, as if I were touching them with my own hands.

I felt the cool metal of the trash can as it lifted off the path and slammed against a nearby tree. The dense weight of the cement bench as it rose—

With Evie still on it.

Her mouth fell open. She gripped the molded gargoyle arm of the bench in terror as her legs dangled a foot above the paved path. Two feet. Three. When I blinked, my vision changed; silver light blanketed the gardens. Somewhere in the back of my head, I knew this was bad. It was night, and I wasn't standing in a protective ward. My mother could—

"Cady!"

My gaze snapped to Lon's. The commanding intensity there was a bucket of cold water over my wayward power. I gritted my teeth and reeled it back in with a growl. The silver light retreated. Half a second later, the cement bench crashed to the ground. Evie cried out as she bounced off and tumbled to her knees.

I struggled for breath as Lon hesitated, then rushed to help Evie up. She didn't look all that hurt, more shocked than anything. I was a little shocked, too. What the hell was the matter with me? Rooke had just finished telling me about my evil mother's crazy outbursts of anger, and here I was, following in her footsteps.

I turned to him with an apology on my tongue and saw the evidence of what I'd just done. Not only was unfiltered awe written all over his face, but the silver light lingering in my eyes was reflected in his glasses, two eerily glowing dots.

"My God," Rooke murmured.

"I'm sorry. I didn't mean . . ." I started, glancing back at Evie. Lon was pulling her up, making sure she was okay as she brushed dirt off her knees.

"Damn me to hell," Rooke swore as we hurried toward them. "What in God's name did Enola do to you?"

"That's what I'm trying to find out."

He didn't say anything else until we were a few yards away. "I truly don't know the exact location of the serpent temple, but Magus Frances said it was in the desert, and your mother would visit it—back and forth in an afternoon—when your parents came to the Pasadena temple, so it can't be that far from L.A."

Maybe not, but we couldn't just roam around Southern California looking for a hidden temple. "You've got to know something else. Mr. Rooke, please."

He clutched his smoking jacket lapels in one hand and shook his head. Then something changed in his face. He halted long enough to tell me one last thing under his breath. "They are snake handlers, like the Pentecostal churches in the South. But they use exotic snakes—big, colorful ones that don't belong in the desert."

Lon didn't say anything until we were back inside the SUV. While he started the engine, I pulled down the visor mirror to confirm what I already knew: reptilian pupils ringed with silver and a halo so bright it cast metallic light across the dash. I slammed the visor back into place as he pulled out of the garden parking lot, heading back toward the residential neighborhood we'd passed through to get there.

"Call Jupe," he finally said in a flat voice. "Get him to summon Priya and find out if he noticed that in the Æthyr."

"I didn't—My tail." I didn't feel it slithering down the leg of my pants in the garden, so that was something. "My horns didn't . . . did they?"

Lon shook his head and flicked a glance at my halo. "Just that. And your eyes. Cady—"

"I know, I know," I mumbled. "I lost control. I don't know what got into me."

But that wasn't really true, was it? I *did* know. I was jealous as hell over a man who wasn't mine. And that was nearly as terrifying as the Moonchild power, which had flared up as fast as my anger and temporarily overridden my good sense.

I dug out my cell phone and stared at the time on the screen. "It's past one in the morning," I told Lon. "Jupe's asleep."

Lon opened his mouth to argue but changed his mind.

"We can check in the morning," I said. "What's done is done. If my mother detected what just happened, there's nothing I can do to undo it."

Traffic picked up as Lon headed into Old Town, where a handful of late-night pedestrians strolled down sidewalks lined with bars and restaurants. Lon was asking me something, what I'd learned from Rooke. But I couldn't concentrate for all the worries clamoring inside my throbbing head. Rooke's insights about my mother. My dead brother. The serpent temple. My screwed-up memories. The jealousy I felt over Lon. The barely restrained power coursing through my veins.

A keening panic gathered in the pit of my stomach.

"Pull over," I pleaded, desperately punching the button to lower my window. Why wasn't it working? Stupid safety lock. "I need air."

The SUV turned sharply off the main road onto a small side street and swung into an empty parking space. I lurched out of my seat and onto the curb, slamming the door behind me. For a second, I thought I might throw up. But after I took a few steps and focused on my breathing, the nausea faded.

I slowed down and rested my hands on my hips, glancing around for any nearby Earthbounds who might spot my insanely bright silver halo. Not a one, but then, I'd only seen one since we left Big Sur. So strange. I'd become used to Earthbounds outnumbering humans in La Sirena; it was easy to forget the rest of the country wasn't like that.

Palm-tree shadows striped the sidewalk below my feet. Lingering scents of expensive tapas and wine hung in the air as I passed the last sidewalk café on the block, which looked to be closing up for the night. Live music pulsed from a neon-lit club across the street. Beyond here, the noise petered out.

Unhurried, steady steps approached me from behind. A few seconds later, Lon's deep voice floated over my shoulder. "You okay?"

"I think so," I said.

"You ready to talk about what happened back there?"

I swung around to face him. "I lost control."

"Did Rooke say something to make you angry?"

"Nope."

"Because you looked pissed as hell."

"Well, you looked like your tongue was going to fall out of your mouth."

"What?"

"Don't play dumb. I saw Evie flirting it up with you."

Lon squinted down at me with a puzzled look on his face. "She was trying to get information out of me."

"*O-o-oh*, she was trying for more than that. And clearly, you weren't discouraging her, because I saw her giving you her phone number. Were you going to drop me off at the hotel while you called her up for a nightcap?"

Lon's head slowly tilted to the side, as if he couldn't believe what I was saying but was trying to make sense of it. I knew at that point that I sounded like a crazed, clingy harpy, but I just couldn't stop myself.

"Her hands were all over you," I said. "You practically had your nose wedged between her breasts. Which weren't real, by the way."

"Whoa," Lon warned as his brows snapped together.

"Don't 'whoa' me. I'm not stupid. I know—" What? What exactly did I know?

My head pulsed as it tried to make sense of the hurt clawing at my chest. I was insanely, painfully jealous, and it didn't match what was in my head. He was not my boyfriend. He was just an overly generous man who'd opened his home to me and taken me in, as if I were some ragamuffin orphan who needed shelter.

I knew this.

But I didn't care. I was still hurt.

"Is that what you like? Women who look like that?" I asked as angry tears stung my eyes. "Can't you manage to spend a couple of days alone with me without sniffing after the first oversexed bitch who shoves her tits in your face?"

"Cady—"

I grunted and shoved at his chest. "I got naked in front of you—I let you take *pictures* of me, for the love of God! Maybe you think of me as just some oddity that Father Carrow foisted off on you, but I have feelings. I have pride."

"Cady, will you just shut up for one second—"

"If you want her so badly, go back and get her. But don't be surprised when she lassos an entrapment spell around your horns. You can't trust magicians."

His lips quivered. "Oh, is that right?"

"Most of them," I corrected irritably.

He burst out laughing. Laughing! And it was the most open, joyful laugh I'd ever heard out of him. I was horrified. Where was the damned moon power when I needed it? Because I really could have used a little telekinesis to pick up the nearby city newspaper rack and bash it over Lon's head.

"Is this just a joke? Am I a joke to you?" I said.

"Oh, Cady, I'm not laughing at you," he said, still grinning. "I'm happy."

"Happy?"

"Very." His hand reached out to touch my hair.

"You're an ass," I said, slapping his hand away.

"Maybe I am, because I damn sure like seeing you jealous."

"I'm not jealous." I totally was. "I'm . . . angry."

"No, you're angry because you're jealous, and you don't understand why."

"That's right, I forgot—you know my feelings better than I do. Screw you."

He chuckled. "You have *no* idea how much I'd love to."

Was he making fun of me? I honestly didn't know. But in case he was, I shoved him again, hard. His eyes tightened as the smile fell away from his face. Crap. Before I could move away, he grabbed my forearms and yanked me closer. "Go on," he murmured in a rough voice near my ear. "Push me one more time."

I tried to think of a sharp retort, but several seconds passed, and all I did was hold my breath and stare at the collar of his jacket while my pulse swished in my temples. When I finally drew in a quick breath, I smelled leather and soap and the intoxicating scent of *Lon*. My body liked that smell quite a bit—so much it temporarily forgot about being angry.

"Listen to me," Lon said in a low voice. "I've got

about as much interest in seeing Evie Rooke again as I do in getting chicken pox, so I hope you pried some helpful information out of her father. And just so we're clear, I haven't touched another woman since I met you."

Oh. Wait . . . "Why?"

He released one of my arms to tentatively trace a lock of hair framing my face. "Because I haven't wanted to." The hand holding my other arm slid around my back and held me closer. "You might have trouble believing this, but I spend most of my time being grateful you're near me or counting the minutes until you will be again."

My heart fluttered wildly. "You do?" I whispered.

"I do."

"Lon . . ." I rested my hands on his chest when he pulled me closer. His heart pounded under my palm. I surveyed his face for some sort of proof. My gaze shifted over the hard jaw darkened with stubble. The long hollows of his cheeks. The narrowed green eyes and the fine lines radiating from their outer corners. It was a heart-stopping, wildly handsome face.

One that I desperately wanted closer to mine.

And as if compelled by my will, that face did come closer.

"Please don't let this be a mistake," he murmured.

His lips grazed mine, light and soft. Seeking permission. I exhaled a shaky breath, and he kissed me. Slowly at first. Reverently. A kiss that would be forgiven with a single Hail Mary. But it was enough to send goose bumps over my arms and a rush of joy through my chest. My arms wound around him as if they'd done it a thousand times. And as I molded my hands to the hard planes of muscle covering his back, he crushed me against his chest.

And just like that, all bets were off.

Tongues tangled. Teeth clashed. We kissed each other like desperate addicts who'd stumbled upon a forgotten stash of drugs, grunting and moaning with pleasure—too lost to care about the headlights that crossed over us as cars sped by or the distant drunken laughter from the club at the end of the block.

None of it mattered.

When I momentarily pulled back to gasp for breath, he dragged his mouth down my neck, kissing me like someone intimately familiar with every architectural detail of my body: the underside of my chin, the pillar of my throat, the shell of my ear, and the hidden alcove of sensitive skin below it. By the time he'd circled back to my mouth, my knees were wobbly, and I was wetter than the ocean.

I don't think I'd ever wanted anyone so badly. If he'd asked me to, I would have stripped off my clothes in the middle of the sidewalk.

He pulled back, chest heaving. "We can't do this."

"Too late," I said with a lazy grin. "I think we just did."

He gripped my jacket tighter, trying to stop our

bodies from swaying together like magnets. "We need to focus. This is a distraction."

"And a damn good one," I murmured, dipping my head to capture his earlobe between my teeth. Christ, he smelled good. He groaned and palmed my ass, holding me against the substantial hardness between his legs.

"Yes," I encouraged wantonly.

"No." He pushed away again and rested his forehead against mine. "I mean it, Cady. This is weakness and . . . complicated. We've got other things we should be focusing on. We need to be on guard, in our right minds."

"Okay, okay," I said, breathless and frustrated.

"Let's just cool off," he said, but that was hard to do when his hands were stroking up and down my back. "Think of something else."

"Like what?" My fingers trailed down his chest, trying to cop whatever feel I could get over his T-shirt. "Something boring like baseball? Margaret Thatcher naked on a cold day?"

"Gonna need more than that," he said with a slow grin, peeling away my straying hand to thread his fingers between mine.

"Hmm, what about all those flying cockroaches in the abandoned cannery?"

"That's better. What else?"

"Smell of wet dog," I suggested. "No—smell of Foxglove after she rolled around in that dead animal carcass she found in the woods."

He laughed. "Christ, that was disgusting."

"I couldn't stop gagging."

"You weren't the one who had to bathe her."

"I held the hose! And I never could figure out what was worse, Foxglove's fur or Jupe barfing all over the grass after he handed you the shampoo."

Lon grinned. "Jupe was worse, hands down."

"Ugh, so gross." I squeezed Lon's hand tighter. "I remember you took two showers afterward, and no one felt like eating dinner. Then we watched that old stop-motion movie with the fighting skeletons."

"*Jason and the Argonauts.*"

"Right. Then . . ." I remembered something else happening after Jupe went to bed, but it was fuzzy. "You were wearing this T-shirt," I said, running a finger over the faded graphic.

Lon blinked several times, almost as if he'd gotten sentimental. "It doesn't matter."

I felt strangely sentimental myself. "I sort of miss Jupe."

"Me, too," he mumbled, so low I barely heard it. He cleared his throat. "But what we need to be thinking about right now is your mother."

Talk about a cold shower.

He cradled my face in his hands. "We're going to find a way to stop her. Come hell or high water, I will not let her take you away from me. You got that?"

I nodded.

He dropped one last lingering kiss on my

forehead, then pulled back and slung his arm around my shoulders. "Why don't we go get some food?" he said, leading me back to the SUV.

"And while we find a place that's open, you can tell me everything you learned from Rooke."

15

Downtown Los Angeles was a twenty-minute drive from Pasadena. And since Lon had spent a lot of time there for work—doing shoots, booking shoots, or catching planes to shoots—he drove us to a hotel he'd stayed in before, a swank building on Flower Street with a twenty-four-hour restaurant inside. Even at two in the morning, a handful of people filtered in and out of the modern lobby, so I donned my sunglasses again.

At Lon's suggestion, instead of heading straight up to our room to continue what we'd started, we camped out on the restaurant's outdoor patio, eating, talking, and using the hotel's Wi-Fi to research our next plan of attack. He stayed on his side of the table, and I stayed on mine. I tried my damnedest not to think about the kiss or how much I wanted seconds. I truly tried. When I occasionally slipped, Lon wouldn't even glance up. He'd just smile to himself and say, "Focus, Cadybell."

Somewhere between all my nonsaintly thoughts,

I managed to tell Lon everything I'd learned from Rooke. But even knowing now that the Naos Ophis group had roots in an ancient Gnostic sect, we still found zero information about a local group online. And I do mean *nothing*. The thought crossed my mind that just because the temple existed before I was born, that didn't mean it still existed now. Because it was one thing if Rooke never found it in the 1980s but quite another if we couldn't now. What doesn't have an internet trail? Either they were an insanely tricksy lot, or we were on a fool's errand.

"Look at this." Lon scooted his chair closer to mine and showed me his laptop screen. "A splinter group of Ophites popped up in Crete in the late 1600s. After a brutal war and the longest siege in history, the Ottomans ousted the ruling Venetians. In doing so, they raided a hidden temple whose congregation killed snakes during rituals. The Ottomans found 'hundreds upon hundreds of serpent-skin banners.' They destroyed the temple, but after studying the Ottoman records, scholars now wonder if the group had combined Ophite beliefs with the older cult of the snake goddess—this one. From the sixteenth century BCE."

He pointed to a picture of two famous Minoan snake goddess statues: bare-breasted women holding two snakes above their heads, one in each outstretched hand. One statue was smaller than the other.

"They're believed to be the mother goddess and her daughter," Lon said.

Mother and daughter. A chill raced down my arms. I stared at the statues and thought about everything Lon had just said. "Rooke said the serpent temple was using big exotic snakes. Where would they get those?"

"Exotic-pet shops?" Lon suggested.

"Maybe that's a good place to start looking."

Studying a map, we pinpointed cities in the area of the Mojave Desert bordering Los Angeles, "Inland Empire" cities such as San Bernardino and Riverside and other places such as Lancaster and Palm Springs. If Rooke said my mother made day trips to the serpent temple from Pasadena, we felt fairly confident gauging how far away was too far.

But when we drilled down for information on the exotic-pet stores that made the cut, only two in our targeted area seemed to carry more than a few chameleons and a python or two. One was a fish-and-reptile wholesaler, and the other was a company that provided trained exotic animals to movie sets. That one mentioned that special requests were "negotiable." Since it opened earliest, we decided to try it first and the next morning drove an hour in rush-hour traffic to Riverside.

No place I've ever been matches the endless urban sprawl stretching over the L.A. Basin, where the sun washes over miles of fast-food drive-thrus, malls, and auto-repair shops, one city bleeds into the next, and everything is connected by a web of busy highways and too-short on-ramps. There's something achingly familiar about the angle of sunlight and the mountains and palm trees, and then you realize it's because you've seen it a thousand times before, in every TV show and movie filmed in this area.

But the farther inland you go, the more you feel a sense of disconnect. And it was in this domesticated borderland between the heart of L.A. and the desert where we spent two hours being bounced around the Hollyweird Animal Ranch. The property was a maze of outdoor enclosures and buildings, and it felt nice to be strolling and breathing fresh air. We saw some brightly colored, beautiful snakes. But when we questioned management about special requests to arrange purchase of exotic snakes, they insisted it wasn't something they'd ever do. "We partner with the L.A. Zoo," the reptile trainer informed us testily. "All of our exotics are brought in by special license, and we're regularly inspected by the state."

Lon confirmed that the man was telling the truth once we were back in the SUV.

"Strike one," I said wearily.

It was almost nine in the morning. Past my bed-time—again. I was tired and cranky, and whatever weight I'd lost in the hospital must have been creeping back on, because the waistband of my skinny jeans was starting to dig into my stomach.

"The other one's in Ontario," Lon said. "It's not far."

We had a better feeling about R&N Reptiles and Aquatics. For one, they'd taken a lot of flak from animal-rights groups who'd found their facilities wanting. Second, they were near the Ontario airport, and as Lon pointed out, most illegal exotic-animal imports were shipped via air.

None of this had me enthused to check the place out. And when I saw the dreary strip-mall building that housed the shop and the dusty unmarked delivery truck being loaded from a dock on the side, my internal creep-o-meter started beeping.

It didn't help that the man loading the delivery truck—who was an Earthbound, the first one I'd seen since yesterday—was shouting profanities at the guy driving it, gesticulating wildly. Looked as if any second they might break into a fistfight.

"We're not here to make friends," Lon reminded me as we drove past the uncomfortable scene and made our way to the front. He parked next to custom aquarium installer, who headed inside through an unmarked door. Seemed he knew where he was going, so we followed his lead.

Row after row of metal shelving stretched over a long room with unfinished cement floors and dim warehouse lighting. Mismatched sizes of glass tanks and metal cages crowded the shelves, most with laminated signs on which were scribbled breed, age, and cost. Hundreds of snakes and lizards, stacked like cargo.

Snakes don't bother me. Never have. But what bothered me now was the sad, shoddy state of the store and the wretched stench. Most reptiles don't have a scent. But their urine and feces do, and that's what I smelled now. Soiled cages that weren't properly kept. It wasn't simply noticeable, it was overwhelming. Two steps inside the door, and I was coughing, covering my mouth with my arm.

"Hey," Lon said quietly, bending his head near mine. "You okay?"

"The smell," I choked out, eyes watering from the sharp ammonia in the air.

"It's a little rough," he agreed. But he didn't seem to be as affected.

Meanwhile, I was seriously wondering if I was going to be sick. "Jesus," I murmured, catching another scent mixed in with all the dirty cages. "Death. Dead snakes in here."

"An operation this big, I'd imagine so."

"This is terrible, Lon."

"I'm starting to understand why the animal-rights groups were up in arms over this." He discreetly pulled up the hem of his shirt to wipe my face. "Can you do this? You could wait in the car."

I shook my head, pushing away nausea. "I can do it."

"You sure?"

"Yeah. Wait, don't turn around." My stinging eyes followed the aquarium installer from the parking lot. He was chatting with a man who unlocked a door behind the front counter. It swung open into a brightly lit room lined with chicken-wire cages, big white plastic buckets, and tied-up burlap bags.

Neon-yellow and green scales flashed from

behind the chicken wire. The door shut behind them. A sign on the door read, OFF LIMITS: EMPLOYEES ONLY.

"They're definitely keeping tropical stuff back there," I whispered.

"That's a good sign, but don't get your hopes up. Let's find a manager."

Breathing through my mouth, I surveyed the cavernous layout with Lon. We spotted someone stocking grungy freezers with vacuum-packed bags of frozen mice. He suggested we wait for one of the owners, Ned, who was apparently the guy who'd led the aquarium installer into the back room.

Five minutes later, Ned approached us at an uneven glass counter that displayed bottles of reptile supplements and medicines. Dressed in a gray polo shirt with the R&N logo on the front pocket, Ned was short and muscular, with a receding blond hairline. Even without Lon's empathic ability, I could tell right away that the man didn't trust us.

Guess that was fair, because I didn't trust him, either. He reeked of lizard piss and cheap, chalky laundry detergent. Something else, too, the death I'd smelled when we walked in. It was clinging to his clothes and trailed from the door in back.

"Are you the couple asking for me?" he said in a guarded voice.

"We are." I forced myself to smile. "You must be the 'N' in 'R&N.'"

"That's right. How can I help?"

Lon gave a fake name and said, "We're looking for something a little different and heard you could help us."

"Maybe, maybe not." He leaned over the counter with his arms spread, hands gripping the edge for support. "What are you looking for?"

This guy didn't seem like someone we could sweet-talk, so I got right to the point. "We've been told there's a Pentecostal church in the desert that handles snakes. We don't care about what they do there, but we're looking for someone in that church—for personal reasons. And we were hoping someone here might've heard of it."

Ned blinked several times and tightened his grip on the edge of the counter. "A church? Can't say that I've heard of anything like that. What kind of snakes do they handle?"

"Exotic," Lon said. "Big and bright. Possibly venomous."

"Sounds like something they'd have to buy out of state."

"Look, we don't give a damn about state laws," I said, struggling not to breathe in when Ned was exhaling. "We're not cops or reporters. We're just looking for that church. You don't have to tell us if you supply them or not. We couldn't care less."

Ned got a little peeved with my gruff manner. "That may be, but I'm not sure anyone here could help you. We don't deal directly to clients. If the church wanted snakes, they'd probably go through a pet store, who'd buy them from us. We get dozens of orders every day, and we don't ask them for the names of their buyers."

"Seems like you might remember orders for exotic snakes."

"Like I said, they'd need to go out of state for that."

"Are you sure? It sort of looked like you had the special orders back there," I said, nodding toward the chicken-wire room.

Wrong thing to say. Ned narrowed his eyes at me. "I'm fully licensed and have passed every state inspection. So if you're one of those Save the Reptiles nutjobs, you can save something else—your own breath."

"No affiliation with any of those groups, " Lon assured him. "What about another reptile wholesaler in the area who might have an . . . interstate business?"

"There isn't anyone else. I service accounts from Covina to Palm Springs to Bakersfield. So maybe you should try L.A.," he said defensively. "And as far as this snake-handling church, I haven't heard of anything like that out here, so I'm afraid I can't help you."

"What about someone else here?" I asked quickly. "Someone in sales, maybe?"

"He's working with a paying client."

"We can wait."

"Maybe I didn't make myself clear. He's working with a client who doesn't pay us to air his laundry. And he's working for a boss who'd fire him if he did.

Now, unless I can place an order for you, I've got work to do."

He pushed away from the counter and gave us one last semithreatening look before storming away. Fine by me. He wasn't going to tell us anything freely, and the stench inside the shop was making me want to hack up all the goat-cheese crêpes I'd eaten back at the fancy hotel. So I told Lon to meet me at the car and then marched back out the front door and took a nice big breath of smoggy air. Give me dusty asphalt over dead reptiles any day.

Dusty asphalt and valrivia smoke, to be exact.

I glanced across the covered entry and saw the Earthbound who'd been loading the truck around the side, the guy who'd been screaming obscenities like they were going out of style. He was leaning against the building with one foot up, the sides of his black industrial lifting brace undone and flapping around his ribs.

Maybe my sense of smell was all screwy from Reptile Hell, but the first thing I thought after the smoke blew away was that this guy smelled . . . approachable.

"Bad day?" I asked.

He glanced at me without moving his head, lazily looking me over until he spotted my silver halo and did a double take. "Very bad day," he said, offering me valrivia.

I waved it away. "It smells wonderful, but I'm too nauseated right now. It's a little overripe inside," I said, motioning at the door.

"*Hmph.* You're telling me." He pushed his dark hair back with one hand while flicking ash with the other. He wasn't a bad-looking guy, maybe a few years older than me. "The owners are cheap bastards who haven't cleaned a cage in years. They hired the secretary's son to do it a couple weeks back, but he's terrified of snakes. Best I can tell, all he does is sweep and take naps in his mom's office."

"Kids," I said conspiratorially.

"The whole place is a toilet. Management, clients, buyers, drivers—all of 'em."

"Well, they certainly didn't help me."

He lifted his chin. "You a new customer? Haven't seen you around."

"Not a customer. *Definitely* not a customer. I'm Cady."

"I'm Ralph." He flicked a look to my halo. "Nice to meet another nonsavage, Katy."

I gave him a nod of solidarity and didn't bother correcting him about my name; I got Katy-ed a lot in the bar after patrons had one too many. "Yeah, I'm just trying to find out if anyone around here knows where I could find a church in the desert, one of those wacko groups that handles snakes."

"Like Parson Payne?"

"Pain?" Dear God. That sounded like some bad BDSM alias.

"Payne," he said, spelling it out. "He's a religious dude who handles snakes out in Joshua Tree."

Halle-freaking-lujah. I could have kissed Ralph

right on the mouth. "That's got to be the one. He buys his snakes from you guys?"

"Every month, like clockwork. He shows up here in his ratty-ass shit-brown Jeep and throws a tantrum if the snakes he's buying aren't just perfect."

"Monthly, huh?"

"Rain or shine. The owners love him because he drops a grand every time, and they don't have to deliver anything. But he never tips for loading, and he's a dick, *and* he's a straight-up freak. His teeth are all fucked up, and he smells like a hippie. Ugh." Ralph shuddered. "Hate that old man."

I tried to hide my excitement, but I was practically busting at the seams with joy. "Wow. He sounds like a real winner. But maybe we're not talking about the same guy. The man I'm looking for buys unusual snakes," I said, giving him my best *if-you-know-what-I-mean* look.

Ralph glanced around as if his boss might be listening. "Endangered Eden boas."

"As in boa constrictor?"

He nodded. "Classified as critically endangered on the Red List. Illegal to remove from Brazil. Illegal to import to the States. One bite from an adult Eden can take down an elephant. And he doesn't want babies. He wants the suckers ten feet long, minimum. The guys in the warehouse say he switches up buying different herps—"

"Herps?"

"Reptiles. They're almost always exotic and venomous. Three months ago, when I started working here, he bought a hundred pit vipers. What he needs with all those snakes . . . ?" He shook his head in quiet disapproval. "I don't even wanna know."

"Well, shit," I said brightly. "That's got to be the guy. You know where his chapel is?"

"Don't know if he's got a chapel or not. He pays in cash, no address on file. Only know he's from Joshua Tree because he keeps an annual park pass on the dash of his car."

Crap!

"But if you want to chat with him, all you gotta do is be at the delivery dock between seven forty-five and eight a.m. tomorrow, before we open. Like I said, the dude never misses a pickup. But don't tell him I was the one who told you. And definitely don't tell the owners." He dropped his cigarette butt and ground it out with the heel of his boot. "On second thought, what the hell do I care? If I get fired, at least I won't have to deal with Parson Payne anymore."

I told Lon everything once we drove away. We made a plan to return the next morning, and after that, I fell asleep in the car. Not gradually, either. One second he was asking if I wanted to head back into L.A., and the next thing I knew, he was standing in the open passenger doorway, unbuckling my seatbelt. I had no idea why I was so tired. It wasn't as if I'd run a marathon or anything. But it was all I could do to carry my bag into the hotel—which wasn't the L.A. hotel. Lon said we could get the same sleep somewhere local.

I agreed wholeheartedly. Especially when he took us to a grand Mission Revival hotel in downtown Riverside that was on the National Landmark list. And I liked it even more when a whiff of clean linen called my name. I managed to stay awake long enough to shower dead snake and dust out of my hair, then collapsed into one of the beds while Lon called Jupe to tell him where we were. Everything smelled so good: the shampoo, my minty-clean teeth, and something else. Something wholly familiar and wonderful. Something nice, nice, nice. It took my fatigue-addled brain a few seconds to recognize that scent as Lon.

He was clearly planning on sleeping in the other bed. And that was . . . normal?

Of course it was. It would be silly to expect him to start sleeping with me after one kiss. One really good kiss. Phenomenal. I wanted another one.

But it wasn't even that. I just wanted him closer for comfort. How weird was that? I watched him for a minute as he slipped off his shoes and socks—no other pieces of clothing, so I supposed that whole casual naked thing was off the menu—and propped up pillows on the other bed. He lounged there on top of the covers and opened his laptop on his stomach.

I flipped over onto my side and, in my mind, willed him to come over to me. That didn't work. I tested the crazy telekinetic power I'd used in the botanical gardens, to see if maybe I could lift his computer. Nope. Not even my phone sitting on the nightstand.

Feeling a little loopy and weary, I picked up the

phone and opened my text messages. Odd. I'd never texted Lon? Of course I had. I remembered texting him on multiple occasions. I certainly texted Jupe all the time. And yep, there. All my texts back and forth to Jupe before I went into the hospital. A couple of months' worth. But no texts to Lon. Maybe I'd erased them by mistake? Oh, well. It didn't matter, I supposed. I'd just start fresh now.

Sent 11:30 a.m.: What you doing over there?

MSG from Lon, 11:30 a.m.: Researching.

Me: You could do that over here.

Lon: You need to sleep.

Me: Don't worry. I'm too tired to jump you.

Lon: A shame. But I don't trust myself.

Me: Come to think of it, I don't trust myself, either. Let's not trust ourselves together. P.S. You smell really good. I mean that in a creepy way. Come over here and let me sniff your skin like some crazy stalker.

Lon: Are you feeling okay?

Me: Be feeling better if you'd just come over here.

Lon: Don't make me call management to restrain you.

Me: I'd much rather you do it yourself.

Lon: **Go. To. Sleep.**

I sighed loudly enough for him to hear me and turned off my phone. But in the midst of making a new seduction plan, I did exactly what he asked and fell asleep. For how long, I didn't know. But I woke up again in the middle of a crazy dream—I was telling Kar Yee that my body was filled with cocktail shrimp, and she didn't believe me—and the curtains over the window were blocking all but a tiny sliver of sunlight. I smelled something nice. And for a moment, I could have sworn I felt a warm hand on my stomach. Which was bananas, because when I put my own hand there . . . nothing.

The bed moved behind me. I rolled over to see Lon's dark figure slipping under the covers on the other side of the bed. My heart hammered inside my chest.

"Hush," he murmured, curling up on his side to face me. "Nothing's happening. Go back to sleep."

I stretched my arm to the middle of the bed—not to touch him, not really. Just to feel as if we were a little closer. A second later, his hand covered mine. "Good night, Cady."

I sank back into my pillow, happier than I should be and unexplainably satisfied. It felt nice to be touching. God, he smelled so damn good. And why all of a sudden? He didn't smell this good yesterday.

Hold on.

After transmutating the first night in Golden Peak, I turned into Superwoman, busting down doors. Last night, I *nearly* transmutated in the botanical garden, and today my sense of smell was radically stronger. Like, ridiculously strong. I concentrated and tested it. I smelled Lon, yes. The sheets. And the dust in the carpet. The window cleaner. The dirty clothes Lon had bagged up and hung for housekeeping to wash.

The ink in the pen by my bed.

Whoa, Nelly. Definitely not normal.

But why smell? It wasn't as if I made a conscious decision to wield a scenting ability. I'd deliberately chosen when I'd gone all Moonchild in the past: I *chose* to save Lon when he was falling off Merrimoth's roof. I *chose* to incinerate Dare. This smelling thing just seemed so arbitrary. Maybe it was like when Jupe was coming into his knack, and he had trouble controlling it.

Knack puberty? Ugh.

Getting used to a single knack was one thing, but I damn sure didn't want a grab-bag surprise ability every time I transmutated.

"What's wrong?" Lon asked, his hand tightening around mine.

"Did you have trouble controlling your knack when you first underwent the transmutation spell?"

"Not that I remember. It was twenty years ago. Your sense of smell's still heightened?"

"You have no idea." I explained my knack puberty theory. "You think that's what's going on with me?"

"I don't know. Maybe it's something else. But your spoon-bending strength faded along with your silver eyes, so if this is another knack randomly manifesting, it'll probably fade, too."

Let's hope so. I mean, it wasn't as if Nose of Bloodhound was some horrible burden or anything. And it wasn't something that put Lon in direct danger.

Not this time. But what about the next time I transmutated?

16

Jupe leaped off the city bus and raced down the sidewalk toward the Bull and Scorpion Lodge. It was 6:55—already dark outside—and Leticia had said Sophic Mass started at 7:00 p.m. sharp. He'd barely been able to persuade the Holidays to let him spend the night at Jack's. But when they'd insisted on driving him to Jack's house after school, he had to make up an excuse to Mrs. Yamamoto, Jack's mom, about why he was rushing off. Then the bus took longer, and he was going to die if he went to all this trouble only to miss the damn mass.

And to top it all off, he expected his dad would call any minute. Dad and Cady were in some city named Ontario, which he first thought was in Canada, but apparently, there was another one near L.A.—who knew? They'd be waking up about now and calling to check in and—

Oh, crap! The door was closing. His long legs gobbled up the sidewalk as he called out to the man at the door of lodge. "Wait for me!"

The man didn't look all that happy when Jupe bounded up the steps, but he let him inside.

"I'm here . . . for mass," Jupe managed between labored breaths.

"First time?" the man asked as he locked the door behind him.

"Yes."

Jupe glanced around and found himself in a dim hallway with a lot of doors. One was labeled as the administrative offices, another as the library. It smelled musty here, which wasn't a surprise, because the décor looked a little *Brady Bunch*, and there weren't any windows. Not much of anything, really. Just a bulletin board above a low table that held a candle and some printed programs.

"Sanctuary's through there," the man said, pointing to a set of double doors. For someone whose job was to greet people at a public event, that guy could sure use some personality lessons. But Jupe was too nervous to care. Strains of exotic instrumental music and the scent of incense floated from the cracked doors. He slowed his breathing and stepped inside.

If he thought the hallway was dim, the sanctuary was black. White taper candles in metal floor candelabras were the only sources of illumination, flickering across a large room with high ceilings. The room was half full. Fifty or so congregants sat in folding wooden chairs on either side of a wide center aisle that led to an Egyptian-looking raised altar at the front. More candles were there, along with some red velvet pillows. The whole thing was enclosed in a sheer, rounded curtain that hung from a half-moon rod and draped to the floor.

For a moment, every occult horror movie Jupe had ever seen flashed through his brain, and he got a little freaked out. What the hell were they going to do on that red table, anyway? And why was that sword up there? Cady's parents had tried to sacrifice her—had Leticia lured him here to gut him like a fish and make a stew of his entrails?

And oh, shit! He just noticed: *he was the only Earthbound here*. No halos. Not a single one. He'd never found himself in this situation back in La Sirena, and he suddenly felt extremely self-conscious. A bead of sweat trickled down the back of his neck.

"*Psst.*"

He swung to the side and saw Leticia sitting alone in a back row to the right. True to her word, she was dressed casually in the same pink hoodie she'd been wearing the first time they met, with her hair twisted up in those messy Princess Leia buns. And when she flashed him a big white smile, he forgot all about his visions of human sacrifice.

He ducked into a seat next to her and dropped his backpack onto the floor. Holy crap, she was way prettier than he remembered—and he'd been remembering her a *lot*. On the bus ride into Morella, he'd tried to think up something suave and classy to say to her this time, but all he could manage was "Uuhh, what's up?"

Ugh.

"We can't talk when the ritual starts," she whispered. "Here. Read this. It'll tell you what's going on." She shoved one of the programs in front of him. When he took it, her hand touched his. Goose bumps spread up his arm.

"Thanks," he said, feeling a new kind of breathlessness coming on that had nothing to do with his race to the lodge. His hand was tingling where she'd touched him, and she smelled like strawberry jam. He wondered if that was her lip gloss, because she had a lot of it on this time, and she hadn't before.

For some reason, that only made him more nervous. His eyes skimmed over the front of the program. Sophic Mass. Some diagrams of a man in ritual robes posing like he was doing lame karate moves. A bunch of poems. A list of saints he'd never heard of. Wasn't William Blake a writer? And since when was King Arthur a saint? This was some crazy shit, and whoa, hold on. Right in the middle of the list was a name that jumped off the page: Saint Sélène the Moonchild.

Cady was a saint?

Jupe opened his mouth to ask Leticia if she knew about Cady, but when he glanced up, he caught her staring. And that made his chest feel warm. It also made him forget what he was going to ask.

"Any questions?" she whispered.

"Are we going to have to sing any hymns?"

She grinned. "You volunteering?"

"You don't want to hear me sing, believe me," Jupe whispered. "The only time I sing is in the car with my dad's girlfriend, and only because her voice is worse than mine."

For some reason, this made her laugh quietly. Then she whispered, "My sister's a good singer. I'm not bad, but I'm not good, either."

The recorded music stopped, and a man in blue robes sat down at an organ near the altar. When he put his hands on the keyboard, a startlingly loud opening chord reverberated through the room.

A soft spotlight in the ceiling flicked on behind them. Jupe looked over his shoulder to see a procession of three robed magicians walking up the front aisle—super-slowly, as if they were in a wedding. The one in the middle was a Latina woman in a wine-colored robe embroidered with symbols. Beneath a weird pointy hat, dark hair cascaded down her back. Between the robe and the funny hat and the tall wooden staff in her hand, she sort of looked like a bishop crossed with Dumbledore. She also looked like the leader, and when she passed by, he glanced back at Leticia and mouthed, "Mom?"

She smiled proudly and nodded. Jupe gave her a thumbs-up before turning his attention back to the procession. Two of the robed people flanked the altar. They looked a few years older than him. Leticia's mom stood in front and said something in a foreign language. Definitely not Spanish. Maybe French. Whatever it was, the entire congregation repeated it. Leticia's mom made a gesture. Everyone stood and repeated the gesture. Jupe scrambled to his feet as a dull panic throbbed inside his stomach. He wished he'd read the stupid program.

The next few minutes were a blur. Leticia's mom switched to English and called out for a bunch of stuff—the names of some pillars, angels, elements. Everyone got up and sat down a billion times. It got a little monotonous, and Jupe's gaze was drifting down to Leticia's breasts. Then the spotlight in the back of the room began moving, and everyone's head swiveled to watch two more people coming down the aisle.

A man holding a spear and a dark-haired woman who was dressed like some sort of Arabian princess or a belly dancer, with a belt of golden coins and a lot of long necklaces. He could almost see through her robe, which was super-distracting. She parted the curtains at the altar and closed them behind her. Now he could just see the shape of her standing behind the curtains. What was she doing back there?

After more ceremonial stuff, the guy used his spear to part the curtain around the altar, and the spotlight fell on the belly-dancer chick. She sat among the pillows on the red table with her legs dangling off, knees spread.

Naked.

Oh.

My.

God.

Naked chick on the altar! Breasts, belly, dark triangle of hair between her legs. As if she didn't even give two shits about the fact that an entire room of people were staring up at her. And the guy with the spear was kneeling in front of her, praying, it looked like, with his face right at crotch level. The bead of sweat that had trickled down Jupe's back earlier suddenly became a waterfall, and—oh, God, *no*—he felt himself getting hard.

Don't look at the naked girl. Don't look, don't look, don't look. How could he not look? It was the first naked chick he'd seen in person. Ever. Well, he once accidentally saw Mrs. Holiday come out of the guest shower naked, but that was *horrifying*.

This was not.

And goddammit, what did they expect? It was a natural reaction. Only it was getting mighty uncomfortable, and he was painfully aware he was sitting next to Leticia. Did she know? How could she not?

He risked a glance at her. She wasn't staring at his dick, thank God. It was pretty dark back here, so maybe he was safe. But then she caught him looking at her, so he forced his eyes back to the naked-flesh carnival at the altar. No good! Ah, crap. He glanced back at Leticia again, and she had a funny look on her face. Like she was pissed, maybe. Or not. He didn't know. How could he think with all this going on?

Just when he thought he couldn't be more freaked out, the people in the seats around him began heading down the aisle. One by one, they headed to the girl on the altar, drank what looked to be wine, and ate some communion-type wafer. Right in front of her, as if they were toasting to her vagina. And maybe they were, who knew? Part of Jupe wanted to find out, and part of him was absolutely horrified to be forced to walk down the aisle with a raging erection.

He couldn't do it. He prepared himself to make up some excuse and bail—just run out of the room and leave. Then he smelled strawberry jam.

"We don't go up there," Leticia's voice said in his ear.

He nearly jumped out of his seat but had sense enough to pull the hem of his jacket down over his pants. "Why not?" he whispered back.

"You have to be a certain degree."

"Temperature?"

"Ranking," she clarified. "For some, you have to be a certain age. I'm not old enough. And you're not a member."

Relief flowed through his limbs. And after concentrating really hard and biting the inside of his mouth until pain shot through him, he was finally able to get everything under control between his legs. He wiped sweat off his brow and exhaled heavily before whispering, "Who is that chick on the altar? Do you guys hire a stripper or something?"

Anger tightened Leticia's face. Her whispered reply was so sharp she might as well have slapped him. "That *chick* is my sister."

The mass couldn't have dragged on any longer. Jupe apologized to Leticia a billion times. And he continued to do so, even when the whole shebang was finished and everyone filed outside the lodge into the old parking lot in back, which had been converted into a patio. Beneath the cover of two battered canopy tents, people gathered around picnic tables and scattered chairs. They looked so normal—moms, dads, teens. A group of smaller kids who hadn't been in the sanctuary burst out of the hallway with a lady who must have been watching them.

Jupe was really confused.

And Leticia was walking really fast. He jogged to catch up to her as she headed to a picnic table outside the tent and plopped down on top of it, settling her feet on one of the attached benches.

"I'm really, really sorry," Jupe said as he approached.

"I heard." She dug inside a neon-green messenger bag that was slung diagonally across her body, pulled out a tablet, and settled it in her lap to read.

"How was I supposed to know?"

"I thought you said your dad's girlfriend went to the main lodge."

"Years ago, before she met my dad!"

"Oh."

"That . . . what your sister did in the sanctuary was just a little shocking, is all."

"She was playing the role of the priestess. It's called a living altar, and there's nothing wrong with it. It's a beautiful ritual that celebrates women's power. It's not some cheap stripper show for a bachelor's party."

"I didn't say—" Ugh. Well, he had kind of implied it. He tried again. "I've got nothing against strippers. Or naked girls. I mean, I like naked girls." Oh, God. *Shut up. Just shut up.* But he couldn't. "Your sister's pretty hot."

Leticia's nostrils flared.

"I'm sure you're even hotter," Jupe said desperately.

She looked horrified. "Naked?"

"No. Yes? No," he said in quick succession. "Wait, have you, uh, played the role of the priestess?"

Her eyes darted to the side. "Of course not. You have to be an adult to participate in the mass. Eighteen."

"That's only four years away. Are you going to—"

"Get naked in front of my lodge?"

Jupe's pulse doubled. Then the thought crossed his mind that maybe Cady had played priestess back when she was active in her lodge, and that made him feel a little squicky. "Never mind," he said. "Can we please not talk about this anymore? I'm already freaked out, and you're making it worse."

"Now it's my fault?"

"Let's blame it on your sister and call it even."

"You're a piece of work, Jupiter." She remembered his name! Jupe grinned, forgetting all the awkwardness for a moment. Until she said, "Who's Kar Yee?"

"What?" How did she know about Kar Yee? All the awkwardness came back and punched him in the gut. "Did you do some sort of spell on me?"

She rolled her eyes. "No, you weirdo. I saw your Facebook profile online. It says your relationship status is complicated, and you've got a bunch of pictures of some woman named Kar Yee. Is that your girlfriend?"

He scratched the side of his neck. "Kar Yee is my dad's girlfriend's best friend. We just tease each other. It's just a joke." Well, most of the thoughts he'd had about Kar Yee weren't funny at all. In fact, they were downright filthy, but Leticia didn't need to know that. *Nobody* needed to know that. "Wait, you looked me up? How come you didn't friend me?"

She shrugged. "I didn't know what kind of person you were. I still don't. I thought you were serious about wanting magical help, but after tonight, I'm not sure you even know anything about it."

"I do," he insisted, smelling charcoal and onions drifting in the air from the grill. "My dad can do a little magick. He's got an occult library that would probably put this one to shame. And his fiancée—"

"I thought you said she was his girlfriend?"

"He bought her a ring, but it's just been hectic. She'll say yes." He hoped. It sure would be easier to say "stepmom" than "Dad's girlfriend" in situations like this. "She's the reason I'm here. I need to help her with a big problem."

"Why didn't she just come herself?"

"It's complicated."

"Like your relationship status?"

"I already explained that." He motioned to the picnic table. She motioned back for him to sit down, so he crawled up beside her, careful to leave a little room between them. From here, he could see the mass attendees talking and laughing under the strings of fairy lights while grabbing drinks out of a big cooler. A couple of other people were bringing covered dishes out of the lodge's back door. One of those people was Leticia's sister, now fully clothed in jeans and a long-sleeved shirt.

That way lies danger.

Fearing a repeat of what had happened to him during the mass, he quickly averted his eyes and glanced down at Leticia's book. A few words were highlighted. "What are you reading?"

"Nothing you'd like," she said, shutting off the screen and closing the cover.

"You're into dragons? Like high-fantasy stuff?"

She shoved the reader into her bag. "Maybe."

"That's cool. My best friend, Jack, reads fantasy. I'm a visual person, so I like comics and anime. Movies."

A long silence stretched between them, until she finally said, "If you want my help, maybe you should start by telling me who your dad's girlfriend is."

He sighed. "I can't do that."

"Don't tell me, it's complicated."

"It's—"

"I already know you're lying, because I looked at all your pictures online. I saw who your dad is. And your mom's a celebrity."

"My parents are divorced."

"I also saw the picture of you and your dad and the owner of that Tiki bar, Arcadia Bell. That's his girlfriend?"

Jupe felt like he was being led into a trap but was powerless to stop. "Yes . . ."

"I asked my mom if she could look up Arcadia Bell in the lodge directory. And she got all weird and freaked out and wanted to know why I was asking and who you were."

Crap. That didn't sound good. "Did you tell her?"

"No."

Jupe bit the inside of his mouth. "Why do you think she freaked out?"

"I don't know," Leticia said, running the heels of her palms over her knees. "But she grilled me about it, and I had to lie and say some kid at school was talking about her. I tried to play dumb, but I'm not sure if she believed me. I don't like lying to my family."

"Tell me about it," Jupe said sourly. "I went to a lot of trouble to get out here again. I'm not sure if I can keep pulling it off."

After a moment, she said, "My mom told me to

leave it alone and forget about it, so I figured it must be important. I sneaked onto her computer after she went to bed and searched the lodge directory myself. It's a list of every member of the order, since it moved from France to the States in the early 1900s. And no one named Arcadia Bell has ever been a member. No Bell at all."

Ah, crap. He was torn between being thrilled that she'd gone to all that trouble out of curiosity over him and panicked that she now knew too much. He'd planned on quizzing her about Sélène Duval, not Arcadia Bell.

"Who is she?" Leticia asked.

"I can't tell you."

"Fine. Then I can't help you."

"Please," Jupe begged. "I really need your help, but I just can't."

She buckled the strap on her messenger bag. "Trust has to start somewhere, Jupiter."

He thought about everything Cady had told him and how she trusted him to keep her secrets. But then, what did her secrets matter if her mother came down from the Æthyr and stole her body? And then there were Priya's warnings and his challenge to Jupe. Priya insisted that Cady's order could be trusted, so it wasn't as if Jupe would be turning her in to the FBI. Jesus, she didn't even do anything wrong—why did she have to keep this secret, anyway?

Maybe the better question was, how could Jupe help Cady if he kept her secret and walked away right now? He needed Leticia's help. And sure, she was pretty and smelled good and had lots of nice curves. Hell, he even liked the way she argued with him. On top of all that, her knee was about an inch away from touching his, and that alone was enough to urge him into telling her anything she wanted to know. But Cady came first, and he really didn't know what other choice he had. One day, he might have a brother or sister who'd look up to him as a hero, but not if Cady's crazy mom won the fight.

"*If* I tell you," he said cautiously, "it might be the biggest, most serious secret you've ever heard. And my family might be in danger if the wrong people find out. Will you promise not to tell anyone? Like, maybe you could undergo some kind of magical oath?"

She turned her head and leaned closer, until her face was right up in his and the scent of strawberry jam filled his nostrils. Her forehead tightened until her eyebrows were almost joined. "A few people in my lodge are under magical oath to protect a big secret. I think that's bullshit. You can't force a person to be loyal. If you're going to trust someone, you trust them until they give you a reason not to. *¿Confías en mí?*"

Jupe's Spanish lessons rattled around inside his head and overlapped with all the Mexican *lucha libre* wrestling he watched on Galavisión. He was pretty sure he understood her question, but he made a mental note to pay more attention in class.

As he cracked his knuckles, trying to make up his mind, Leticia's knee touched his thigh, warm and insistent. He glanced down between them. After a moment, he pressed his leg against hers in answer. She didn't pull away. When he lifted his head and looked into her eyes, all at once, he decided he *did* trust her, and not just as a last resort.

So he licked his lips and spoke in a low voice. "Have you ever heard of the Black Lodge slayings?"

17

If I thought that after sleeping all afternoon a few feet away from Lon, I might wake up and accidentally find myself in the middle of a lust-bleary romp under the sheets—and admittedly, that's *exactly* what I thought—I was w-r-o-n-g. He'd already gotten up, showered, given our dirty clothes to the maid, gone to the gym, and scouted out the on-premises restaurant where we could eat our early-evening breakfast.

Overachiever.

"I know we didn't get enough sleep, but we've got an entire night to get through until we can head back to the reptile store tomorrow morning," he told me before I'd even sat up in bed. "So I think it would be best if we spend what time we can outside the room, so we aren't tempted."

"Tempted to . . . ?"

"To fall asleep during the night," he clarified.

"Oh."

A girl might think she was being avoided. This

girl certainly did. But I didn't say anything. Nope. Not a word. I did, however, leave the bathroom door wide open when I got dressed, during which I *did* hear him swearing under his breath before he announced loudly that he'd meet me downstairs in the lobby when I was ready to eat.

My smell-o-rama knack was still alive and kicking but not half as strong as it was before I slept, which was both a relief and a shame. It was working well enough to make me reject the food our waiter brought out and order something different. And after we wasted time window-shopping at a mall until it closed and then nearly falling asleep in a midnight showing of a crappy horror movie that even Jupe would have hated, I found myself able to identify a unique scent wafting from Lon. Not all the time. Just when I tried to play footsie with him under the restaurant table. Or when I walked too close to him. Or when I raised the movie-seat arm between us and leaned against his shoulder.

I wasn't certain, but I thought that scent was a little amorous. Sure, it crossed my mind that perhaps I was projecting my own wants, but by the time we'd sat around in an all-night diner caffeinating ourselves and doing all the research two people could do on a crappy internet connection and no sleep, I was willing to take the risk that I was right.

It was past five by the time we made it back to our hotel suite. Sunrise was more than an hour away, but soon after, we'd have to leave for the reptile shop.

I kicked off my shoes and headed over to Lon, who was looking miserable, flipping through channels in the sitting area of our room.

"Where's the tarp?" I asked.

"Why?"

"Because I want to practice transmutating."

"I don't think that's a good idea."

"Oh, really? Because you were all gung-ho about it back in Golden Peak. How am I supposed to learn to control it if I don't practice? I think that was your argument."

He stared at the TV, stewing. "That was before random knacks started appearing unexpectedly."

"Afraid I might suddenly develop the knack to read your thoughts? Oh, wait. That's right. You already do that to *me*."

His eyes narrowed to slits. "Don't be a smart-ass."

"Give me the tarp."

"No."

"Fine. I'll practice without it." I began unbuttoning my jeans, watching his gaze hover over my fingers for a moment until he groaned and got out of his chair to dig through his luggage.

"Here," he said, tossing the folded tarp to me. "Be stubborn, see if I care."

I retreated to the marble-tiled bathroom and called out to him as I snagged a boxed sewing kit the hotel provided along with a plethora of fancy shampoos and lotions. "I'm not the one who's being stubborn. You've been avoiding me all night, and you won't talk about the kiss. Makes me wonder if you regret all that stuff you said in Pasadena."

Indecipherable grumbling answered me. I strolled back into the sitting area and pretended not to look at Lon as I inspected the sheer curtain behind him, one that covered a patio over a dark palm-lined courtyard.

"What are you doing?" he asked.

"Finding a place to pin this up. It would give me some freedom to walk around without worrying I'll smudge up the symbols. Since you're watching TV, I'll hang it up on the other patio by the beds."

His gaze darted to my unbuttoned jeans. I think. Maybe I imagined that. "No room to walk around back there," he said. "You might as well do it here. I can sit somewhere else."

"Makes no difference to me." I told myself to keep my feelings guarded, but it really wasn't a problem, because I was actually getting downright pissed about his bad attitude and unwillingness to talk.

I unfolded the tarp and stepped up on the chair to close the heavier blackout drapes over the sheers. Then I wrestled the tarp up, accidentally smacking Lon in the head as I did.

"Sorry," I mumbled.

"Give me the corner."

He held it up as I anchored it to the drapes with safety pins from the sewing kit. A strong tug could pull it down, but as long as I didn't manhandle the thing, it would stay. I dug out my caduceus and could have sworn I heard Lon mumble, "Please be careful," as I siphoned electricity and kindled enough Heka to charge the tarp.

After it fired up nice and bright, giving me solid protection from the floor almost all the way up to the ceiling, I said, "Why are you being so weird?"

Instead of answering me, he just walked around the sitting area, holding his hand up to test the magick. "How far you think this'll extend? Never mind, I stop feeling it here." He moved a love seat there to mark a boundary. "Don't go past the back of this."

"If you regret it, just be a man and say it." I pushed my jeans over my hips and kicked them aside when they dropped to the floor. "I'd rather it be out in the open so we can move past it."

"I don't regret it."

Aha! Must keep satisfaction in check. Maybe he was far enough away that he couldn't hear me. I kept my back to him and pulled the clip out of my hair. "Then what gives? Was it not as good as you hoped, and now you're having some doubts? Not feeling it?"

No response.

I supposed there was really no reason to get naked like I did in Golden Peak—we weren't inspecting my markings again, unfortunately. However, there was also no reason to be uncomfortable in front of someone who had already seen all of me, so I left my panties on and did the girl trick of unhooking my bra under my tank top and pulling it out of my sleeve.

Then I took a deep breath, shook out my hands, and transmutated.

My vision turned to silver. My hearing went weird. And that familiar coolness spread over my skin, along with the strange itch of my horns growing and the disconcerting pressure at the small of my back as my tail pushed out over the top of my black bikini underwear.

"Just hold steady, as you are," Lon's voice said over my shoulder with forced calmness. "Don't try to reach for anything more than this. You're doing great."

I inhaled slowly, making sure I felt no connection to the Moonchild magick. It was fine. I could tell the difference when I pulled moon energy. It was like pulling electricity, something that fired up my innate power. I knew I could do some magick without kindling Heka; therefore, I could definitely hold this form without tapping into the Æthyr.

"You know, we're friends," I said, catching a glimpse of him behind me in a mirror that hung near the drapes. He was discreetly fidgeting with something around his neck. What was that, and why was he being sneaky? Sneaky and obvious, because I could tell by the angle of his stare where his eyes were. I flicked my tail to be sure. Uh-huh. Just what I thought.

He cleared his throat. "Yes, we're friends."

"Good friends," I said. "So, just like you advised me in Golden Peak, if you're having some physical problems, you know you can tell me."

His eyes met mine in the mirror. He didn't respond.

"It's probably natural for a man your age to have a few issues," I taunted. "You shouldn't be embarrassed to see a doctor if you're experiencing . . . dysfunction."

The air shuddered.

Flames flared up over his shoulders—a fiery crown, topped with stunning horns that spiraled into place on either side of his head.

Arrow, meet bull's-eye.

I spun around to find him leaping over the loveseat barrier as if it was a trivial inconvenience. He landed with a thud in front of me. My heart thumped so madly inside my chest that I nearly dropped my serpentine form. And when he grabbed my shoulders as if he was going to shake the living daylights out of me, I could smell the arousal all over him, and it thrilled me to no end.

"Happy, are you?" he said, reading my thoughts as he lowered his face to mine. "Think you've won? You think you can break me?"

"Yes," I whispered.

"Let me tell you a little story. I sat in a fucking hospital looking at a body that was black with blood and bruises, with shattered bones poking out of your flesh. I didn't know if you were going to live or die. And when Mick put you under and you didn't wake up, I didn't know if you ever would—or what condition your brain would be in if you did. I nearly lost my mind grieving over you. And I nearly lost my spirit beating myself up over it, because it was my fault."

"Lon—"

"I introduced you to Dare. *I* brought that horror into your life. *Me*," he said in a hoarse voice. "And if you died, I didn't want to live. But I didn't fall apart. I sat there night after night for weeks, praying and hoping and believing you'd be okay. And now that I have you back, I will do whatever it takes to make sure you stay okay. So you can tease me all you want, but I *will not* budge."

I inhaled a shaky breath and fought back tears. Way to go, Bell. Now I felt ashamed and confused and angry, all at once. And I hated him for it.

"You hear all that?" I bit out.

"I hear it."

The steely grip on my shoulders loosened, and before I realized what was happening, he was running a hand down my arm, down my scaly skin. When he got to my hand, he entwined his fingers with mine and pressed my palm right over the straining fly of his jeans. He was hard. Big. And hot as damnation against my too-cool transmuted skin.

"Feel that?" he said. I couldn't answer. "Every time you give me one of those coy looks of yours. Every time you wrinkle up your nose in that snarky little way of yours. Every time you brush up against me 'accidentally.' Yes, I knew exactly what you were doing, and I've been in hell all day long."

I whimpered. But when I tried to get a better feel of things, he tore my hand away. "Not going to break me. Come here." His arm swung around my back. He dragged me to the sofa and sat, pulling me down to straddle his lap. "You think you're making a connection to the Æthyr, you tell me that very moment, you hear me?"

I nodded, not really understanding what I was agreeing to. Then he let out a long breath and looked me over. His fingers lightly stroked over my arms. The insides of my elbows. My palms. He splayed his fingers over my stomach, up my sides, his index fingers hooking beneath the thin fabric of my tank top and pushing it up, up, up, notching it over my breasts, which rose and fell under his languid scrutiny. He traced the long, flat scales between, and when his thumbs stroked over my nipples, I planted my hands on his shoulders and gasped as if I was dying.

And maybe I was a little. Dying, or living for the first time since I'd left the hospital, it was hard to tell which.

His hands circled to my back. He stroked down, down, down my spine . . . until his touch grazed over my tail. For a moment, I was caught between a weird, unexpected embarrassment—he was touching territory no one had touched, not even *me*, barely—and an ecstatic anticipation, for exactly the same reason. But when his fingers slid to the underside of my tail, I forgot all of that. Waves of pleasurable chills rolled in, ebbed, and rolled in again as he stroked down the length of it, bringing it around between us to see the rings of black and white stripes.

"Amazing," he whispered as it curled around his hand and wrist. "So goddamn amazing."

Before I could respond, he shifted his free hand to my leg and slid his way up to my inner thigh, eyes intently fixed on mine. "I'm going to touch you now. Can you handle this?"

Holy freaking Harlot. My senses went bananas.

"It's sort of a forest down there," I warned, panicking at the last second.

"Fantastic," he murmured, as if I'd just given him a birthday present, then pushed my panties aside and slipped his fingers between my legs.

If all the rest of it was good, this was divine. He touched me as if he'd aced Pleasuring Cady 101. I mean, seriously, he wasn't messing around. No awkward searches, no guesswork, no fingers going everywhere but where they should. Where had he been all my life? I couldn't have done this better myself. And all the little whispers of encouragement he gave were the icing on the cake.

I wanted to hold back and make it last, but I got greedy fast, and before I knew it, I was bowing off his lap, cheek bent to his, every muscle straining. And in my ear, his low voice said, "Come for me, Cadybell." That was it. I tipped over the edge and cried out, utterly and completely lost.

It took me a few seconds to come back down and

a few more for the heat of his proficient fingers to slip away. At that point, the only thing on my mind was returning the favor. Well, first it was a whole lot of *Holy shit, that was amazing* and a little bit of *I can't believe that just happened*. But next, when I was able to think properly, I slowly reached for him.

And that's when I got the boot.

"Go on and shift back down," he said in a strained voice, gently but firmly ejecting me from his lap. "We need to be ready to leave in a half hour and pick up our clothes on the way out."

And as I dazedly pulled my clothes back into place and watched him disappear into the bathroom and lock the door, I realized something that made me sad.

During everything that had just happened, he'd never even kissed me.

18

If I thought the Pasadena kiss was the elephant in the room, it was a mouse compared with our little predawn tête-à-tête on the love seat. And maybe because we were barely speaking after it was over, we efficiently got ourselves ready to leave on time . . . only to have rain-slicked roads and an overturned eighteen-wheeler make us late.

But by the time Lon and I had inched through the detour with a million other cars and found our way back to Reptile Hell, it was 8:15 a.m. A quarter hour past the time this Parson Payne guy was supposed to show for his snake pickup.

I squinted past the windshield wipers as Lon flipped on his turn signal and spied an empty loading dock. No way had we traveled half the state to follow Wildeye's notes only to be stymied by a random traffic accident.

An old dark brown Jeep Grand Cherokee pulled out of the parking lot—one with blooming rust spots, a dented fender, and the back windows covered in peeling do-it-yourself tinting. It most definitely qualified as "ratty-ass."

"There!" I shouted to Lon as the Jeep turned onto the road in front of us. "That's him."

"Are you sure?"

"No one's at the loading dock. No Jeeps in the parking lot. And look, there's a giant wooden crate in the back—you can see it through the cracks in the window tint."

"Shit."

Lon swerved back into his lane and trailed the Jeep through Ontario.

Through Riverside.

Through San Bernardino.

And into the desert.

A steady rain fell on the SUV as we continued east on I-10 through miles of flat, lonely land. Thousands of white, leggy turbine windmills stood sentry between the freeway and long chains of crinkly mountains in the distance.

"He's going back to Joshua Tree," Lon finally said.

"No sense in turning back now."

He nodded in agreement and kept driving.

So far, no new random knack had popped up to replace the super-smell, so that was good, I supposed. But now that the sniffing was gone and our normal conversation had gone off like old cheese, all we had to occupy our time on the drive were the radio and the dreary rolling landscape.

Yippee.

Two hours passed, along with my bedtime. I knew Lon was tired, too. Nothing to do except buck up and hope this was worth it. The rain gradually stopped, but the ominous dark clouds hung around. Signs for Palm Springs appeared, but we turned north, skirting around the western edge of Joshua Tree National Park. The rough ground was barren except for spotty clumps of desert grass and outcroppings of burnished wind-hewn rock; the park's ubiquitous namesake, with its twisted branches and spiky tops, dotted the landscape between.

Somewhere before we'd hit the oasis community of Twentynine Palms, the brown Jeep pulled off the freeway onto a side road. If the land was lonely before, it was pretty much depressing here, and it was harder to stay far enough behind the Jeep that we weren't noticed. A few houses and buildings stood near the turnoff. But a couple of miles past the last gas station, the Jeep turned again, this time onto a dirt road. It dead-ended after a mile.

The Jeep slowed to enter a long unpaved driveway, guarded by two crumbling stone posts. And arching between them was an old painted sign that had been turned upside down: SOPHIA RANCH.

It wasn't the only sign. Several no-trespassing warnings were posted around the gate and on the weather-faded fencing that banded the property.

"Christ, I really don't like this," Lon mumbled.

The Jeep came to a stop just outside the gate. Maybe to check the rickety mailbox. Lon pulled up next to him and lowered his window halfway. Cool air rushed across the front seat. The Jeep's driver's-side door creaked open. I craned my neck to get a glimpse of Parson Payne and instead found myself looking down the barrel of a shotgun.

Lon raised his hands.

"This is private property," a rough voice said from the Jeep.

"I can see that," Lon answered evenly.

"You followed me from Ontario."

Lon kept his hands in the air. "We just want to ask some questions."

"I don't think I'm in the mood for chatting."

I raised my voice to be heard over the wind. "Please. Are you Parson Payne? We need to talk to you about an occultist who visited here twenty-five years ago. Her name was Enola Duval."

The shotgun lowered, and the man leaned out of the Jeep. I saw the halo first. Dark green, the darkest halo I'd ever seen. My mother was conferring with an Earthbound? She hated Earthbounds. Not that she could see their halos—most humans couldn't. Only me. And in hindsight, I supposed my humanity was up for debate at this point.

"We're trying to track down the origins of a ritual," I added. "We know she spent some time here, and we were hoping you might remember some things."

I shifted so I could see the man better. The disgruntled warehouse worker at the reptile store wasn't wrong: Payne was an ugly son of a bitch. Leathery sun-damaged skin rippling with wrinkles. Long white hair pulled tightly back into a long braid. In his seventies, I guessed. When his dark eyes flicked from Lon's halo to mine, surprise blazed across his face. Just for a moment.

"Who are you two?"

"I'm Butler," Lon said. "This is Miss Bell."

Payne blinked several times and then tossed his shotgun into the Jeep. "Storm clouds followed us from the city. Come on through to the house before they break. We can talk there."

Lon raised his window and idled the SUV, waiting for Payne to lead the way. "We need to be careful," he said to me, without moving his gaze from the road. "He was shocked to see you."

"Did he recognize me? Could you tell by his emotions?"

"I don't think so. But keep in mind that we don't know the last time he had contact with your mother. They could've been friendly all these years."

The flat land became rockier and dipped into a small canyon. A large, flat-roofed adobe-style house sat at its entrance, surrounded by several other smaller bungalows, which all looked run-down and unoccupied. The compound was backed by a ridge of enormous boulders that stretched into deeper canyon walls in the distance.

Next to the main house, the Jeep backed into a carport otherwise filled with scrap metal and a variety of junk. I watched Payne exit his car and wondered if he was going to retrieve the illegal boa he'd bought. But he just marched to the house's front door and stood there waiting while Lon parked at the side of what might have been a nice driveway fifty years ago.

"No other cars here," Lon murmured. "You think he's alone?"

"Don't know, but he left his shotgun in the Jeep. And hey, at least he's not a magician."

"Earthbounds can dabble," Lon reminded me as he opened the center console and fished around for something. "And we don't know his knack or who he's got on his side. If he was friendly with your mother, he might be friendly with other magicians."

"Believe me, I couldn't be any more leery right now."

"Stay that way." Lon found what he was looking for, a holstered handgun. Beneath his thin leather jacket, he clipped the holster to his belt. "And be ready to shock the shit out of the good parson if he does anything that sets off warning bells."

Biting cold cut through my jacket as we battled the wind to meet up with Payne, who led us inside the adobe home. And once we were inside, I saw it wasn't a house at all but a lobby—at least, it had been at one time. Wooden cubbyholes and hooks for room keys lined the wall behind a registration desk. Signs with arrows pointed the way to private numbered bungalows and rooms down a hallway that stretched out of sight. Old brass luggage carts sat in the corner, loaded with storage boxes near a door labeled BAR AND RESTAURANT.

Touches of old-fashioned California-meets-Mexico rustic décor graced the walls. Everything smelled of dust and smoke.

"The ranch used to be an inn," Payne said as he strolled to an enormous stone fireplace in the center of the room, where he knelt on a woven rug to light a fire. A chandelier made of antlers hung from rough rafters above. "Back in the '40s and '50s, Hollywood writers and producers vacationed here. But in 1967, a family of five was murdered in one of the bungalows. Rumor was that the killer was living out on the property. They never caught anyone, and the ranch never recovered. I bought it for pennies in 1978. That was a couple years before I met Enola, actually."

"How did you meet her?"

Payne stood up from the fledgling fire and squinted at me as he brushed off his knees with gloved hands. His clothes seemed too big, as if they were hanging off his bones. Maybe he'd lost a lot of weight recently. "I met her in L.A. at a book signing in a New Age bookstore on Melrose. She wrote something about the origins of ritual in Greece and Italy—*Ritual Mysteries of Antiquity and the Search for Knowledge*. She had some interesting ideas about Gnostic cults. They were mostly wrong, but she vehemently defended them. I invited her to stay at the ranch. It wasn't open to the public, but we had a handful of people stay from time to time, interesting people who were dialed into the current."

"Nonsavages, you mean."

He nodded. "Occultists, pagans, philosophers, writers."

"Did she know you were—"

"Son of the Serpent?"

"Earthbound," I corrected.

"One and the same," he said, flashing me a disconcerting smile. His teeth, dear God—the middle six on the top had been filed to points. "And no, not at first. Like most humans, she wasn't gifted with the sight. But she eventually believed."

Wood crackled in the fireplace. "She was a member of Ekklesia Eleusia," I said.

"Oh, I'm well aware of that."

"What did she do when she was staying here?"

"She talked. Soaked up knowledge. Connected with like minds." Payne braced one arm on the mantel and watched the hearth. "She'd recently lost a child, so she was looking for solace, she said. Reflecting on the meaning of life."

Reflecting, my ass. Reflecting on how she could fix her Moonchild formula, maybe. But the way he talked made me think he wasn't all that sympathetic to my mother, either.

He glanced above my head, studying my halo. "You might not understand that, because you're too young to have children of your own, I'm guessing. Just how old are you, my dear?"

Out of Payne's sight, Lon lifted his hand for my benefit, but I didn't need the warning. The old man was speaking in riddles, not telling us anything of substance. If he was bold enough to ask my age, he had a good idea I was Enola's daughter. Which should be an advantage to me—for once—because he was supposed to be my mother's ally in some sort of capacity. But I couldn't get a clear read on his feelings about her. And that, frankly, gave me the willies.

I did my best not to let it show and merely smiled at his question before asking one of my own. "When was the last time she stayed here?"

"Oh, I imagine it's been twenty-five, twenty-six years." His mouth curled into a taunting smile.

Shit. He definitely knew who I was. "Why did she stop coming?"

"A busy woman like Enola Duval?" he said, voice thick with sarcasm. "I imagine she had people to see. Things to do."

"You never saw her again?"

"Something always kept us apart."

What the hell did that mean? I couldn't figure out if lack of sleep was screwing with my instincts, but I had a feeling this man hated her guts as much as I did.

"You *do* realize what eventually became of her?" I said.

"The Black Lodge murders? Oh, yes. She and her husband were quite the media darlings for a while there, weren't they?"

Indeed. We stared at each other until I couldn't hold his gaze. "Is your temple still operational?" I said, glancing around the cavernous, dust-filled room. "Seems quiet around here."

"When I first bought the ranch, before Enola Duval graced my doorstep, there were days when this room was filled with people and conversation. Most of my original flock is old or in the ground. But as long as I'm still standing, it's functional."

And he still bought snakes on a regular basis. Big, expensive ones. Where were they? From the look of this shabby lobby, there was no indication these walls had seen anything but neglect and hard times. "Did Enola ever do any magick for you?" I asked.

He snorted. "She demonstrated a few . . . tricks," he said, spiraling his gloved hand in the air. "And she offered to work in trade, but I refused her."

"Trade for what?" Lon asked in a low voice, speaking up for the first time since we'd entered the building.

Payne blinked at Lon as if he'd forgotten he was there. "Now, that *is* a good question, brother," he said. "For the answer, I'd have to show you. Would you care to see my temple?"

19

We warily followed Payne out one of the back doors into a covered breezeway. Lon's face was a stony cliff. One hand twitched over the bump beneath his jacket, the other protectively held the back of my neck. I wished like hell he was transmutated so I could communicate my thoughts to him. Even more, I wished I could read his thoughts. What was he reading from Payne?

The breezeway opened up to a stone path that circled the eastern group of bungalows, some of which had boarded-up windows or junk piled in front of the doors. I scanned the grounds for signs of other people and saw no one. Only a curving pool, mostly hidden by a dilapidated wooden fence. A few broken boards allowed me a quick peek inside as we passed. Lightning streaked across the dark storm clouds, illuminating piles of beer bottles on the cement patio surrounding the pool. A hose hung limply from the broken diving board, and the pool itself looked half-filled. The dark surface of the water rippled unsettlingly.

But we weren't headed there. Payne was leading us away from the compound, toward the rocky cliff walls of the canyon, where another rounded adobe-style structure jutted out from the cliffs. Half clay, half sienna-colored stone, the temple looked as though it had been built in stages by a madman who'd run out of funds halfway through construction. But Payne assured us that this wasn't the case.

"A sacred spot for the Serrano tribes who'd settled the oasis before the miners came in the nineteenth century," he shouted back to us as his shoes kicked up dust. "I extended what was already built."

The first thing I noticed when we were a few yards away was tire tracks leading to a small utility cart with an attached trailer. What did Payne haul out here? My mind jumped to the boa constrictor in the back of his Jeep.

The second thing I noticed was the spider web of carvings that covered the clay walls. Sigils. Strange ones, reminiscent of the spells Lon and I had uncovered last Halloween when we were tracking the Sandpiper Park snatcher and ended up going toe-to-toe with Duke Chora, the demon my mother recently murdered in the Æthyr.

The temple's carved symbols had to be Æthyric. And the closer we got, the more I was certain their purpose was to keep the temple hidden. How that was possible, I wasn't sure, because they weren't lit with white Heka or with the pink magical light I associated with Æthyric magick.

A stained-glass window was set into the clay wall above a wooden door—it looked like a figure of some sort, but it was hard to tell with no light behind it. Payne took out a set of keys to unlock and open the door. Darkness lay inside. No way in hell was I walking in there. But Payne opened a rusted box on the wall and removed a metal striker, which he used to light two oil lamps inside the door, exposing the first few feet of the temple entrance's dusty mosaic-tiled floor. And spelled out in the broken chips of earthen tile were the words we'd been chasing: NAOS OPHIS.

"Come on in," Payne said. "No live serpents in here today, don't worry. Might find the occasional rat or a lizard or three. The scorpions don't come out in the day."

As he circled the outer walls lighting lamps, Lon and I hesitantly stepped inside. Kerosene and a strange, leathery scent filled my nostrils. The room was larger than I expected, shaped like a dome. A ladder led to a wooden balcony circling the walls beneath the rounded ceiling, and rough beams crisscrossed from one side to the other, from which hung something that looked like Spanish moss, dangling in clumps.

I scanned the shadows. No real furniture here, just three pews facing a sunken fire pit in the center. A couple of display cabinets with glass doors stood against the walls near some odd paintings of snakes devouring cities. Serpentine dragons. A human woman giving birth to a litter of cobras.

Storm-gray light filtered in from glass windows above the balcony. And now that Payne had lit more lamps, I began to be able to see better what dangled from the balcony and the rafters.

Not Spanish moss.

Preserved snake skins.

Hundreds and hundreds and hundreds, tacked up with nails. All shapes, colors, and sizes. This was the leathery smell in the air. Bile rose in the back of my throat.

"Would you like to hear a story?" Payne headed to the far end of the room and climbed stairs onto a wooden dais, where he began lighting candles at an altar. "The Great Serpent traveled down from the Æthyr to see the new world. He settled in a tree in a lush garden, only to have his nap interrupted by a man and a woman. The Serpent was intrigued and tried to converse with the couple about his world, but the man was jealous and forbade the woman to speak."

Candlelight illuminated a sculpture sitting at the back of the altar, as tall as a person: a clay tree whose trunk was being strangled by a massive snake with arms and the head of a man biting an apple. Crude renditions of what could only be Adam and Eve cowered below the branches.

"But the woman was curious," Payne continued. "And she came to the Serpent in secret and willingly offered herself to him. And from her womb was born Sophia, the essence of wisdom. Mediatrix between the two worlds. A gift to all humans. But when Sophia grew to be an adult and started giving her knowledge to the people in this world, the man saw that she wasn't blood of his blood. He saw the Serpent's light in her, and he knew what the woman had done.

"In his petty jealousy, he tried to snuff out Sophia's light. So the Serpent hid her inside a copy of himself, a green snake in the grass. And he told that snake to go out into the world in secret, carrying Sophia's light in its flesh. And the Serpent gave the snake venom, to protect itself from the evil man."

I'm not sure if Lon thought Payne might be referring to him in an abstract sense, but he immediately stuck his hand inside his jacket and quietly thumbed open the strap on his holster. Not good. If I was going to get any information, it had to be now.

"Aren't you an evil man?" I asked Payne.

"I am a being of light trapped inside a human body. Therefore, I am filled with sin. But I partake in the Serpent's gift regularly to cleanse myself." Payne waved his hand to the snake skins hanging above us. "When I consume their bodies, I gain the essence of Sophia's wisdom. The more I consume, the closer I am to home."

He was eating them.

Eating the snakes.

"Is that what Enola wanted from you?" Lon asked, recovering more quickly from that gruesome information than I could. "To find a way to bring Sophia back to life in a human body?"

He spun around to face me. "Enola feigned interest in Sophia, but what she really wanted was Sophia's gift of knowledge." He opened a box on the altar and removed something, then turned around to show it to me: a ripped fragment of parchment framed in gilded glass, a little bigger than his hand. I was too far away to read the writing on it, but the calligraphy looked old.

"What is that?" I asked.

"Take a look," he said, holding it up for me.

My heart sped. I glanced at Lon. He quietly took out his gun and disengaged the safety. I took a step closer. Just a step. Just so I could see better.

"This is all that's left, this small piece. For hundreds of years, my family has kept this. Hundreds of years, and Enola stole it from me within a few months of knowing her."

"What is it?" I repeated.

"It is the Invocation of the Great Serpent."

All of my muscles tightened. "A summoning ritual?"

"To call down the Lord of the Æthyr onto this plane. The Father of Wisdom. Eve's lover."

I'd never heard of such a thing, and surely this, much like Payne's religious fervor, was overstated. But if it had a rare magical seal or some bit of wisdom that might help my mother tweak the Moonchild ritual, I could see why she'd want to steal it.

"It's not the only written record of the Invocation," he expounded. "There are older copies scattered around the world, but this was the only one in the States. And it is sacred knowledge that the Serpent gave to Sophia, so that she could call him back to this plane in secret. But this time, it wasn't an evil man who wanted to erase the Serpent's gift—this time, it was an evil woman who wanted to abuse it."

"Enola, you mean."

After pocketing the gilded frame inside his jacket, he turned to face me again while tugging at the fingertips of his gloves. "The Moonchild experiment. That's all she wanted to talk about, her precious child of the moon, and how the ritual was wrong—how she could give me untold wealth if I'd only let her borrow the parchment. I refused. She stole it from me. And then she cursed me."

Agitated, he threw his gloves onto the altar and held up his hands. They were a horrific sight, mangled and covered in scar tissue. It looked as if fire had melted off all the flesh and his body had barely been able to regrow enough skin to cover his finger bones.

His voice was low and filled with bitterness. "If I get within a mile of Enola, I burn from the inside out. The pain is the worst torture you could imagine. My extremities go first." He yanked up his pants leg to reveal the top of a prosthetic foot inside his boot. "I lost this one the last time I tried to see her, about a year before the Black Lodge slayings started. I've tried to have her murdered, have hired other people to do the deed. They never came back, so I eventually gave up."

"That's impossible," I said. "There's no such magick."

He chuckled. "Having been a victim of it, I must politely disagree. Enola was a master at finding lost magicks and doing what other magicians could not, which is what drew her to my work. I found that out later. You see, we didn't meet by chance—she'd had someone invite me to her book signing. She'd arranged everything, all so she could get her hands on the parchment."

"For her Moonchild experiment," I said, thinking aloud. "She used your invocation to alter her own ritual, so that she could call down a demon into her womb."

"Not a demon. She wanted to create something new."

"Like Sophia?" I asked.

He violently shook his head. "Sophia was the sun. Mother of Wisdom. She was made of golden light, like her father, the Light Bringer. What Enola wanted was a spirit of darkness. The essence of the moon. A creature of *silver*."

He paused at the edge of the dais and pointed a scarred, bony finger at me. "You, wicked child, are not anything like Sophia."

He knew. Of course he did. He knew the minute he set eyes on my halo. And although Mr. Rooke had been wrong when he told me in the gardens that Payne was a friend of my mother's—Payne might have hated my mother as much as I did—he wasn't wrong to warn us that we were treading dark waters in seeking his temple.

Payne was a threat. And we were in grave danger. Every cell in my body screamed this, even before Lon's gun rose in the air to aim at the snake handler.

But I was closer to uncovering my mother's secrets than I'd ever been. And a strange sort of fog was descending inside my sleep-deprived head, like the calm rhythm of a silent lullaby.

"What am I?" I demanded, swaying on my feet.

Lamplight chased shadows over his gaunt figure. "You are an abomination."

Lon's gun clattered to the tile floor. I spun around to see him collapse. He didn't make a noise when his body dropped.

Was he unconscious? Dead? I couldn't see any blood, and I heard no gunshot. Was he drugged? I felt drugged. But we hadn't eaten anything.

I fell to my knees at Lon's side. And as I reached for him, I slipped into darkness.

We'd underestimated the potential peril of Payne's knack.

20

In complete darkness, I smelled the snake skins drying in the rafters. That's how I knew where I was when I woke. The temple was as black as coal, except for a soft rectangle of light falling over my shoulder. I groaned and pushed myself up to sit, wincing at soreness in my cheek and jaw. I must have landed on my face when I fell.

Right after Lon fell.

"Lon?" I patted the floor around me, searching for him as my eyes adjusted to the darkness. But he wasn't there. Panic flooded my veins. "Lon!"

No response. Where was he?

And where was Payne?

The blackness slowly gained texture, and I could make out gray shapes in the dark: the edge of the dais, the clay statue of the serpent with Adam and Eve, the fire pit to my side.

I was alone.

Swinging around to search the shadows, I glanced up to find the source of the light. It was the stained-glass window I'd noticed earlier. I could see the image now. It was a beautiful woman with flaxen hair standing in front of an apple tree. Sophia. She was nude, and her body was covered with golden snake scales.

Like my body.

My other body.

Only mine was black and silver.

"Lon!" I shouted in desperation, pushing myself off the floor. What had Payne done with him? I stumbled around in the dark, looking for a door or a closet or a secret entrance into the cliffs, any place I'd missed before. But there was nothing, not even up on the balcony. I shuffled to the entry and tried the door, but I supposed I'd already known I was locked inside.

Do not panic. Do not. Just think. How long had I been out? Was it still storming outside? I listened for howling wind but heard nothing. Phone. Okay, good, yes. I'd check my phone. I usually kept in in the right pocket of my jeans, but those were getting tighter by the day, so I'd moved it into my jacket . . .

Not there. Not in any pocket.

Gone.

The bastard had taken my phone and locked me in this godforsaken temple. Maybe my mother hadn't been so wrong in hexing him; when I got a hold on his scrawny snake-eating neck, I might just burn him from the inside out, too. But I had to get out of here first. And if the door was locked, I'd get out the hard way.

I carried an old wooden chair across the tile and dragged it up the ladder, hefting it onto the balcony with a grunt before I followed. A few snake skins fluttered to the floor below. The balcony boards were worn and creaky. I had just enough room to walk and did my best to watch my step as I hugged the wall and headed to the stained-glass window of Sophia. I counted out loud and hoisted the chair in the air.

"One, two . . ."

The first swing only cracked the colored glass. The second busted out Sophia's legs. By the fifth or six—I lost count and just started pounding at it— half the glass was gone. So was half the chair. I used the back of it to knock out a few more pieces before I tossed it out through the hole I'd made. Then I looked outside.

Not stormy anymore. It was night. I'd been locked up here since . . . early afternoon?

A few pieces of broken glass tinkled to the ground below. The utility cart that had been parked here earlier was gone, its tires having left trails in the damp sand. God, it was farther down than I'd thought. And jumping into broken glass wasn't my idea of good smarts. But I forgot all about that when a distant shout ripped through the dark desert landscape.

Lon!

No more waffling. I kicked away glass with my shoe and leaped out the window. Glass smashed under my feet as I hit the ground. The impact reverberated through my calves. I lost my balance and had to throw my arms out to stop myself from face-planting. Broken glass bit into my palms. I cried out and surged to my feet, wiping my bloodied hands on my jeans.

Lights twinkled from the bungalows across the canyon. There. That was the direction of Lon's shout. Wasn't it? Sound did funny things in the canyon. But it was where the tire tracks led, so I took off toward the main house. Chilly night air whipped my hair behind me as I raced over the rocky land, moonlight aiding my steps. The compound seemed twice as far as when we'd walked out to the temple. Adrenaline and anger pushed me to quicken my pace.

I sprinted until I thought my lungs would burst. And when I was a few yards away, I slowed to a jog so I could better hear my environment. Where did Payne have Lon? Inside the main house? Lights shone through the breezeway out back. More lights in the carport on the far side. And inside the enclosed pool. And in one of the bungalows. Too many lights, and I couldn't hear anything but the blood pounding in my temples.

Inside the main house—that seemed to be the logical place. But I needed a weapon before I stormed in there. If Payne had taken my phone, he'd certainly confiscated Lon's gun and grabbed his own shotgun out of his Jeep. Gasping for breath, I surveyed the area, looking for something I could use. A board, a pipe, a shovel—anything at all.

Splash.

What the hell was that? I swiveled on a heel to track the source of the noise. My gaze lit on the wood fencing penning the pool. I quieted my heavy breathing and listened harder.

Splish. Plop.

The hair on my arms rose. Was Lon inside the fence? A familiar scent wafted past my face. Acrid. Funky. Gamey. And something else. Something I'd smelled once when I was a kid living in Florida. Memories of a school trip flashed inside my head. St. Augustine. The horrible musky smell of an alligator farm.

I circled the wooden fence until I spotted the pool's entrance. Closed but not locked. Heart racing, I lifted the latch. Rusted hinges creaked as I slowly opened the gate and peered inside. A single kerosene lantern sitting on a round table lit the kidney-shaped pool. Old 1950s-looking chaise longues and patio chairs were haphazardly stacked in one corner, a tangled heap of metal legs surrounded by empty white plastic buckets. Empty beer bottles lined the fencing near the gate.

"Good of you to join us," a voice called across the pool. Payne. I could hear him, but I couldn't see him.

I snatched up one of the empty beer bottles and wielded it like a dagger as I searched the shadows at the other end of the pool. "Where's Lon?"

"Right here," Payne called out. "Would you like to say any final words? He's got a minute or so left, I'd say."

"Lon!" I shouted.

Payne's dark silhouette shifted behind the diving board. "He's lost control over his vocal cords, I'm sorry to say. The Eden boa's venom paralyzes within a minute, so don't feel too bad about getting here in time. He was a goner the minute you smashed my window."

A lighter shape dragged behind Payne's dark figure. And when he stepped out of the shadows, I saw what was happening.

Payne had stripped to the waist. His grizzled torso was darkly tanned and covered in hundreds of tiny white scars. And held up a few feet from his body was a massive, golden yellow snake. Longer than him and fatter than my thigh, it hung from a long pole, a set of metal tongs encircling the scaly flesh behind its head. The bottom half of its length was wrapped around a second piece of piping that extended from the tongs.

Payne's scarred stomach became sunken with every labored breath, and it looked as if his scraggly frame might collapse from the weight of it. "Eden boa," he said in a strained voice. "Named for the bright red apple shape on the back of its head. One of the rarest snakes in the world, and terribly venomous. I'm afraid she's taken a nip out of your friend."

My knees weakened.

It couldn't be true. Payne was lying. Lon was—

On the diving board. I saw the gold in his halo glinting like glitter. He'd been laid out on the board, his arms dangling limply over the pool. His body jerked once, as if he was convulsing. Then . . . nothing.

For a moment, I forgot everything else and made a move to race toward him. Then I remembered Payne's knack. Hard to save someone when you're hypnotized. And I had no idea how far his range extended, but from my recent years of experience facing dozens of knacks in my demon-friendly bar, I'd guess that it didn't extend this far.

"Come closer, child," Payne said. "How can you tell this poor man good-bye from all the way over there? Don't worry, I won't let her bite you, too. You can say your last words in peace. It's clear that you must care for each other in some manner or other, because he called for you before the venom took hold."

"You're insane!" I shouted, pacing along my side of the pool as I tried to decide what to do. Then I looked down. The pool was half filled with dank water, the source of the musky stink. Dark shapes rippled on the surface.

"Mind the edge," Payne said. "Cottonmouth water vipers from Florida. They've got a nasty bite that will cause you to lose large chunks of flesh. They say fatalities are rare, but everyone I've ever thrown in there has proven otherwise."

This couldn't be happening. I didn't give a shit about his pool of vipers—I was too busy panicking about Lon. Could this all be a sham? Was Lon just hypnotized and Payne only screwing with me to get me closer?

But I'd heard Lon shout. All the way across the canyon, I'd heard it. Lon doesn't shout. Hell, Lon barely forms complete sentences some days. And was I going blind, or was his halo fading? I thought so, but I wasn't sure. I just wasn't sure!

And yet.

Even without those fragments of evidence, no way was I risking his life on an *if*.

Better to risk mine instead.

I exhaled a fast breath, calling out to the so-called abomination inside. Sound warped, and the landscape fell away. Magical current shifted under my skin as the transmutation began: the cool rush of scales, the prickly nudge of my rows of horns, and the slithering weight of my tail busting its way through the back pocket of my jeans.

No protective circle to keep my mom at bay. I paused for a moment to listen, remembering how it was back before my hospital stay, when she would tap into me. But I heard no strange whispering. No French-accented voice calling my name. At least, for the moment. Better take advantage of it while I could.

I blinked, and my surroundings returned. A sea of silver dusted the pool and the desert beyond. But it was the look on Payne's face that held my attention. Absolute disbelief.

It wouldn't last long, and I wasn't immune to his knack in this form. So if I was going to get closer to Lon, I needed to take Payne down first. I knew this. But power coursed through me, from my fingertips to the agitated slap of my tail against the cement. And I didn't know if it was the heat of the moment or if what had happened between Lon and me earlier was affecting my good sense, but I was done with being careful.

I tossed the beer bottle and heard it crash somewhere behind me as I stalked around the viper pit. What a foul fucking mess. What was the matter with people? I was sick to death of crazies who had zero respect for anything outside their own selfish motivations: Dare, my mother, the owner of the reptile shop, and now this lunatic.

But if he thought he was taking Lon away from me, he could think again.

"Get thee back!" Payne shouted, thrusting the golden snake in front of him like a shield.

"Oh, but I thought you liked serpents. You want to slice open my belly and eat me, too?"

Payne gulped for air and then began chanting something low and quiet. And just as I had in the temple, I felt that same *whoosh* of sleepiness. No way in hell was I going down again.

One moment I was striding toward him. The next I flew like an loosened arrow. I didn't even feel the cement beneath my shoes, just the slice of cold wind through my clothes, and I was in his face. The flattened head of the golden snake reared back. I knocked the metal contraption from Payne's hands. Both it and the snake sailed through air and struck the wooden fencing, which collapsed under the weight and toppled backward as if it had been struck by a wrecking ball.

"Aeyyhhhh!"

Payne stumbled a step, shouting hysterically as his eyes widened in terror. And I might have almost felt sorry for the old bastard had I not caught a glimpse of Lon's limp body on the diving board. And that just sent me into a rage.

"Holy Light Bringer," he prayed to the night sky, "protect me from this monstrosity—"

I clamped a hand around his throat and squeezed.

He reached behind his back and pulled out Lon's gun. The cold muzzle slammed against my forehead. Half a second, and I'd be dead. But half a second was all I needed to jerk my head around and knock it away with my horns.

The shot exploded over my shoulder.

Out of my peripheral vision, I saw the gun swinging back around. I didn't even think about it. I just let go of his neck and pushed with my mind.

The gun dropped. And Payne sailed backward . . . and backward, until he was flailing in midair over the pool. His disbelieving eyes met mine one last time.

And I dropped him.

The descending scream was muffled by the eruption of snake-filled water that shot several feet up into the air when his body hit the surface.

Let his ill-kept vipers do what they wanted. I

frankly didn't care if the crazy asshole lived or died. All I cared about was wrapping my arms around Lon's legs and tugging him back to safety. Back to me, where he belonged. But God, he felt so heavy as I pulled him onto the wet cement. So heavy. Not moving.

I barely heard Payne flailing around in the viper pit. Barely heard his gurgling screams. Because I was too busy listening for Lon's breath. Lon's heartbeat. It wasn't there. And something much worse: his halo had faded away.

21

No breath. No heartbeat. No halo.

And still, my mind fought it.

Lon couldn't be dead. This wasn't happening. It was a trick of Payne's knack. Never mind that I'd never seen a knack do this. Maybe he'd amped it up somehow, with something like Dare's bionic drug.

And even as my panic-fueled mind was trying to rationalize all this, the frantic splashing in the pool had slowed and finally stopped. Payne was dead. His knack would stop working on Lon.

Which meant . . .

The golden snake *had* bitten Lon.

But where? Not on his face or neck. Not his hands. I lifted his shirt and saw nothing there. Legs. Arms—

Arm. There. Two ragged holes in his thin leather jacket, just above his left elbow. The pale brown leather was stained with blood.

The jacket was too tight to remove without effort. I reached inside his jeans pocket and fished out his pocketknife, right where he always kept it, next to his car keys. Guess Payne hadn't bothered to confiscate Lon's stuff as he had mine. I supposed he'd counted on Lon being too paralyzed to be a threat.

Dare had once thought that about me.

Never assume.

I used the pocketknife to saw open the cuff of his jacket and sliced up the sleeve, splaying open the leather. Jesus. No wonder I couldn't get the jacket off— the bite was already swelling. Okay, think, Bell. Think. What did I know about snakebites? Only that you were supposed to cut them open and suck out the venom. But what if the venom had already stopped a man's heart? Removing the venom wasn't going to help that.

CPR. I could do that. Kar Yee and I had both learned it for the bar. After dropping the pocketknife, I pinched his nose and puffed air into his mouth. Once. Twice. Then I tried compressions on his heart. One, two, three—

What the hell was I doing? Screw CPR, I had something better.

Tapping into Payne's electricity, I found a fat pocket of current nearby and reeled it into my body. It surged and sank inside me like the tide rising over a dry beach. I held it for a moment, letting it kindle my Heka. Then I pressed my palms over Lon's heart and zapped him.

Electric pain shot through my arms as Lon's chest seized.

"Lon!" I shouted in his face, as if that would help.

Breathe, dammit! I pinched his nose again, but when I fitted my mouth over his, he jerked and gasped for air.

"Oh, thank God," I said, silvery tears blurring my sight.

His eyes opened, but he didn't see me. He was struggling for breath. His body wasn't moving.

Venom.

Fuck.

I started to slice open the snakebite on his arm. Were you supposed to do this or not? I couldn't remember! But when I set the blade against his skin, I stopped.

All knacks. I had all of them, including healing. And if I could perform metaphysical surgery on Yvonne to dig out a damn spell, then removing venom had to be possible. Somehow.

Wrapping my hand around his injured arm, I closed my eyes and pushed my consciousness inside him. If I was afraid I wouldn't know what I was looking for or how to find it, I was wrong, because the venom was as bright as neon in fog. It didn't belong. And it was everywhere. Unlike what I'd done to Yvonne, I couldn't just rip this out.

In my panic, the only thing I could think to do was picture my hand as a magnet and the venom as one of those Wooly Willy toys, the one with a magnetic wand that could be used to create a beard or a mustache made of metal fillings over a drawing of a man's face. If Lon lived, we could laugh about it later.

Come to me, I thought, willing the venom out of

him. *Leave this body.* I repeated it like a mantra, over and over, not giving a good goddamn if it was tipping my crazy scales to be talking to some animal's body fluid. I cared about nothing but the sound beneath my ear, where I'd laid my head on Lon's chest to hear his heart. How remarkable it was that I fit so perfectly there, in the dip of his breastbone. I had the oddest feeling of déjà vu. As if it was the most natural thing in the world for me to be lying there on top of him. As if I belonged there.

Please. I'll do anything, please.

Christ. One kiss and a hand job from the man, and I was ready to give away my soul to keep him alive. But I didn't have long to dwell on that, because two things happened at once.

Something warm slid against my hand.

And beneath my ear, Lon's chest rumbled. He was coughing.

"Lon!" I pushed myself up to give him room.

His halo bloomed around the crown of his head. Alive! Most definitely alive. He cracked open his eyes and looked surprised to see me. In a rough voice, he asked, "Where is he?"

"You're not dead," I said stupidly. Then I started blubbering like a maniac.

"Hey, whoa." He strained to pull himself up.

"Don't move," I said through the tears. "Your heart just stopped, you idiot. Oh, Jesus, that was—" My hand was tingling. I loosened my grip on Lon's arm to find blood-tinged liquid dripping off my hand.

The venom, hell's bells. Well, at least it distracted me from crying. I wiped it on the side of my jeans—they were ruined anyway, what with the new tail hole.

Lon reached up to swipe a thumb under my eyes. "Where's Payne?" he asked again.

"Dead in the viper pool. We're safe."

Despite my protests, Lon sat up and inspected his wound. The swelling was already going down. "You did this?"

"Well, not the biting part, but yeah. I just—"

"How did you get out of the temple? I heard glass breaking."

"I jumped."

"Cady! Jesus. You can't do that. Are you okay? Are you feeling any pains?"

"Just my knees. My God, I'm not some precious porcelain doll. I healed myself in the hospital, as you kindly reminded me before you gave me that angry orgasm in the hotel room."

He made a strangled noise. One hand clamped around the back of my neck. He pulled me close and kissed me firmly. "You saved my life," he said against my lips.

"Technically, I brought you back to life. Or, at least, back from the brink of death. Not too shabby for an abomination," I said with a tight smile.

He made a low noise as his gaze moved over my face. "You're the most beautiful thing I've ever seen."

"Please don't make me cry again."

"Your mother—"

I shook my head. "I haven't heard her. But I probably shouldn't stay like this much longer. Tell me how you feel. Are you tingling? I don't know if I got it all. Should I try to heal you some more? I don't want your skin to turn black and fall off, and what about your heart? Does it feel right? I'm not—"

"All right, already. Enough with the questions. You sound just like Jupe."

"But—"

"I'm a little light-headed, and my arm hurts like a motherfucker." He rotated it and flexed his fingers. "But I can move it, which is something I couldn't do about ten seconds after Payne forced that damned snake to sink its fangs into me. Where the hell is that thing?"

"Somewhere over there." I gestured toward the downed fence. "Payne took my phone. Do you have yours?"

"I'll tell you if you get off me."

"Oh," I said, slightly embarrassed, as I rocked away from him and teetered on one knee.

"Don't be. I like you on top. And for the record, it wasn't an angry orgasm." The corners of his mouth quirked up in a dirty little smile that made me fall backward onto my ass. Which hurt. In a weird way. It took me a second to realize I was sitting on my tail.

He lifted a brow.

"I . . . better shift back down," I said.

His face sobered. "I think that's a wise idea."

My sight and hearing returned to normal when I concentrated and pushed away the Moonchild body.

Meanwhile, Lon found that he did, indeed, have his phone. "A million and one texts from Jupe," he murmured. "And it's almost midnight? Jesus fucking Christ. We lost *hours*."

"Half a day," I confirmed, looking around the pool. I searched the dark water for Payne's body and couldn't find it. That gave me the creeps. I didn't want to dream about his bloated corpse popping out of the viper pit.

Lon grunted behind me. He was having trouble pushing himself up to stand. I helped him to his feet and encouraged him to lean on me.

"Maybe we should find a hospital," I said.

"I'm fine," he said in a weary voice. "Just a little woozy. Need to rest."

Which probably meant he was about to die again but was too stubborn to admit it. While helping him keep his balance as we skirted the wretched pool, I spotted Payne's abandoned coat and shirt on a nearby patio table. My phone was there, too. And Lon's wallet. I grabbed both, then remembered something and peeked inside Payne's jacket pocket. Jackpot. The gilded frame with the parchment fragment was still there. I snagged it.

"Let's get the hell out of here," I said, eager to get to a safe place where Lon could rest and I could do a little old-fashioned magick. "I'll drive."

It only took a few minutes to get him into the SUV, and a couple more for me to change into an extra pair of not-ripped jeans. And while we argued the pros and cons of making an anonymous report to the police about Payne—from a pay phone, we decided—I drove us to the nearest decent-looking hotel in Twentynine Palms. It was somewhere between acceptable and shady, but on the plus side, it was clean and quiet, with an all-night diner across the parking lot.

"You need to sleep inside the ward," Lon mumbled after I'd checked in.

"What?"

"The canvas tarp. You can't fall asleep outside it. Not after what you did tonight. How long were you transmutated?"

"A while."

"If your mother noticed, she'll know you aren't in a coma anymore and might try to tap into you when you're asleep. It's a wonder she didn't while you were hypnotized."

Yes, I supposed he had a point. And he sounded frustrated with me that I'd put myself in this situation, but I couldn't fathom why. I wanted to say, "Hello, I saved your life, dumbass," but I didn't. We both knew it was the only choice. And the tarp might be an inconvenience, but if it kept my mom out of my head, I had nothing to complain about.

After helping Lon into the room and calling to check in with Jupe, I soon discovered that being passed out for several hours under Payne's hypnotic knack didn't count as actual rest. We both felt as if we'd been awake for two days straight. I grabbed a first-aid kit from the SUV and cleaned up Lon's snakebite, which was definitely better, thank God. I also fetched us something to eat from the diner. When I got back to the room, Jupe called.

He reported that Priya had noticed my transmutation in the Æthyr. Big-time. The Hermeneus spirit had unfortunately lost track of my mother, so he didn't know if she'd also noticed. But I guessed it had panicked him so much that he'd immediately appeared to Jupe and told him. Jupe had been freaking out that he couldn't get in touch with us. Poor kid sounded frazzled, and this made me miss him. And made me wish something fierce that we were back home.

Back at Lon's home, I mean. Not mine. I got that weird rush of déjà vu again and continued to feel unmoored, even while I gathered some random supplies from the motel room and began assembling a servitor.

Servitors are Heka boomerangs, roving balls of focused magical energy that I can shoot out into the world. They're able to perform small, mindless tasks: remote viewing and spying, information gathering. And in this case, I hoped it could track down a single sheet of paper.

I needed a physical vessel to anchor the Heka. Back at home, I kept a supply of crudely sculpted clay dolls for this purpose. Since I had no clay dolls at my disposal, I used Lon's pocketknife to carve a small bar of hotel soap.

"You sure that's going to work?" he asked.

"We'll find out."

While he ate, I broke open Payne's gilded frame and removed the parchment fragment.

If my mother had stolen the parchment this fragment belonged to, I was hoping a servitor could find it. No way in hell she would have gotten rid of something that valuable, especially if she used it to rework the Moonchild spell. I hoped that finding it would finally give me some solid insight into the Moonchild spell.

Which would, in turn, shine a light on how I might reverse it.

Using the parchment fragment as a "scent" for the servitor to track, I performed a simple life-giving spell on my crudely carved bar of soap. The resulting servitor didn't look like much, just a loosely humanoid shape made of light. Once charged, it emerged from the soap doll like a fairy light and floated on its merry way to track down the original parchment . . . and maybe the Moonchild spell.

It might take hours, it might take days, but if the other piece of the parchment existed, the servitor would find it and come back to show me where it was. I allowed myself to be cautiously hopeful about this prospect.

And it was the only real lead we had, other than the last line from Wildeye's diary page: "3AC 1988." Lon and I had puzzled over this since we left Golden Peak, trying to see how—if—it fit together with my Arcadia Bell alias, but to no avail.

As I wrapped the servitor soap doll inside a washcloth and tucked it into my overnight bag, I thought about everything Payne had said in the temple, all his crazy beliefs about the Serpent and Sophia. After all of that, I really didn't know if it got me any closer to understanding what my parents had planted inside me during my conception. Was I half human, half demon? Or some sort of Frankenstein creation that was greater than the sum of my parts?

One thing I was sure of: all that garbage about Sophia being Mother of Wisdom was a crock of shit. Which probably meant the whole Mother of Ahriman thing was likely an inflated title of no value. All that time spent with Payne, with Rooke, chasing Wildeye's ghostly trail, only to be sent all the way back around the proverbial game board with no real gains: go directly to Jail, do not pass Go, do not collect $200.

Weary and frustrated, I stepped into the bathroom to wash remnants of soap off my hands. When I'd finished, I came out to find the anti-Enola canvas spread over one of the beds. Stretched on top of it was Lon, fast asleep. His shirt sat in a heap on the carpet with his belt, and the top button of his jeans was unbuttoned, but it looked as if that might have been all he could manage before he gave up and passed out. He still had his shoes on.

I watched him for moment. I wasn't worried; his halo was bright, and his chest rose and fell in a comfortable, steady rhythm. I'd have been content to watch him all night. Mainly because he was alive and okay. But the longer I watched him, the more I found that assessment taking a decidedly nonsaintly detour as my eyes followed the line of golden hair bisecting a very fine chest straight down to the unbuttoned button of his jeans.

Damn.

After tugging off his shoes, I stripped down to my T-shirt and pulled the sheet over both of us. He didn't even wake up. At least it gave me a chance at a closer peek. Just a little harmless perusal. Or lustful ogle, whatever. My gaze wandered over lean muscle. Really nice arms. Really nice everything. Oh, and there was something I'd seen before: the scar over his ribs where his ex-wife, Yvonne, had stabbed him the day they got divorced. And on his neck, the scar he'd gotten at Halloween from Duke Chora's blade. I'd never seen so much blood.

Christ. I'd been through a lot with him.

Gingerly, I reached for the scar on his neck and traced it with the tips of my fingers. A thin silver chain stretched above it. Funny. Lon wasn't one to wear jewelry. Whatever was on the chain had swung to the other side of his neck and was buried in his hair. I arched my arm to retrieve it, careful not to wake him as I slid it to the front of the chain.

A ring.

An engagement ring.

Tiers of rectangular stones surrounded an elongated emerald-cut diamond. A fairly sizable one and damn heavy. The setting was geometric and sleek, very classy and modern. The diamonds alone had to have cost a pretty penny, but it was what lay inside the center stone that made it priceless.

Lon's halo. Gold-flecked green swirled inside the stone. Demons who could afford it hired a gemplexer, a sort of chemist who could siphon off a bit of halo and trap it inside certain gemstones. It was more than a little expensive and enormously romantic to offer a piece of yourself to someone else.

My throat tightened. Was this Yvonne's engagement ring? God, if he'd been wearing it all these years, was he holding a torch for her? Or maybe he just kept it because he didn't want a piece of his halo ending up in a pawn shop. Wanting to believe it was the latter, I slid the ring back where it was, out of my sight. Then I curled up against his side and held on to him as if he were mine.

22

Late Sunday morning, while Cady and Lon were sleeping in Twentynine Palms, Jupe tried one last code on his dad's library door. The fingerprint mechanism could be bypassed with a numerical master code, but the system only let you try three wrong codes before locking it down for twenty-four hours. Which was exactly what was happening now—the flashing red lights told him he'd failed again before the keypad shut off.

"Goddammit," Jupe muttered. "What is the code?"

"Jupiter?"

Crap. The Holidays were already back from church.

"I'm just getting something in the studio," Jupe called back as he quickly strode down the hallway and popped into his dad's photography room. He scanned the tables, looking for the "something" he was supposed to be getting as his phone buzzed.

He glanced at the screen. Leticia.

His heart leaped inside his chest. He fumbled

with the screen to answer it, nearly dropping the phone in his haste. "Hello," he said a little too loudly.

"Hey, it's me," Leticia's voice said in his ear.

He nearly melted into the floor. "Hey. What up?"

"You busy?"

"Maybe, I don't know." That's it, nice and smooth. Chicks liked it when you acted reserved. That's what his friend Jack always said, anyway.

But Leticia didn't sound all that happy. In fact, she sounded downright pissed. "Look, are you or aren't you busy? Because I'm about to do you a big favor, but if you don't have time—"

"I have time, I have time!" he said quickly, then regretted sounding so eager.

She didn't seem to notice. "My sister is about to drive into La Sirena. Her boyfriend lives there."

"Okay . . ." Jupe wasn't sure what that meant, but he really didn't want to think about Leticia's sister any more than he had to.

"I'm coming with her," Leticia finally explained. "Our grandma lives in La Sirena. She used to know the Duvals when she was grandmaster of the lodge before my mom took over. I thought maybe we could get some information from her."

"Man, I don't know. I'm already feeling guilty about telling you about Cady. I'm not sure if it's a good idea to bring someone else into this."

"Look, my grandma is pretty cool. She and my mom don't get along, so you don't have to worry about her blabbing anything."

Jupe thought of his own grandmother, Gramma Rose, who was ten kinds of awesome, so maybe Leticia was right. Maybe he could trust someone else. He certainly wanted to. As much as he hated to admit it, the problem seemed bigger than something he and Leticia could handle alone.

Plus, he really wanted to see Leticia again. Like, *r-e-e-eally* wanted.

"Okay," he said, blowing out a long breath. "Let's do it. Where and when?"

"She lives in the Storybook Retirement Cottages near the Village. The condos across the street from the amusement park, the ones that look like Hobbit houses."

"Oh, yeah! I know where that is." And the Holidays wouldn't say no to driving him there to meet up with Leticia. Come on, a retirement home? How much more unsexy and innocent could *that* be? Unless you were Jupe, in which case, it was the sexiest thing he'd ever heard in his life, because he'd get to be alone with Leticia. Sort of.

"Meet me at the front gate in forty minutes."

And he did. The Holidays were totally fine with driving him there, just as he'd suspected. But when he tried to race out of the minivan, they weren't having it.

"Hello," Mrs. Holiday said from the passenger seat, rolling down her window to get a look at Leticia. She was wearing her pink hoodie and jeans, but today her dark hair glittered with tiny pins shaped like pink roses. The T-shirt beneath her hoodie was a mildly disturbing cartoon image of a princess slaying a knight while a dragon looked on in approval.

"Jupiter, aren't you going to introduce us?" Mr. Holiday said from the driver's seat, leaning next to Mrs. Holiday to peer out the window.

"Oh, uh, yeah. This is Leticia Vega. I met her . . . through Jack," he lied. "She's from Morella." He wiped his sweaty palm on his jeans. "Leticia, this is Mr. and Mrs. Holiday."

"Nice to meet you," Leticia said.

Jupe should have stopped there, but he was nervous. "They're my godparents, and they live in a house on our property. They're not really man and woman, obviously. It's a long story. But they're married. They're lesbians."

Oh, God. He was talking way too much again.

But Leticia just lifted a brow at him before saying to them, "That's cool."

Mrs. Holiday smirked at him. She knew he was uncomfortable—she always knew. And she loved torturing him. It was practically her hobby. "Well, it's lovely to meet you, Leticia. We're headed to the farmer's market down by the boardwalk. We'll swing back here in an hour to pick you up, Jupiter. Exactly an hour." She cut him a look that clearly said that if he wasn't standing right there, she'd take away his laptop and phone. Again.

"I'll be here. Later." He quickly turned his back on them and strode toward the gate with Leticia, wincing when they tooted the horn twice as they drove away. Finally.

They walked through the main gate of the retirement community. She was right; the buildings really did look like overgrown Hobbit houses, with their round windows and sloping green roofs. They'd been there since Jupe could remember and fit in with the fairy-tale vibe of the Village.

"Sorry 'bout all that," he mumbled.

"Don't be. They were nice." She leaned closer and sniffed the air near his face. "Are you wearing cologne?"

"Aftershave."

"Oh."

He only really had to shave, like, once a month, but she didn't need to know that.

"It's pretty strong." She reached up and touched the skin near his mouth that he'd nicked with the razor.

"Oww," he said, but he was too happy that she was touching him to notice the pain all that much. And he wanted to touch her back, but when she caught his eyes wandering to her breasts—which wasn't his fault, really, because the dragon's eyes were positioned in exactly the right places—he decided it was probably best to keep his hands above her neck. So he poked one of the rose pins in her hair. "What's all this?"

"I like to experiment," she said defensively, jerking her head away from him.

"It looks nice. Kinda different. I like weird things."

Her face scrunched up, like maybe she was unsure how to take a compliment. So he smiled at her; she loosened up and smiled back. "Thanks. I guess I like weird things, too."

"Yeah?"

"I'm here with you, aren't I?" she said with a big grin that made her cheeks plump up prettily.

Jupe's insides twanged like an out-of-tune guitar string. His own smile slid into something that felt like it was verging on stupid, but he didn't care. She liked him. He liked her. This was the single greatest day of his entire life. He couldn't wait to tell his dad and Cady and his Auntie Adella. And he was even sort of glad the Holidays had seen Leticia, so they could confirm how hot she was in case no one believed him. Maybe he could sneak in a picture for good measure.

"Here's my grandma's place. I called her this morning, so she's expecting us. But I didn't tell her what we wanted, so let me do the talking." Leticia lifted a brass knocker shaped like a frog and banged it. Then she rang the doorbell three times. "She doesn't hear so well."

After a few more bangs on the door, it finally swung open. A tiny gray-haired woman stood in the doorway. She was sort of round like Leticia, and they had the same big brown eyes. She was dressed in what the Holidays called upscale loungewear, just old-lady sweatpants with a matching pullover top.

They didn't look good on the Holidays, and they didn't look good on Leticia's grandmother. But the last time he'd pointed that out, he got bitched out. So he wisely kept his mouth shut.

"*Mija*," the old woman said, hugging Leticia tightly. "What a good girl you are to come see your *abuelita*."

Leticia pulled back and stepped to the side to introduce him. "This is my Grandma Vega, my dad's mom. Grandma, this is my friend, Jupe," she said in a loud voice. "The one I told you about on the phone."

"What kind of name is that?"

"It's short for Jupiter," he said, extending his hand.

Her grandmother accepted it and squinted at him, looking him up and down as she shook. "You didn't tell me he was a black boy."

Oh, hell, no. Did she really just say that?

"Excuse me?" he said, snatching his hand back.

Leticia flashed Jupe an embarrassed look. "No one cares about those things anymore, Grandma."

"I know, I'm too old to understand how the world works," her grandmother said with heavy sarcasm. She glanced at him. "You a mulatto or just light-skinned?"

"Mulatto?" What was this, nineteenth-century New Orleans? Who the shit said that anymore?

"It's called biracial, Grandma."

The old woman shrugged. "I was only curious. What do I care? At least he's not Salvadoran." She glanced at Jupe. "You drink juice?"

What was the matter with this woman? Was this a trick question? "Uh, yeah?"

"Then I suppose you can both come on in and sit down."

As she wandered off to a small kitchen, Leticia grabbed his hand and dragged him into a tiny living room decorated like a beige beach house. Not exactly what he expected from an old magician who used to run an occult order. "You didn't tell me your grand-mother was a racist," he murmured. "Is she going to call me the N-word, too?"

Leticia looked supremely mortified.

"She's not racist, she's just old and opinionated," she argued weakly. "Okay, well, at least she's an equal-opportunity racist. She talks trash about white people, too. She even calls my father a *pocho* because he only uses Spanglish. She claims he's too American and shames their family back in Ensenada."

"And why does she hate Salvadorans?"

"Something about a political dispute that's, like, two hundred years old. I don't know. But when I was ten, she went to jail for starting a fistfight in a Safeway parking lot with a woman who had an El Salvador flag on her car."

Jupe restrained a laugh. "Holy shit!"

"Shh," Leticia said, giggling as she covered her mouth with her hand.

"*Santo mierda!*" he said, correcting himself in a muffled voice. He'd learned that one from a dubbed Spanish version of *Animal House* on Univision, and using it now reinforced his suspicion that the things he learned from watching TV had more real-world applications than the crap he learned at school.

"No, no, no!" Leticia whispered. "She hates swearing."

He peeled her hand off his mouth and grinned down at her, quickly tracing a line down the center of her palm with his finger. Jesus, her skin was soft. When she didn't pull away, he traced it again. "You have a long life line," he murmured.

"I do?" she whispered back.

"I can read palms pretty well." He couldn't. But a couple of months back, he'd gleaned the basics of palmistry from a 1960s library book and had since been using it as an excuse to touch the hand of every girl in his class. All of that practice had been worth it for this fleeting moment with Leticia. Especially for the way she looked up at him, all breathless and lazy; her lips parted, but no words came out.

Just when it was getting good, shuffling footfalls behind them made him drop her hand like it was a hot potato. Just in time, too. Leticia's grandmother set a tray down on a shell-covered coffee table and offered them each a can of mango juice with straws. When she leaned over, he saw a pendant around her neck with the same symbol he'd seen on the altar— the real one, not Leticia's naked sister—at the lodge. A unicursal hexagram.

"Now, what do you want to chat about?" she said, sitting down in a recliner with her own can of juice.

They sat across from her on a couch that seemed to suck Jupe's body down into it.

Leticia kicked off her flats and drew her legs up. "Like I said on the phone, Jupe isn't a savage. He attended Sophic Mass last week."

"Who was the acting priestess? Cristina?"

Leticia groaned under her breath. "Yes, ma'am."

"Why your mama allows that, I'll never understand. Mark my words, that girl is going to end up in some pornographic film."

"Grandma!"

"Oversexed girls like her shouldn't be priestessing. In my day, all the women took turns, young and old. It wasn't a beauty contest, it was sacred honor. Now Cristina's talking about fake boobs."

"Mama told her no."

"Today maybe. But Cristina will wear her down. Spoiled brat can't even bother to get out of the car and say hello to me," she grumbled before narrowing her eyes at Jupe. "If you think my baby granddaughter here is going to get a boob job one day, you can think again."

Part of Jupe wanted to tell the crazy old woman that Leticia's boobs were awesome already, but mostly he was just freaking out. His Gramma would go Godzilla on him if he so much as made a joke about chicken breast. "My dad's a photographer, so I've seen a lot of plastic surgery. Natural's better."

"I couldn't agree more," the old woman said very seriously, raising her juice can in confirmation.

Now Leticia looked freaked out. She quickly changed the subject. "Grandma, I told Jupe that you used to know the Duvals back in the day."

"The who?"

"Duvals," Leticia repeated in a louder voice. "You know, the serial killers."

Her grandmother's face brightened. "Oh, the Duvals. They weren't killers." They were, but Jupe didn't argue. "That was just talk from savages, trying to destroy our order. The Duvals were celebrities. But I don't talk about people in the order with outsiders."

"But this is important."

"I said no. And you promised me you wouldn't tell your mama I knew the Duvals, but here you are, telling a—"

"A what?" Jupe said, sudden anger flaring inside his chest.

"Outsider," she finished sourly.

Leticia and her grandmother immediately began conversing in angry Spanish, the speed of which was way too fast for Jupe's junior-high Español skills to follow. And the more they fought, the worse he felt for Leticia. She was really trying, but every point she made was quickly Whac-A-Moled down by the old lady.

After weeks of fending off the temptation to use his knack, he made a split-second decision to make an exception. This was important, after all. He was doing this for Cady. And for his future brother or sister. And for Leticia.

Triple hero.

He took a deep breath and interrupted the grand-mother-granddaughter throwdown. "Mrs. Vega," he said in a loud voice, his persuasion turned up as high as he could crank it. "You can trust me, and you want to help us by answering all our questions about the Duvals." When he opened his eyes, both females were gaping at him, so he added in a knack-free voice, "Right?"

Grandma Vega's shoulders relaxed. She looked a little dazed as she said, "You don't look untrustworthy."

"I can keep a secret like nobody's business," he assured her.

"I suppose there's no sense in holding on to se-crets about the dead, is there? What do you want to know?"

Cha-ching! Pride and victory zinged through him. Well, until he noticed Leticia staring a hole into the side of his face. Crap. Dealing with humans was rough. Not for the first time, he wondered how open Leticia was to the concept of Earthbounds. Cady once told him that some of the people in her order were believers, so maybe she was cool about it. You never could tell. Jupe had the Nox symbol all over his social media, but if Leticia knew what it meant, she hadn't said anything.

Her grandmother was waiting for an answer, so Jupe put the Earthbound dilemma out of his mind for the moment and said, "So, yeah, umm, how did you meet the Duvals?"

"I first met them when I visited the main lodge down in Florida, back in 1979 for the annual summer solstice ritual. Everyone loved them. They were practically superstars of the occult world. And I met their first child, the boy. I can't remember his name."

They had another kid? Cady had a brother? This was brand-new information to Jupe.

"Anyway, he died in the mid-1980s—"

Oh.

"—so he must've been around two then. Strange child. I babysat him one afternoon, and he bit me so hard I had to have three stitches on my hand." She pointed it out, but Jupe couldn't see any scars.

"Is that the only time you saw them?" he asked.

"Oh, no. It was after the boy died that I saw them next," she said, leaning back in her chair with her juice can. "Imagine my surprise when I bumped into them at Gifts of the Magi."

Jupe glanced between Grandma Vega and Leticia.

"A magical supply shop on the highway between Morella and La Sirena," Leticia explained. "It closed down a few years ago when the owner died."

"Got it," Jupe said. "So, wait, they were here in the area? Were they visiting the lodge in Morella?"

Leticia's grandmother slurped the last of her juice and shook her head. "That was the surprise. If they were on official business, they'd be staying in Morella at the lodge. It has guest rooms for traveling dignitaries. Makes it easier when other members come down from San Francisco or if the caliph visited, may the gods rest his soul." She kissed her hexagram pendant in tribute.

"So if they weren't visiting the lodge on official business, why were they here?"

"They had a winter home in La Sirena."

Jupe frowned. "Are you sure we're talking about the same Duvals? They're from Florida."

"Enola and Alexander," she said, grunting as she pushed herself out of the recliner. She shuffled across the room to a bookshelf and removed a worn photo album before plunking it down on the coffee table. "Where is it . . . ?" She paged through thick black sheets of old photographs affixed with paper corners. "Here we are. Mrs. Pendleton took this of us—she was the Gifts of the Magi owner who died a few years back. That's me, in the middle."

Jupe squinted at a three-by-five photograph taken inside the magical supply shop. He recognized the Duvals instantly from pictures in the true-crime books he'd read about the Black Lodge murders. They looked uncomfortable and were flanking a much younger Grandma Vega, who was smiling from ear to ear.

She tapped the photo with a long fingernail. "They made me promise to keep their winter home hush-hush because they were busy writing a book and didn't want people from the order popping over and interrupting them. Understandable, of course. And I kept my word."

Jupe leaned closer to read the squiggly handwriting

on the bottom of the photo: "The Duvals, January 1989." Crap! That was the year Cady was born . . . only, she was born October 1. He knew, because her driver's license had her fake birthday, but she'd told him her real birthday back when she first started dating his dad. Jupe counted backward from October 1. Nine months would be January, the same time her parents were here in La Sirena. What did this all mean?

"Hold on," he said. "They spent January 1989 here in La Sirena. That's what you're saying?"

"Yes, but that was only the first year, right after they'd bought the winter home. They came back the very next winter solstice with their new daughter, the Moonchild. She was only three months old, I believe. I was the first person outside the main lodge to see her in person," she said proudly.

Cady! She'd seen Cady as a baby. This was crazy. Jupe's mind was speeding off in ten different directions at once. He'd come here expecting to get some information on summoning a demon and ended up uncovering something Cady herself didn't even know. "So you saw them twice? In 1989 and 1990?"

"And every winter after that. They wrote their books here because it was peaceful," the old woman said. "They usually came by themselves, especially after their daughter got older. But every year around the holidays, I'd have breakfast with them at that vegetarian diner near the farmer's market. Well, that is, until they died in that terrible car accident with their daughter seven years ago."

She chuckled to herself and closed the photograph album. "You know, I could've sworn I'd seen them last year at a gas station on the north end of Ocean Avenue, but Leticia's mama said that was impossible. And she was right, of course. Can't see dead people, can you? My eyes aren't what they once were."

Santo mierda.

23

I was dreaming about shrimp again. This time, Lon was showing me how to catch them with a fishing pole in a stream. But while he was struggling to reel one in, I walked away and found myself in a strangely familiar field. Tall grass. Wildflowers. And standing in the middle of it with her back to me was a tall, leggy woman with graying hair.

A terrible anxiety came over my dream body.

The woman turned around and smiled triumphantly. "*Ma petite lune.* You are awake."

Snapping out of sleep, I tumbled off the bed in a cold sweat. Several panicked moments ticked by as I jerked my head around, looking for my mother in the shadows, unsure of where I was. Or *when* it was . . .

Twentynine Palms. The cheap motel. Two in the afternoon.

Daytime. The safe time to sleep. So that was only a dream. Right? I pushed off the floor and looked at Lon. He was stretched out on the bed, softly snoring.

His halo was still healthy. But when my gaze slipped over the rumpled sheet, I found the problem.

I'd forgotten to charge the ward.

No protection. I had slept without any protection, and now my mother knew I was no longer in a coma. Worse, she'd managed to tap into my dreams *during the daytime*.

Mad at myself and scared, I sat on the floor next to the bed and wilted into a shaking mess. My breathing quickened. It didn't take long before I was hyperventilating and nauseated. I stuck my head between my knees and tried to count myself into a calmer state. The mattress creaked. A warm hand smoothed across my shoulders as Lon settled on the floor beside me.

"What's wrong?"

"What *isn't* wrong?" I said before telling him what had just happened.

He listened, rubbing circles on my back, while I talked into my knees. When I finished, he exhaled a long breath, and said, "Cady—"

"What am I going to do, Lon? I'm out of ideas. I don't know what to do next."

"*Cady.*"

I looked up at him. He pointed in front of us. A ball of cotton-candy-pink light hovered in the air above my overnight bag. My servitor! That was fast. Too fast? We both watched the pink light disappear inside the bag, heading back into my soap doll.

"I need your pocketknife again."

I both dreaded and couldn't wait to see what it had found. I pulled out the soap doll and wasted no time drawing the series of symbols that would trigger the servitor to spill its contents. I only needed a tiny bit of Heka to charge the retrieval spell, so I stuck my finger in my mouth and rubbed saliva over the scribbled sigil while stabbing the carved bar of soap.

Cool energy surrounded me as the servitor's collected images unfolded. Like a psychic film, it replayed the spell's journey: leaving the hotel room last night, floating into darkness. Then it sped up in a flash of blurry light, the shift making me dizzy until it settled on its final destination.

A forest, heavily wooded. A dirt road. A dark green house sat at the end of it, the roof covered in leaves and pine needles. Dozens of white antlers hung around the door. A hunting lodge? No identifying house number. No mailbox. No signs. The image moved through the door like a ghost to show the inside of the house. A spacious great room with a rustic fireplace. Sparsely furnished. Dark. Blinds drawn.

I strained to see anything that might indicate location: mail, calendar, family photos, letterhead. But no. Nothing and more nothing. It was the blandest, least personal house I'd ever seen.

"Come on, give me something," I murmured, as if that would help. It wasn't sentient; the images were already prerecorded, so to speak. What I saw was what it had retrieved. I hoped it would move into another room where I might see something more—magnets on the refrigerator or a takeout menu on the counter. But the servitor's metaphysical lens only moved to the far end of the room, where an oversized grandfather clock sat near the fireplace.

Deer and trees and wood nymphs were carved into the massive wooden base. A stag's antlered head jutted above the gold clock dial. A terrible familiarity washed over me at the sight of it. Some dusty, long-forgotten memory cowered in the corned of my mind.

I'd seen this clock before.

The servitor's gaze bobbed and floated down to the bottom of the clock. In a swift movement, it pushed forward and ghosted through the base, but there was nothing but darkness. Darkness, and more darkness, then—

Pop!

The servitor's transmission ended, leaving me sitting on the hotel floor with Lon's pocketknife stuck into the bar of soap.

"What did you see?" Lon asked, squatting next to me.

"A house in the woods, no cars. I couldn't even tell where the woods were—Oregon? Maryland? Florida? I don't know. There was nothing identifiable, Lon. Just a grandfather clock. But maybe that was the clue the servitor was trying to show me. And it's weird, but I think I remember it from when I was a kid."

"Your parents' house in Florida?"

"No, that's long gone. And we didn't have a grandfather clock. Maybe I saw it somewhere we went. Another house."

"Family vacation?"

"We never went on vacation." Like, never. And strange, but the word *vacation* triggered a whole other nagging feeling inside my brain, that déjà vu sensation. Plane tickets. Skiing. Mountains. Christmas. Where the hell was this all coming from? Someplace more recent? I couldn't piece it together.

"Did you ever visit anyone?" Lon pressed, unaware of my warring memories. "Friends of your parents? Another lodge, maybe?"

"They never took me anywhere. They were gone half the time, traveling."

Lon's phone rang, tearing me out of my brain strain. He slid his fingers over the screen to answer the call. Even with the phone against his ear, I could hear Jupe's urgent voice. Then Lon said, "Hold on." He put it on speakerphone and held it between us.

"Cady?"

"I'm here," I confirmed. "What's wrong?"

"You guys need to come home," Jupe's voice said. "Right *now*."

24

Nine hours later, after speeding our way across the state, we sat on the most comfortable sectional sofa known to mankind, in the cleanest-smelling, coziest home in the world. Stack stone and pale wood. Soft rugs. Black-and-white photographs. Large plate-glass windows and sliding doors that looked out onto a covered patio and a redwood deck and the dark Pacific beyond.

If I could, I'd never leave Lon's house. Ever. In the midst of the shitstorm that was my personal life, his home felt safe and familiar and good—so good it helped dull the shock that trickled through my body like medicine dripping down from an IV.

"Are you sure that's everything Mrs. Vega knew?" Lon asked. "You positive she had no idea where this winter house was located?"

"I'm sure," Jupe said from my side, then reluctantly added, "I used my knack on her."

Lon's jaw twitched. "Why doesn't that surprise me?"

Jupe's long legs were folded up against his chest. He leaned hard against my shoulder, smelling faintly of coconut oil and chamomile, while Mr. Piggy sniffed his bare toes. I knew he was still worried that he was in trouble for sneaking around; considering Lon's simmering, barely restrained anger and this latest confession about his knack, I was pretty sure a long grounding was in Jupe's future.

But I personally wasn't mad at the kid. Confused by what he'd learned from Mrs. Vega? Oh, yes. Very confused. Which was probably why I couldn't stop holding his hand. I craved comfort, and he was the only thing between sanity and a whole lot of travel-weary, sloppy-ass tears.

"I made Mrs. Vega not want to tell anyone about our visit and what she told me and Leticia," Jupe added.

"How did you meet this Leticia?" Lon asked. "She doesn't go to school out here."

Jupe's groan was so low I felt it more than heard it. "She kind of, well, she goes to school in Morella. I sort of, kind of, met her . . . well, it doesn't matter."

God, he was the worst liar in the world. I forced myself not to laugh as I tried to put a face to the name. I wasn't sure I'd ever seen Leticia Vega; I'd only ever talked to Grandmaster Vega on a handful of occasions. I never attended the Morella lodge as a member; I only went to them for help when I needed it. "She's your age?" I asked.

A dreamy sort of daze breezed over Jupe's features. "Uh-huh."

Oh, boy. I'd seen that look before, whenever Jupe was in the same room with Kar Yee. "So she's cute, huh?"

Slow grin.

"And she's helping you, so she must like you."

He teased, "I mean, who wouldn't like all this?"

"I'm not liking you much right now," Lon complained.

"But—"

"Don't even bother," Lon said. "You'll be telling me whatever it is you're lying about tomorrow when we sit down with the Holidays and get everything out in the open. Count yourself lucky we've got more important concerns at the moment."

"When you say it like that, I don't really feel all that lucky," Jupe mumbled.

Lon snorted. "You and me both, son."

Foxglove jumped onto the far end of the sofa and sneaked her way over to Lon's lap, stretching her front paws over his thighs. He mindlessly scratched her behind her ear, let out a slow breath, and slunk lower on the couch, staring at the ceiling.

Damn, he looked exhausted. All that driving today didn't help. I'd checked his snakebite a couple of times when we stopped for gas or a restroom; it was still tender and a tiny bit swollen, but at least his skin didn't feel numb anymore.

The way he was sprawled on the couch pulled his shirt tighter across his chest. I could just make out the bump from the ring hanging around his neck.

I hadn't asked him about it, but God, how I wanted to. I guess he must have heard this in my emotions, because he hassled me the entire ride up here about my memory problems.

But as he told Jupe, we had bigger concerns.

"My parents' 'winter home' has to be the house in the woods," I said to Lon.

"What house?" Jupe asked.

"None of your business," Lon said.

"But I helped," he insisted, his gaze swinging from Lon to me. "I know you're both mad at me, but I did help. Right?"

Maybe it was the pitiful note in his voice or the earnest squeeze of his fingers around mine, but whatever it was, it turned me into a sucker. I slung my arm around his shoulder. "You helped," I assured him, pulling him closer.

Lon slanted me a ticked-off look, but he needn't have bothered. I could feel the agitation rolling off of him in waves. So I was babying Jupe. Big deal. He really did help, even if he had to sneak around to do it. And who could blame him? We—that is, I mean, *Lon*—ran off and left Jupe alone for a week. That was the same shit my parents pulled on me all the time. Especially during—

During the holidays.

Every Christmas. They left me every December and returned a month later in January. And all that time, they were here. Here! How was that even possible?

"Time for bed," Lon said to Jupe.

"It's only eleven, and I haven't seen you both all week."

Lon pushed off the sofa and headed toward the sliding doors. "Cady and I need to talk."

"But I helped," he protested. "I might be able to help some more."

"Come here for a second." Lon flipped on the outside lights and stepped onto the patio.

"Crap," Jupe mumbled.

"Buck up," I said. "It'll be okay."

He gave me a unnervingly grave look. "Will it?"

I stared into his bright green eyes, with all those dark, fanning lashes. His uncertainty and worry were almost palpable—almost something I could hear as clear as his voice—and it had nothing to do with whatever punishment he feared from his dad. He was scared for me. *Me*. And for us, and the future. And I wanted more than anything to assure him that he was worried for no reason, that everything was fine, and nothing ever went so horribly wrong that it couldn't be fixed. That life was easy, and if you worked hard enough, you'd get everything you wanted. If you did right by others, they'd do right by you. That both humankind and demonkind were intrinsically good, and people you respected didn't disappoint you, and no one would ever break your heart.

None of that was true.

But unlike him, I was an excellent liar.

"Trust. Me," I enunciated firmly, pressing my forehead to his. "Everything will be fine."

"Okay."

"Okay," I repeated.

"I really do like your eyes all silvery like that." He'd already told me twice, after freaking out about them when we first pulled up to the house.

"Yeah, well, I'll like them better if your dad and I can use this new information to stop my mother."

"Me, too."

"You did good, kid. Now, go on. Your dad's waiting."

He let out a long-suffering breath and eventually broke away to meet Lon on the patio. I watched them through the glass as Lon slid the door shut and talked to him. Lon's face was intense, but he wasn't angry. Not in the least. He was talking rapidly, speaking in a voice so low that I couldn't hear anything through the door. And as he talked, Jupe's stubborn expression fell away and was replaced by a taut anxiety.

When Lon paused his rapid-fire, one-way conversation, Jupe flicked a look in my direction. Pity? What the hell was Lon telling him?

Feeling like a third wheel, I left them to their father-son conspiracy and brooded my way to the cool oasis of the kitchen. It looked the same as it had when we'd left it, with its white subway tile and Lon's neatly organized, well-used cooking tools.

I raided the fridge for something to make me feel better and devoured two sweet clementines in a matter of seconds. Thank God for yoga pants; I'd given up on public decency halfway between Twentynine Palms and La Sirena, when I'd forced Lon to pull over so I could change out of those horrible skinny jeans in a McDonald's bathroom. And with all my new-found stretchy yoga-pants freedom and my grumpy mental state, I decided I didn't give a damn and ate two more clementines. Lon walked in and caught me stuffing the last segment into my mouth.

As I tossed the mound of peelings into the garbage, I had the distinct feeling he was concerned. Maybe he'd never seen a grown woman attack a piece of fruit as if it was her last meal. But whatever he was thinking, all he said was, "Jupe took Foxglove upstairs for the night, but maybe we should set up camp in the library, just in case he tries to listen in."

As I wiped my citrus-sticky hands on a kitchen towel, a bottle of vitamins sitting on the counter caught my eye. The label bore a colorful sketch of a woman whose curvy body was filled with fruit and vegetables, so I assumed they were the ones he'd been foisting on me. Idly, I started to turn the bottle around to see it better, but Lon snatched it out of my hand and shoved it into a kitchen drawer.

"You have the page from Wildeye's journal?" he asked suddenly.

O-o-o-kay. Why was he so flustered? I mean, he didn't look it. He looked mildly irritated, staring at me with his perpetually narrowed eyes, but that felt like a false front. As if he knew that *I* knew, he quickly strode off toward the library. "Bring it with you. Let's look at it again and make sure we've covered all our bases. We need to use this time wisely."

He was probably right about that. I grabbed the journal page out of my purse, then headed past the kitchen into the first floor's southern hallway. At the end of the corridor, Lon was grumbling at the fingerprint lock as he punched in an override code. "That little bastard's been trying to get in here."

I thought about all the dangerous magick Jupe could get his hands on, but Lon confirmed that the break-in attempts weren't successful. Score one for expensive technology.

Once he got the door unlocked, I shuffled inside, smelling musty old paper and leather. I'd almost forgotten how much I loved the scent of old books. Lon switched on the frosted art deco pendant lights, illuminating the hundreds of rare occult tomes that lined the walls from floor to ceiling. I plopped down on one of two overstuffed armchairs that faced each other in front of an unlit fireplace in the back of the library. Lon took the other seat, eyeing me cautiously.

"What?" I asked, sinking my toes into the soft rug as I slumped in my chair.

"Nothing."

He seemed anxious, which was completely out of character for him. I studied him as he cracked open his laptop, trying to determine why he was so edgy.

"So," he said, pausing for a long moment as the computer booted up. "We know your parents stayed in a house here every winter. And we know they shopped for magical supplies at Gifts of the Magi."

"You knew that shop?"

He nodded. "My parents knew the Pendletons. Not well, just as people around town. The husband died the same year as my father. The wife ran the shop until she passed—four years ago, I think."

Before I moved to Morella, then. Which explained why I'd never heard of it. "And there were no other occult shops in town?"

Lon shook his head. "That one only survived as long as it did because it was halfway between Morella and La Sirena, which drew business from the city. La Sirena is seventy-five percent Earthbound. Most Earthbounds don't want anything to do with an occult shop."

"Makes sense. But it doesn't help us pinpoint where that winter house might've been located."

"Jupe said all Mrs. Vega knew was that they said it was peaceful, and they wrote there. Your caliph never gave any hint whatsoever when you moved to California that your parents vacationed here?"

"He didn't know."

"Are you sure?"

"He wouldn't have kept that from me. No reason to. Grandmaster Vega didn't know, either, or she would've said something. After everything we've seen over the last week, I think it's pretty obvious my parents spent a lot of time outside the order's radar."

He grunted his agreement.

"The house I saw in the servitor's upload had a lot of antlers tacked up around the front door. My parents were vegans."

"Vegan serial killers."

"They ate that way to keep their bodies pure, not out of respect for animals. My mom believed it kept her Heka reserves sharper. But what I'm saying is that they weren't hunters. Maybe they were renting that house from someone who hunted, or maybe it was a hunting lodge of some sort. Where do people hunt around here?"

"North of my property, away from the coast."

"Maybe we can start looking there."

He nodded and began searching on his laptop, seeing what came up in the way of cabin rentals with nearby hunting. "You wanna take a look at the photos on this rental website and see if you recognize anything?"

I got up and sat on the padded arm of Lon's chair to study the small photos of the rentals he pulled up. He smelled nice. Not as nice as he'd smelled in the hotel a few nights ago—God, how I wished I had access to that scent knack all the time—but pretty damn good for someone who'd spent a good part of the day riding in a car. And for someone who'd just been super-anxious and twitchy, he was awfully relaxed.

Until I stretched my neck as he turned his head, and my skull butted into his cheek, sending a quick jolt of pain through my head. "Oh, sorry," I said, chuckling at the awkward contact. "You're scratchy, by the way." I ran the backs of my fingers over the golden-brown stubble dusting the lower half of his face.

The contact was shocking.

Not physically. Something else.

It was as if I'd been listening to a radio station that wasn't quite tuned, and that skin-to-skin contact flipped it to the right frequency. Suddenly, everything was loud and clear. I just didn't know what I was hearing. Not right away. It sounded like this:

Happy-content-happy-longing-thrill-happy.

I nearly fell off the arm of the chair when I realized what that meant.

25

"O-o-oh!" I stammered.

"What? Do you recognize this house?" Lon's eyes widened as I wrapped my hand around his neck to stop him from moving away.

"No, it's not the house," I said, sounding mildly delirious.

Surprise-confusion-worry-worry

"What?" he said again, a little louder, trying to wiggle out of my grip.

"I can hear you!" I shouted gleefully.

PANIC-CONFUSION-PANIC.

"You can hear my thoughts?"

"No, I can hear your emotions. Your knack—this is what your knack feels like. Jesus! It's amazing!"

He jerked out of my grip and stood up, all in one motion. "You can hear me?"

"Well, I could, when we were touching."

Eyes on me, he set his laptop on a small table next to his chair, nearly missing the table altogether. "You can't now?"

"A little . . . I think. It's hard to tell." I vaulted off the chair to follow him. "Are you panicking?"

"Hell, yeah, I'm panicking. Are you"—he backed away a step—"sure that's what's going on with you? Is this like the fork bending and the smelling?"

"Oh, yes. But this is so much better. You never told me how wonderful it is."

He backed up another step. "It's not always wonderful."

"I think I was hearing Jupe on the sofa—I just didn't realize what was happening. But it's definitely stronger now. Either that, or I'm just really attuned to you. Can you hear certain people louder than others?"

"Yes."

I grinned. "Let me just—"

"Hold on, now—"

"—touch you again. Stay still."

"This isn't a good idea."

I stalked him as if he were easy prey. "Why?"

"Because it's a distraction."

"Maybe I need one," I said, sobering up for a moment. "In case you haven't noticed, life hasn't been all that good to me lately, and this has been a particularly shitty week."

His features softened. "Hasn't been all bad."

"No, not all bad." My breath came a little faster. "A couple of highlights come to mind," I said as I reached for him.

He sidestepped me and hid behind the chair. "Let's be sensible."

"Boo. You're just afraid of me hearing your emotions, and that's not fair. You get to hear mine all the time. Turnabout's fair play."

Indecipherable curses fell from his tightened lips. He glanced around as if he was trying to figure out an escape plan. I took that opportunity to leap onto the chair cushion and grab two fistfuls of his shirt.

"Ahhh," I said triumphantly as I tipped toward him. "Don't try to run again, or I'll have to use my youthful vigor to catch up with your weary old-man bones."

He snorted but didn't pull away. "You've probably got a knack for that."

"Probably. I'm going to try to read you now. Ready?"

"No."

I ignored that and clamped my hands on his shoulders, making a fuzzy connection with his emotional rumblings. "Amazing. I can *just* hear you. It's the direct contact that really does the trick, isn't it?"

His Jupe-like dramatic sigh confirmed. "Go on, then."

I slid my hands up to his neck so I got some skin contact. It turned up the volume from one to ten. "Wow. Just . . . wow."

After a moment, he said, "What do you hear?"

"You're still a little panicky."

"You would be, too," he complained.

"But you're curious, too."

"Of course I am. The last empaths I knew were

my parents. It's been years since anyone could hear me."

"Does it bother you?"

"You tell me."

I calmed myself down so I could listen in better. "Wow, this gets really jumbled. It's hard to tell whose emotions I'm feeling—mine or yours. Whoa." I sank a little further into the chair cushion and wobbled until my knees hit the back of the chair, putting me just above his eye level.

He slid warm hands around my waist to steady me and said, "You learn to sort that out with practice. Other people's feelings have a different frequency."

"You're . . . a little unhappy. But resigned. Wait, you're not really unhappy. You're embarrassed?"

"Uncomfortable," he corrected, smoothing one hand up my back, then down again. "Not unhappy."

That hand was distracting me. "You're worried about something. Oh! I heard that. Right about the worrying, for sure. Why are you worried?"

"Do I really have to list it all out for you? Or have you already forgotten everything that's happened over the last twenty-four hours?"

Good point. "I'm trying to forget, at least for a few minutes. So don't remind me. And hush, I'm trying to listen."

"Yes, ma'am," he mumbled, wrapping his arms around me a little tighter. Which felt damn nice. He made a short chuckling noise near my ear, so I guessed he was listening to me, too. I had to adjust my position to keep a hand on the back of his neck. "What else do you hear?" he asked.

"Let's see. Your feelings aren't as loud now. Or . . . well, that's not exactly right. They're loosening up? It's like a slower rhythm or something. I can't read it as easily. And . . ." He ran his fingers through my hair and pushed it off my shoulder, combing it several times down the back of my neck. "Oh, that feels nice," I mumbled as goose bumps broke out on my scalp.

"What else?"

"It's really hard to listen while you're doing that."

"Try."

"Okay, I hear something. A twang. It's sort of, well, not anxious. It's too calm for that. But it's got a similar urgency. Just lower-pitched. What is that?"

"That," he said, grazing my ear with his lips, "is the sound of my willpower breaking."

His mouth opened on my neck. Hot, wet, pulling kisses that made me forget all about his feelings and my feelings and every shocking thing I'd learned that day. My breasts pushed against his chest as I melted into him, turning my head to give him better access. He took it. And more. While his mouth was busy setting fire to my throat, his hands trailed down either side of my spine, following the curve of my lower back until he palmed my ass and gave it a slow squeeze.

"You want me," I murmured, excited by the

scrape of his whiskers against my cheek as I angled for a proper kiss.

"You think so?"

"I can hear it." I shifted all my weight to my knees so I could tip forward to press closer. "Jesus, I can almost feel it."

"Is that right?" He pulled me tight against his hips until his erection butted against me. "You feel it now?"

My pulse doubled. "I don't know . . . it's hard to tell from this angle. And last time, you wouldn't let me touch you long enough to really know for sure."

"You win. Let's try again." He pried one of my arms off his neck and guided my hand down between us. He pushed into my palm as I stroked him through his jeans. Whatever teasing taunt he'd been ready to wield morphed into a low moan.

"That feels promising."

"Promising?"

"I'm not totally convinced."

"I can hear the lie, Cadybell," he whispered against my cheek, making me shiver.

"Oh, that's right," I whispered back, giving him another rub before my fingers sneaked up to his belt buckle. "Show me what a lie sounds like. I want to hear one, too."

"Mmm." He dragged his mouth against mine and kissed me slowly. "I'm not attracted to you in the least bit, and I haven't spent the last week in agony, wanting to touch you."

"Oh?"

"I haven't thought about how soft your skin is or how sexy it is when your eyes tilt up at the corners when you laugh or how obscene your ass looks in those pants—and I definitely did not come close to pummeling that trucker who was watching you bend over to reach the bottled water in the convenience store at Bakersfield."

Oooh. That explained the foul mood he'd been in during that leg of the journey home. "You didn't?"

"Nope." He kissed me a second time, deeper and slower, his tongue rolling with mine as I briefly halted my struggle to unbuckle his belt. "And I definitely didn't have any fantasies about pulling over outside of Bakersfield to throw you into the back of the SUV so I could tear off those damned pants and screw you senseless, because I've got caveman genes that make me want to mark you up with my scent so everyone knows you're mine."

An equally primal satisfaction squeezed my chest.

"And lastly, I am not wondering"—his arm tangled with mine as he slid his hand beneath both the waistband of my yoga pants and my panties—"just how wet you are right now."

"*Ungff.*"

"My," he murmured in a controlled voice.

But I could feel the thrill that shot through him, as clear as the bright pleasure zigzagging between my thighs as he leisurely stroked me. The way he was making me feel, the way his feelings sounded in my head . . . God, it was all so damn good.

Too good. I lost track of my balance.

All of my weight suddenly shifted toward him—my weight and the chair. Lon's hand flew out of my yoga pants; his arm tightened around my waist. He stumbled, carrying me with him as the wobbling chair tipped completely backward and slammed against the floor.

"Shit!" I slid down his body and got my footing, twisting in his arms to make sure I hadn't knocked his laptop onto the floor. I hadn't.

We both laughed a little. Then he said, "Maybe that's a sign that we should stop." But I could still hear him, and he damn sure didn't want to stop. Good thing, because neither did I.

If I was being totally honest with myself, I could only think of a handful of men I'd ever truly wanted. Fewer still whom I'd wanted to spend time with outside of bed. But Lon was a rare beast. I wanted every bit of him, from his deadpan way of communicating and his unswerving loyalty, to his ex-surfer-boy long hair and devilish good looks. I wanted his surprising wit and his grumbly, slow-burn anger and his long, lean body.

I wanted all of him, and I wanted him all for myself in the most desperate way possible.

My gaze rose to meet his, and I stared into heavy-lidded green eyes blazing with a hunger that was almost intimidating. He was trying to hold himself back, to rein it all in, but this time, it was a losing battle. He knew it. I knew it. And I heard the moment he cracked.

He kissed me as if he meant it—no slow tease, no detailed exploration, just his mouth on mine, hot and possessive. The hands that had softly stroked me were now pulling off my clothes as if they were on fire. He had me naked in seconds, mumbling, "Finally," as if it had taken him hours. I got his belt unbuckled and tugged at the buttons on his fly while he urged me around the fallen chair and onto the rug. He sprang into my waiting hand, hot and thick and proud. I wrapped my fingers around him, enjoying the hissing sound his breath made when he inhaled sharply through gritted teeth.

"Jesus, that feels good," he murmured.

"My thoughts exactly."

"Fuck. I'll never last if you keep that up. Come here."

We sank to the floor, and after his mouth blazed a southward trail from my breasts down my stomach, I bowed off the rug and roughly grabbed his hair—first to keep his face between my legs, then to push him away. I, too, wasn't going to last.

"Lon," I begged. But I didn't need to. He knew.

His body covered mine. He hooked one of my legs around his waist and hiked it higher, spreading my legs wider with his knees. When I felt him nudge my center, I thrust my hips upward and welcomed him inside.

Joy-joy-joy!

Relief-relief-relief!

Whether I was hearing him or experiencing my own feelings, I couldn't tell anymore. Emotion and pleasure emulsified until I couldn't separate one from the other, his from mine, mine from his. There was only his driving weight above me and the intense, raw thrill that bloomed between us.

When he spread his knees wider, I twined both my legs around his and dug my toes into his calves, pinning him from below. With his weight braced on one forearm, he used his free hand to cup the back of my neck and pull my head up to meet his, pressing his forehead to mine. His long hair tickled my cheeks.

"You hear that?" he asked between huffed breaths.

"Yes," I whispered. "I hear us."

Exhilaration shot through me, and just like that, everything picked up speed and violence—his hips, my shaking muscles, and the urgent release we were both chasing.

He begged me; I threatened him.

He warned me; I cursed him.

And I knew the exact second he was lost, when he couldn't hold back. His forehead pushed against mine hard enough to bruise, and I felt all that strength crumble under the free fall of his surrender. And it was so good, watching him come, so sweet and disarming and brutal, that I forgot about my own racing needs, just for a moment. Just long enough for me to be caught off-guard when my own orgasm came at the tail end of his.

It was almost as if my body had forgotten how to do it right and that it, too, was surprised. Then it felt as if the floor dropped out beneath me. I clung to Lon as if I were dying. It was so intense it was almost painful, and I was half afraid I'd broken something. But when the last shudder ran through me, I collapsed in a pile of relief, satiated and thoroughly wrung out.

Lon didn't say anything. He just rolled off onto his back and took me with him, settling me on top of his chest, penning my legs between his, as if we'd done this a million times. He held me loosely and kissed the top of my head as it fell against his neck.

The lingering, pulsing pleasure that steadily thumped through the middle third of my body made me forget my own name for a long moment. But somewhere in the distance, in a deep, quiet place inside him, I heard something. It spread like warm honey, slow and unmanageable, a wild thing that had no center or borders. I didn't know what it was, but it grew so loud that I was overwhelmed by the unexpected strength of it. I felt the wet tickle down my cheeks before I realized I was quietly crying.

And then he said something that turned my world upside down.

A simple thing. Innocuous, almost. A sentiment

that clearly just slipped from his lips. A casual confession that was an outgrowth of the thing I could already hear him feeling.

He said, "Jesus fucking Christ. I've missed you so much."

And that's when I absolutely knew something wasn't right inside my head.

26

I slid to my side, heart hammering in my chest, and stared at him. "What did you say?"

Had I not been wielding the empathic knack, I might have believed his poker face when he said, "Hmm?" God, he was good. Better than I ever realized. Because behind his languorous façade, his emotions were going haywire, practically screaming *Oh, shit!* in my face.

My mouth dropped open. "We've had sex before."

"Cady—"

"My screwed-up memories . . . that night I can't remember before our road trip. Did we have sex that night?"

"No." He was telling the truth.

"But we've had sex before," I said, putting a palm on the center of his chest.

He closed his eyes and let his head loll on the rug. "Yes."

"Not just once. Lots."

His panic slowed and trickled into heavy resignation. "I haven't kept count."

"Try. How many?"

"Once or twice a day, four or five days a week, give or take . . ."

"Mother of God. Since when?"

"Six months."

I covered my mouth with my hand. "You haven't taken me in like a refugee. I *live* here."

"Since October."

My brain fired through all the missing pieces of my memories, thinking back to the first day of our road trip, when he was quizzing me on the way to Golden Peak. "Oh. My memory loss isn't a holdover from my coma, and I didn't get drunk that night."

He groaned, exhaling heavily as he draped a forearm over his eyes. "No."

"H-hold on. This has the stink of dirty magick all over it. You did a memory spell on me!"

"It wasn't my idea."

Anger flared. "Whose idea was it, then?"

He lifted his arm briefly to squint an accusing look at me.

Crap. I bit the inside of my mouth. "I asked you to?"

"Argued it until I couldn't see any other option."

Oh. That *did* sound like me. "Why?" But as soon as I said it, I knew. "My mother. To keep you out of danger." But that didn't seem like Lon. He was too proud, too selfless, to care about his own safety. The only person he'd worry over would be—"And Jupe.

To keep Jupe safe, too." That sounded right, but there was something he wasn't telling me.

"The spell is temporary," he explained. "We wanted to keep certain things out of your mind in case your mother tapped into your dreams. And since she did exactly that last night, and the spell was active, then I guess it was the right decision. I just didn't know it would be so broad."

"You didn't expect me to forget about us."

"We didn't expect that. *We*."

Right. Because this was my idea. "Why didn't you just tell me?"

"Because I didn't want to risk you remembering everything."

"Like now."

He grunted.

I fell onto my back beside him and stared up at the pendant lights dangling from the library's ceiling. Had I done this before? Had crazy monkey sex with him on this rug? It was surreal to think about and gave me a nasty headache. Yep. That was magick, all right. Pretty freaking good magick if I hadn't realized it until now. Then again, Lon always could work a decent memory spell.

My arm bumped his. I immediately heard an erratic mix of angsty emotions, from regret to begrudged resignation to something that felt a lot like guilt. And that's when the other emotion jumped back into my head, the warm-honey feeling I couldn't identify before, only this time it had an undertaste of *ache*.

I pushed up and leaned over his face, pulling his arm away from his eyes. "Lon Butler, you're in love with me."

He reached up and ran his fingers along my clavicle. "Nope."

"Liar."

"You're just some girl who shows up for dinner and ends up hogging all the covers."

"Double liar."

"And you aren't in love with me, either. You just stick around because I've got money and a nice cock."

"It is pretty nice," I admitted.

Merriment sparkled behind his squinting eyes. "You seem to be fond of my kid, too, but I really can't figure that one out."

"Well, that's . . . that's—"

My mouth fell open again. I kicked my leg over his hips and straddled him.

"Where is it?" I said, reaching for the chain around his neck.

He grabbed my hands. "Hold on, Cady."

"No, *you* hold on. Let me see it. Now."

We wrestled for a moment, but he finally gave in and scooted it around the chain from where it had twisted to his back. There it was. That big-ass stone swirling with gold and green.

"I saw it last night, when you passed out on the bed after the snakebite. I thought it was Yvonne's."

"Yvonne's ring was normal," he said quietly.

"No halo."

"No halo. And she 'lost' it a couple of years before we got divorced, which probably meant she sold it for drug money. But either way, it's long gone."

"Oh."

"Mmm-hmm."

I felt the grin coming on, and I just couldn't stop it. "That's my ring."

"I have no idea what you're talking about." He calmly shifted me from his stomach to his thighs so he could sit up. The ring swayed on its chain.

"It's beautiful," I whispered.

"You think so?" Oh, the feeling of pleased satisfaction that fluttered through him. I could enjoy him feeling that for days and never get tired of it.

"I'm sure I've oohed and ahed over it already."

One brow lifted. "Not quite."

"I turned you down?"

"Christ, I hope not."

"Oh, shit. You haven't asked me yet."

He confirmed my horror with a clucking noise. "Things have been busy around here, in case you haven't noticed. I'd originally planned to give it to you in France a week or so ago, but our trip got waylaid."

Holy shit. That was the reason for the déjà vu sensation I felt when we were talking about vacations. "You gave me plane tickets for Christmas. The French Alps. We joked about it—sex vacation."

"You remember that?"

"Barely." I squeezed my eyes shut and groaned. "Oh, Lon. I'm so sorry I spoiled it."

He wrapped his arms around my lower back. "I'm not. To be honest, I'm—"

"Relieved."

He chuckled. "Yes. Very good."

"Mmm." I stared at the ring. I couldn't help it. I'd never been the kind of girl to pore over wedding magazines and dream about square-jawed princes whisking me away to some fairy-tale white-picket-fence home. But the ring was pretty dazzling. "I've never seen anything like it."

"I wasn't sure what you'd want, but I couldn't see you wearing something precious or girly."

"It's beautiful." Had I said that already? My cheeks warmed. "And bizarre that I can't remember anything that made you want to give it to me in the first place. I'm sorry all of this spoiled your plans."

He took in a deep breath through his nose. "I bet a lot of couples have wondered, if they'd met under different circumstances, perhaps they would've taken a different path and never ended up together. And in a way, you got that opportunity. You chose me twice. If that's not meant to be, then I don't know what is."

I swiped a couple of quick tears from under my eyes. "Well, when all my memories come back, I hope you'll still want to give it to me."

"I will," he assured me, but I heard a little disappointment behind his words and knew I'd hurt his feelings. "I can wait. There are other . . . practical things to consider."

"Like what? I hate to break it to you, but you're

going to be sadly disappointed if you're expecting a dowry. I have no cattle or acreage to offer."

"No cattle?"

I laughed. "I can give you half my share of the profits from the Tahitian pinball machine at Tambuku. And maybe—"

"Maybe . . . ?"

Oh, shit. I leaned over Lon to reach the side table and got my fingers on Wildeye's wrinkled journal entry.

"What?" he asked.

"3AC 1988," I said, staring at the page. "Jupe said Mrs. Vega first met my parents in La Sirena in January 1989. What if they bought the winter house instead of renting it? Not '3AC' but '3 AC.' Three acres."

"Three acres purchased in 1988," Lon murmured. He lifted me off his lap and rolled over to pull down his laptop. "If that's right, there's a public record of it."

It didn't take long to search through the state's land-sales records, and there was nothing under Duval. But a few minutes later, under a search in the county's real estate archives, he found a two-bedroom house on a three-acre plot of land about fifteen minutes north of Lon's house. It sold in December 1988 to an E. Artau.

A misspelling that cut off the last letter in Artaud. Enola Artaud. My mother's maiden name.

The land's previous owner was listed, and when I saw the name, I forgot how to breathe.

The party who sold it to her was Ambrose Dare.

27

The SUV's headlights illuminated the white antlers nailed around the front door of the hunting cabin. The property was nestled in some heavily wooded foothills bordering a popular hunting spot that had become popular over the last couple of decades for wild boars. The house, we learned, was built by Dare's father in the 1940s. Dare had sold it to my parents for a dollar.

It was almost two in the morning. Lon cut the engine and transmutated, listening for any signs of life before we stepped out of the car. The heavy silence felt deceptive. I half expected to be attacked by a ghost—Dare's or my mother's. Or maybe some golem my mother had constructed to guard the house.

Nothing.

"Look how the SUV's wheels cut into the gravel." Lon shone a flashlight in one gloved hand and motioned with the sawed-off shotgun in the other. Now that we were home, he'd traded the handgun for his beloved vintage Lupara. I usually hated the noisy thing, but I wasn't complaining tonight; we might need it. "No other cars have been out here for a long time. And the front steps are covered in dead leaves."

He was right. The place looked as if it hadn't had human contact in a while, at least since autumn. In fact, the only active life I could detect was an owl hooting somewhere in the distance and a subtle glow of warding magick twining around the house.

"You see it?" I asked Lon, whispering as if I could be heard out here, miles away from the nearest paved road. I wrapped my fingers around his flashlight hand and tilted it toward the edge of the front porch. "White Heka disguised by the white paint in the trim. Bet you anything that's lead paint or there's lime powder mixed in to hold a charge."

He grunted. "But those are just extensions. Where are they anchored?"

Good question. We stepped closer and got our answer: the heart of the ward was hidden in the white antlers decorating the front door, which were delicately carved with magical symbols. Clever. But not extraordinarily sneaky. And not extraordinary warding magick, either, just a standard spell that would give the owner a brief mental image of anyone who crossed it. Not half as complex as the ward Lon had built around his house.

"It's a distraction," I murmured. "Anyone looking for the symbols or the Heka signature can find it, but it's hidden *just* well enough—"

"To make someone cocky enough to think they'd outsmarted it. An ego stroke."

"Exactly. There's more magick inside, I guarantee you."

"But your servitor didn't show you any magick."

"That's what worries me," I said. "I don't want to get caught in another landslide."

"Maybe I should go in alone and scout it out first."

"Just because you've given me hundreds of orgasms I don't remember doesn't mean you have to be my knight in shining armor. We go in together." I shook the can of spray paint I'd purloined from Lon's garage and sprayed a nice fat line of blue over one of the ward's extension lines. The Heka powering the front of the ward evaporated. Good enough to get us onto the leaf-strewn front porch, and, once there, I sprayed down the antlers and dismantled the rest.

"Electricity's still on," I said, surprised when I reached out for current and found plenty.

"Makes sense if they came here every winter. They've probably got automatic payments coming out of an account that hasn't been drained yet. They didn't exactly have time to close everything out when you sent them across the planes. Might have a small fortune tucked away somewhere that technically belongs to you now."

"I wouldn't touch their dirty money with a ten-foot pole," I murmured.

Lon handed me the gun and the flashlight long

enough to splinter the doorframe with a crowbar and pry open the front door. Then he slowly swung the door open. Dust motes danced in the flashlight's beam as he shone it inside.

"Empty," he said, searching the entry for more magick.

He found a light switch and flipped it on. I was eager to confirm that the interior looked the same as it had in my servitor-powered vision, but I couldn't see past his broad shoulders.

"Come on," he said, motioning for me to step inside. Why was I so wary? My parents weren't here, and Dare was dead. There was nothing to worry about but months-old magical traps that may or may not still have enough charge to be effective. I stepped over the threshold as he continued to talk. "Stay close behind me, just in case—"

I never heard him finish.

Within a blink, he vanished. I was standing in the entry of the house alone, and everything was coated in the silver sheen of my moon magick, only I hadn't used it. I hadn't tried, hadn't felt any indication it was coming, and I wasn't transmutated into my serpentine form. But Lon was gone, and I was alone. And it was . . .

Daytime.

Silver-tinged sunlight slanted across the floor from a window I couldn't see. But this was definitely the same house my servitor spell had shown me.

What the hell was going on?

A knock sounded behind me. I whipped around and found the door closed. Someone was knocking on the other side. I backed away, stumbling further into the house, and glanced around in a panic. Same great room, same fireplace.

Same enormous grandfather clock.

And sitting on the floor at the base of the clock was a large gated playpen, a bigger version of Mr. Piggy's. No hedgehog in this one. Inside sat a little girl. A toddler with dark bobbed hair and thick, straight bangs. She was humming to herself while shuffling wooden puzzle pieces over a tiny play table.

And she had a small, pale halo swirling around the crown of her head.

Quick footsteps and whispers drew my attention to a hallway at the back of the room. I nearly tripped over my own feet in my panic but managed to duck behind a chair before they saw me. I recognized the voices a moment before I peered around the back of the chair and spied two people striding past the fireplace toward the door, arguing in French.

Mom and Dad.

I clamped my hand over my mouth to stop myself from screaming.

Impossible! But there they were. Not ghosts, not memories. In the flesh, just as real as I was. My mom was dressed in a skirt and a striped top—one I knew was navy and white, even though my silver sight didn't show it; I remembered her wearing the outfit in photos of book signings. My father wore his usual button-up Oxford and slacks. And they were so young. About my age, I thought. Which meant—

The girl in the playpen had to be me.

Seriously, what the hell was going on?

The knock on the door came again, this time more insistent.

"Coming," my mother cooed before she and my father momentarily stepped out of sight. The overly friendly male voice of the visitor boomed through the walls.

"Enola and Alexander," the voice said. "Hope you don't mind me dropping by unannounced. I was on my way home from San Francisco and thought I'd take a detour to see if you'd arrived in town yet.

"We have," my mother said in her heavy French accent.

"May I come in?"

"Of course, of course. Come on in." That was my father and his used-car-salesman voice. The one that made you feel as if you were the most important thing in the world, until you heard him use it on someone else and realized he was only playing you.

I held my breath, listening to them stroll into the great room. From where I was crouched, I could see the grandfather clock and Little Me in the playpen. The girl didn't see me. I didn't know if this was because I couldn't be seen or because she was too busy watching the adults across the room. Was I reliving a memory? I certainly couldn't recall this house at all, so that seemed impossible.

"Can I take your coat?" my dad asked. "I'd offer you a drink, but we haven't had a chance to refill the pantry yet."

"No, that's fine. I can't stay long. Just wanted to check in. Make sure we were still on for Monday."

"We are here, no?" my mother said, not bothering to hide her irritation. "Have we given you any reason to think we would not be?"

"My wife's tired. The flight was a little rough."

"No need to explain," the voice said. "I just . . . ah, there she is."

Footsteps approached. Little Me's head tilted upward as she quietly watched the visitor walking up to the playpen. She wasn't frightened, I didn't think, but she wasn't speaking, either. She just stared up at him, mouth drawn in a tight line, assessing him. Was I this cold and calculating as a child? Was this really me?

"Hello, Sélène," he said to her.

I let out a shaky breath, waiting to hear her voice, but she didn't reply.

"Are you shy, pretty girl?" he asked. "Do you remember me? I met you last winter, when you were just a year old, but you've grown so much since then. I barely recognize you now, but I see you are looking more like your beautiful *maman*."

"We've taught her not to speak to strangers," my mother's voice said bluntly.

"Ah," he replied. "Probably wise. The world is full of crazies, and she's . . . quite the prize, your little Moonchild."

My mother made a sharp, unhappy noise.

"As we've told you before, we prefer that people don't know we're here," my father said, as if he were her interpreter. I immediately remembered Karlan Rooke calling him my mother's apologist. "So please don't use that title around your own people or anyone in town. I'm afraid we must insist on that, or the deal is off."

"Strong words, Alexander. But I understand, and you have my word." A man's hand came into my view as he reached over the playpen's gate and pointed at the scattered puzzle pieces. "What are you playing with there? Astrological symbols? My. Already the great magician, I see. Following in your parents' famous footsteps."

"Naturally. She is a Duval."

"And your first child, so I'm sure you'll spoil her rotten."

Not the first. If this man only knew . . .

"Don't worry, I will not tell anyone about her," the man said, standing so that I could only see the toes of his polished shoes. "But I would advise you not to parade her around La Sirena. Back home in Florida, the chances of her encountering one of us are slim, but here? The locals call this area Earthbound Paradise. If the wrong demon got a glimpse of her, he might decide she's rare enough to warrant his interest."

"What do you mean by that?" my mother snapped.

"I mean that I'd advise you to find a babysitter in Florida for your little moon muffin when you come to work for me next year. Bring her here at your own risk."

"Is that a threat?"

"I'm sure it's not a threat, darling," my father said.

"I'm paying you for your magical skills, and quite handsomely. If you want me to continue funding your publishing career and paying for all those first-class plane tickets to France, then you'll keep family and work separate."

"If I were you, I would watch myself, devil. I can do things to you that you never knew were possible. And if anyone touches my property, I will punish you."

"Is *that* a threat, Mrs. Duval?"

"We will continue to honor our working agreement only as long as it is beneficial to us. Incur my wrath, and you can kiss your Succubus-summoning circles and your magical potions good-bye."

"Don't worry," he said. "I foresee a long, prosperous working relationship between us. As long as you perform your work to my satisfaction, I will not tell your order that you're moonlighting for a demon. And if you ever believe I'm not compensating you fairly, we can renegotiate our terms. Now, if you'll excuse me, I'll be on my way home. I'll see you at the Hellfire caves at nine a.m. sharp on Monday. You have a lot of work to do before the solstice."

Shock was a knife through my gut. And as his

footsteps trailed away and the front door shut, my world closed in on itself, pieces of shattered memories collapsing under the weight of too many seemingly random paths converging.

My parents worked for Dare. They were Dare's paid magicians.

They constructed the summoning circles in the Hellfire caves.

That's why they were in La Sirena.

No such thing as coincidence.

The engine of a car roared to life outside the house, and soon after, Dare was gone.

"He saw something!" my mother said excitedly, her mood jumping from anger to glee. "Did you hear him? The filthy Earthbounds will steal the child because they will see something rare about her. She must have the marker. He saw a nimbus of light around her head."

I heard a muffled noise. My father was kissing her. Then he gave a little shout and said, "We did it, my love! I knew it was right this time. I felt it."

"Let us call my guardian to confirm that the halo has appeared," she said in a controlled voice. "The day I trust demon swine is the day I roll over and die."

28

"Cady!"

I blinked, and Lon's face appeared above mine in full color. No silver light. I shoved him away and flicked a look around the room. I was back in the present. The great room was empty. No playpen. No toddler me. No parents.

"Are we alone?" I asked.

"What the hell just happened?"

"I-I don't know," I stammered. "A time warp? Or a memory came to life. I was here in this room twenty-some years ago. I saw my parents, and I saw . . ."

He swiveled me back around to face him. "Saw what? Did we set off a magical trap? I don't see any Heka or spellwork."

"Did I transmutate?"

"I suddenly couldn't hear your thoughts. I turned around, and you were standing there like you were in a trance. Your pupils—"

"What?"

"Your pupils disappeared. Just silver. You wouldn't wake up."

"How long was I out?"

"A minute?"

"Holy . . . Lon, I relived something that happened in this room. I walked around and watched myself as a two-year-old girl." I looked around and pointed to the far corner. "There. I hid behind that chair. I watched the whole thing like it was actually happening. I don't know if it was induced by some sort of knack. What is it when people can see in the past?"

"What did you see?"

"I saw how my parents found out I had a halo. I always thought it was Scivina who told them—"

"Your mother's guardian?"

"—but Scivina only confirmed it." I grabbed the front of his jacket and pulled him close. "The person who first saw it was Dare. My parents were working for Dare."

Lon paled.

"They built the glass summoning circles in the Hellfire caves. They were doing winter solstice work. My God, Lon. They could've done some of the transmutation spells."

"Not mine. I already told you who did mine, remember? Merrin's brother."

That's right. I knew this. A small relief lifted me; I really didn't want my parents to have put their evil hands on Lon. "Dare told them not to bring me here anymore, which must've been why I started spending

Christmas alone in Florida. They were working for Dare and keeping it secret from the E∴E∴.."

Lon pulled back and paced several feet, swinging the Lupara at his side. "I couldn't have ever been introduced to them. I would've recognized them when the Black Lodge slayings first hit the news. But they were working for Dare, and Jupe told us that Mrs. Vega saw them every winter until they faked their deaths. That means they were working for Dare while I was still active in the Hellfire Club."

"God, I'm going to be sick."

"No, you're not." He stopped pacing and forced me to look up at him. "We aren't done here, Cady. Your servitor saw this house. The snake handler's stolen parchment is here."

"Right," I said, taking a deep breath. The grandfather clock. I looked across the room and flinched. To the right of the fireplace, where the servitor had shown me the carved clock—where I just saw it in my vision of the past—there was . . . nothing.

"The clock is gone," I said. "It was right there."

"Are you sure?"

"Yes!"

"Maybe it was moved."

We rushed over to the empty spot and looked for scuff marks on the floor or a secret panel or door in the wood wall there. Nothing. Not a goddamn thing.

"How is this possible?" I said, nearly in tears. "The servitor doesn't show me things that happened in the past. It has specific magical instructions. If it showed the clock to me before we drove home from Twentynine Palms, then that means it was here earlier today."

"Cady. Put your hand here."

He was holding his hand near the empty spot. I did the same.

"What is that?" he said. "Something's there."

"Holy—You know what that feels like?" I tapped the sleeve of my coat. "Ignore."

"What?"

"One of my tattooed wards. Ignore." I left him there for a moment and raced back to the front porch to retrieve the can of blue spray paint. "Fucking genius. How the hell did they turn it into a permanent spell? And where's the Heka? Move out of the way."

I shook the can and tried to gauge exactly where the clock had stood. Then I sprayed the wall. Like a shaded pencil mark exposing a pen imprint left behind on a pad of paper, the paint stuck to the air and revealed a hidden form.

The grandfather clock.

"Amazing," Lon murmured when I'd sprayed enough to give us a rough idea of its shape. He touched his gloved hand to a still-invisible spot uncoated by paint. "I still can't feel it. Just the strange sensation from before. The spell's still active."

"No telltale Heka, no sigils. Oh, of course. It's not on the front."

"On the back," Lon said, setting the Lupara down on the fireplace. He felt around the clock's invisible side, mumbling as he tried to get a good hold on it. After several tries, he grunted loudly and pulled. The massive clock moved an inch. God only knew how much it weighed, but now that he had some wiggle room, he got a better grip on it and slowly pulled one side away from the wall.

"Anything?" I asked as he peered behind it.

"Invisible, just like the rest of it. No Heka."

"Has to be. Oh! On the *inside*, Lon."

He moved back so I could spray the back side of the clock, and there it was: the outline of an imperfect rectangular panel that had been cut into the bottom half of the backing. Lon pried it off with the crowbar. Soft white Heka glowed on the inside of the panel for a moment before it fizzled and faded away to nothing.

The clock materialized right in front of our faces.

"Ha!" I shouted.

"Fucking brilliant," Lon agreed before peering inside a dark cavity at the base of the clock's back. He reached inside and retrieved a metal container about the size of a safe-deposit box. "This must be it. Here."

I took it from him and set it on a console table. Lon cocked the Lupara and aimed at the box while I took a deep breath and opened the hinged top.

Nothing jumped out. No magick sigils or Heka anywhere in sight. Only a pile of papers, a couple of notebooks, a box of red ochre chalk, and an envelope with a stack of bills, both American and old French francs.

"These haven't been in circulation since the 1990s," Lon said, removing his paint-stained gloves.

"Maybe that means this stuff hasn't been touched since I was a kid."

"They probably hid it all when Dare started poking around in their business. What's that?"

I cracked open one of the notebooks—just a plain old composition notebook with a cardboard cover. My mother's perfect penmanship covered the pages. French words, variations of magical sigils.

"Experiments," Lon said, able to read some of the French. "Mostly failures. Look at the dates. This is before you were born."

"And after they'd killed my brother. Were there . . . other children?"

"No, but not for lack of trying. Here's a home pregnancy test result, negative. And here again, the next month." He flipped through pages and stopped on one, turning the notebook to read the page horizontally.

A chart. It started on my date of birth. Lon read it aloud, interpreting the French for me as he went.

Sélène Aysul Duval: Notes and Observations

3 months: No reaction to 100 V, perceptible distress at 5000 V.

6 months: No reaction to 1000 V, perceptible distress at 7500 V.

9 months: 10,000 V burned skin; taken to hospital for treatment; no internal damage.

"Jesus," I whispered. They were experimenting on me?

15 months: Shocked Alex with kindled current when he reached for her. Continues to defend herself when prodded. We are extremely hopeful now.

18 months: Charged first spell successfully.

27 months: Scivina confirms halo.

5 years: Caliph's nanny called police about suspected abuse. Adapting standardized parenting techniques in attempt to make S. more socially acceptable. Induced brain hemorrhage in nanny. Wiped caliph's wife and children's memories.

7 years: Able to charge adept 6 level spells. Shows interest in summoning.

8 years: Kerub demon summoned for Walpurgis identified S. as "Mother of Ahriman."

9 years: Magical health of S. far exceeds first Moonchild experiment. Becoming rebellious, studying magick in secret, stealing books from lodge's library. May need another major memory wipe.

10 years: No Moonchild powers demonstrated during ceremony. Rumors circulating within order. Third memory wipe on caliph. Hiring private nanny for winter months.

11 years: Alex found documentation of previous Moonchild abilities remaining dormant until puberty.

13 years: First menses. No Moonchild powers.

14 years: Incident at school required another memory wipe.

15 years: Alex fired from day job. Have tried Moonchild ritual six times this year. Doctor says I may be unable to conceive again. Beginning secondary plan to siphon power. Unsure what to do about S.

16 years: Magical ability markedly increasing. Dare still asking about her, so still have hope that all of this was not in vain. Alex says we should consider selling S. to Dare, but I am not ready to give up on her quite yet.

"Selling me to Dare?" I murmured, surprised I could even be shocked by the depth of their depravity anymore. "What else?"

"That's where it stops."

I tore the book out of his hands and flipped to the next page. Blank, just as he said. "Sixteen years old," I murmured. "That's when the Black Lodge slayings started, so that last entry must've been the last winter they worked for Dare."

"And after they faked their deaths and sent you packing with a new alias, they found out you were worth hiding from Dare after all when they uncovered the old grimoires in France."

"Yes," I said quietly. "Must have been a joyous day in the Duval household when they discovered that the so-called age of magical maturity brought out the Moonchild attributes, not puberty. All they had to do was wait until I hit twenty-five and slit my belly open."

"But we stopped them."

Or delayed the inevitable, but I didn't voice my negative thoughts.

Lon picked up the second book, a journal. This one had a black leather cover embossed with a sigil on the front. "My mother's personal sigil," I said, running my finger over it. "Huh. A variation, actually. This star shape at the base is new."

"Or maybe it's an older version," he said, and opened the journal between us on the console. "More spells. Christ, it might take hours to go through, but this might be what you need. I think these could be the Moonchild rituals. The dates range from 1978 to 1988."

"I don't need all of them. What's the last one? The one that applies to me."

He flipped toward the end of the notebook and stopped at a drawing marked with a date nine months before I was born.

The Moonchild ritual.

"It's a diagram for the ceremony," I said, running my finger over the precisely drawn layout. "Here's the main circle, the altar, the cardinals . . . Jesus, Lon. Doesn't this look familiar?"

He let out a slow breath through his nostrils. "It's the same ritual setup as San Diego."

"Exact configuration. And look, a directional compass. A house and a road."

We stared at it until Lon turned the diagram and pointed toward the road we had used to get here. "*This* house, Cady. The road we drove in on."

He was right. "They conceived me here," I murmured. "Behind the house."

He flipped the page and began reading to himself.

"What? Is that the ritual?"

"Looks like more of a statement of intent. Almost as if she was writing it for one of her books, like maybe she thought of publishing it one day."

"What does it say?"

"Give me a second, and I'll tell you," he murmured.

While Lon read to himself, I anxiously thumbed through the rest of the paperwork. More loose pages in French that I couldn't read. A photocopy of a Moonchild ritual from the 1800s with red lines crossing out entire chunks of the text. A page containing a woodcut print of a pregnant woman with the head of a sun and a pictorial map of the world below her. It was labeled *GEHEIME FIGUREN DER ROSEN-KREUZER, 1785*. Gothic script above the woman's sun-disk head said: SOPHIA.

I opened my mouth to tell Lon, but when I picked up the paper, I saw what was on the bottom of the box.

The torn fragment of parchment stolen from the snake temple.

Invocation of the Great Serpent.

It was in English, and the calligraphy and old spellings were mostly readable. It wasn't a ritual, really. No instructions about laying out this or that protection circle, no binding or ward.

It was a prayer of sorts, a set of sacred words to call down a powerful, godlike being from the Æthyr. A strange summoning seal was crudely drawn in the center of the parchment, like no demonic seal I'd ever seen. And as I read to the end, skipping over the mumbo-jumbo, I realized something important.

This was not for summoning an Æthyric being

into a circle for a chat. Nor was it a spell to draw down the creature's essence into a womb to create a Moonchild.

It had nothing to do with a conception ritual.

It was a set of instructions to call down this creature into a living human body.

A male body.

Not my mother but my father.

Dazed and disbelieving, I let go of the parchment and watched it drift back down into the box, then glanced up to see Lon's gaze lift from the fallen page. He cupped my cheek with his hand, and I heard his emotions echoing mine.

"The Moonchild ritual was just meaningless ceremonial bullshit," I said. "All they did was invoke this serpentine being into my father. Any magician with half my skills could do it. All my mom did was have sex with my dad while he was possessed by some kind of nocturnal proto-demon creature."

"Cady . . ."

"Don't you get it? Priya said all I had to do was figure out what kind of magick my parents used and remove it, but he was wrong. How can I reverse this? I'm a stew of psychotic human and demon DNA."

Lon didn't deny it.

Tears burned my eyes. I backhanded the metal box off the console, sending my parents' cache of money flying, and roared at the pain that shot through my knuckles. When Lon tried to reach for me, I stormed away and headed to the hallway I'd seen in my vision, where my parents first appeared. It branched off to two bedrooms with nothing in them but stripped mattresses. Empty closets. Another empty room with traces of red ochre chalk on the wooden floor. An avocado-green kitchen that looked as if it hadn't been updated since the 1960s. I strode through it, opening cabinets and drawers, flinging silverware across the peeling countertops. Nothing and more nothing. Not a damn thing but old grease splatters and a door that led to the backyard. I unlocked it and marched outside.

Remembering the diagram my mother had drawn, I strode through dead grass and made my way through scraggly underbrush to a clearing ringed with winter-bare trees.

Here it was. A February moon shone down on the place where they'd made me. I stared up at the dark sky. No magical hot spot or carefully designed ritual space. Just a plain old clearing on some property they'd bought out of convenience, where rich old men hunted wild boars for sport.

I heard Lon's boots crunching through the brittle grass and sighed as he stopped by my side and stared up at the sky with me.

After a few moments of silence, cold night air sent a shiver through me. I stuck my hands into my pockets. "All of this was for nothing. I spent my entire adult life on the run to protect them, and they didn't need protecting. And when I finally decide to start living my own life, what do I do? I come *here*. Of all the places in the country I could choose, I come right back where it all started. How sick is that?"

"Cady—"

"I've been running in circles, and I just can't get away. I send them to the goddamn Æthyr, and she's still got her nasty claws in me. I feel like a puppet that can't shake the puppet master. Was I drawn here because she's still puppeting me? Am I still Sélène?"

Lon was silent for several moments. "You may not feel it now, but you love me. You're fucking crazy about me, and you're crazy about Jupe. So maybe you were drawn here because *I* needed you and because my boy needed a mother."

I swiped away tears, unable to respond.

"Or that could just be coincidence," he said, looking back up at the sky. "Maybe you were drawn here because you're the only person strong enough to stop Enola."

"Maybe," I whispered.

"I'll tell you one thing I know for certain. When I read that chart she made of your life, I didn't see a puppet. I saw a girl who shocked her own father in self-defense, who was rebellious and had to be carefully controlled. A girl who was a threat to them, even when she was a child. So despite whatever your mother chose to call you, you've never really been Sélène. You've always been Cady. Be that girl now. Be *yourself*. Enola Duval has no power over Arcadia Bell."

I stared up at him, breathing hard and tamping down chaotic sentiments. "You know, you're probably my favorite person in the entire world right now," I said, trying to be lighthearted about what he was making me feel. And *oh*, the intense emotion that radiated from him when I said that. Strong enough to make me suck in a startled breath. Whatever it was, it cut through my remaining indecision.

Shutting out my surroundings, I yanked up my coat sleeve and stuck my finger in my mouth. Then I swiped saliva across the white-ink tattoo on my inner arm to charge Priya's homing sigil.

"Priya, come," I commanded, willing my guardian to appear.

The air fluctuated a few feet in front of me. I backed up and watched a slim, bare-chested figure step out of the night, all silver skin and dark, spiky hair crowned with a halo of black smoke, with shiny black wings folded behind his back. A beautiful sight and a massive relief to see him again, unharmed and whole.

"Mistress!" His black eyes blinked rapidly, as if *I* were the one who'd materialized in front of him. "I am so happy to see you. So very happy."

"The feeling is mutual, my friend."

He pushed back a lock of black hair that had fallen over one eye. "Why did you summon me? You should be using the Kerub's boy . . ." He trailed off and flicked an unhappy look at Lon before offering him a begrudging nod in greeting. "You shouldn't be calling me directly," Priya corrected. "It isn't safe."

"I know. But I need you to deliver a message for me. Can you do that?"

"Of course. Anything."

"First, I want to show you something."

I willed the transmutation to come, trying my best not to tap into moon power as silver coated my vision and my body began changing. I caught my tail just in time and guided it over the stretchy waistband of my yoga pants—much easier than jeans—letting it coil around my wrist as it grew.

Priya's jaw dropped, flashing me two rows of pointy silver teeth as he gaped at the change. Then he dropped to one knee, black wings rustling as the tips dragged over the ground. "Mistress," he said as he bowed his head.

"Look at me, Priya."

His face tilted up to meet my gaze. "Mother of Ahriman. Your word is my command."

"Then I'm commanding you now. Go to my mother in the Æthyr. Don't identify yourself. Just deliver her a message."

"Anything."

"Tell her if she wants me, she's going to have to come down here and face the monster she created."

"Mistress, please, that is unwise. I believe she is close to uncovering how to cross the planes."

I thought of my mother's embossed sigil on her journal. There was a reason it was altered and a reason she'd kept that version hidden from the rest of the order. And when I considered every revelation I'd uncovered in that evil metal box of hers, this small detail might be the most important.

I knelt down in front of Priya and grasped his taloned hand in mine. "I don't give a damn whether she's learned to cross over or not." I leaned close to his face and whispered, "I'm going to summon her psychotic ass down here myself."

29

The following night, just before sunset, Jupe watched the red taillights of his father's black pickup truck disappear down the back road of their property. Cady had gone with him. She was in a really weird mood. All Dad said was that the two of them were doing important magick and warned Jupe not to leave the house under any circumstance until they got back. The Holidays would be there in about an hour to lock down the house.

Jupe knew this had to do with Cady's mom. But Dad wouldn't tell him anything, which sucked, big-time. Imagining all the things that *could* be happening had to be ten times worse than knowing. Plus, when he got home from school, he saw they had a bucket of pig's blood from a slaughterhouse outside of town.

Major shit was going down. Scary shit.

Like he was going to just sit around here and jump at shadows? Screw that.

He had a good idea where they were headed, because the back road was a half-mile long and only really led to three places: Mr. and Mrs. Holiday's cabin, an open-air shed, and the beach at the bottom of the cliff. No way would the Holidays let Dad anywhere near their cabin with blood. That left the shed and the beach. Sand and blood seemed like a messy combination, and it might rain tonight, so he was betting on the shed, because it was covered and walled in on three sides. Apart from a tractor and some tools, the thing was empty.

Before he sneaked down there, he would call up Priya to find out if he knew anything. But first he called Leticia to give her an update on what was happening. Leticia was at the retirement Hobbit house, a.k.a. Racist Grandma Vega's apartment. His original plan was to meet her there, but when all this shit starting transpiring, he'd asked her if she could come here instead. And as his dad's pickup truck's engine rumbled down the hill, Jupe's phone chimed with her answer. He held his breath.

MSG from Leticia, 6:40 p.m.: **Grandma Vega fell asleep. I've got two hours before my sister picks me up. I could take a taxi to your house if you tell me how to get there.**

Hot damn.

It took her about twenty minutes. No way would Dad ever forgive him if he allowed a taxi across the house ward, so Jupe met her at the electronic gate and let her in after she paid the driver. Tonight she wore a fur-trimmed gray vest over her pink hoodie, and her hair was back in the messy buns behind her ears. She stuck her hands into her pockets and smiled at him as he punched the close button on the gate.

Foxglove jumped up on her. "Down, Foxglove, you damn freak. Sorry, she's just extra friendly. She won't bite or anything."

"Hello, Foxglove." She bent low and held out her hand. After a quick sniff, Foxglove gave it a good approval lick. Leticia scrunched up her nose and wiped her hand on her jeans as she stood.

"You wrestle a wolf for that vest?" Jupe asked, using it as an excuse to look her over freely without seeming too creepy.

"It's fake fur. Stop looking at my boobs."

Dammit. Best not to admit anything. He walked her up the gravel road toward the house. "It's only seven. Your grandma goes to bed that early? Mine stays up past midnight."

"Whoop-di-freaking-doo. And no, she usually doesn't go to bed that early. I gave her wine at dinner."

"Damn, Leticia! You don't play."

"Watch yourself, Jupiter," she said with a sly smile. "I know all sorts of ways to manipulate you if I want to."

"Maybe I want to be manipulated."

She shoved his arm and made him stumble off the road.

"Hey!" He laughed and pretended to shove her back, but she raised an eyebrow in warning, so he gave up on that idea.

She whistled as they crested a hill and crossed the house ward. "That's your house? Whoa. Your dad is loaded. That looks like something out of an architectural magazine."

"We're not *crazy* rich or anything. He inherited this property from his parents. It's just that my dad's an artist, so he likes things to look good."

"My dad's an engineer, so our place is pretty nice, but it looks like every other house on the block. This is cool. Your dad has good taste."

"Wait until you see inside." Jupe unlocked the front door and held it open for her. "But I'll have to give you a tour another time. We only have forty-five minutes before the Holidays show up, and there's something I want to show you."

She gave him that little judge-y eyebrow tilt as she slid past him, smelling of strawberry jam and shampoo, and he almost lost his mind. If they'd had more time, that house tour could have gotten her inside his room. But as it stood now, he was just happy she was here at all.

"Tell me more about this big thing you've been texting me about," she said as he led her into the living room, which was a bad idea, because now she was looking at his baby pictures.

"I'm not a hundo percent sure, but I think Cady and my dad are doing a summoning down at my dad's workshop."

"Wow." She glanced out the patio window, looking nervous. "Where's this workshop?"

"In a shed on the other side of the cliff. We can get there in five minutes if we walk fast. But here's the part I want to show you first. Have you ever heard of a Hermeneus spirit?"

"Sure. Guardian angels. Everyone's heard of those."

"You don't have one . . . do you?"

She shook her head. "Grandma Vega used to, but it died. I heard it, though, a couple of times when she called it. It's sort of spooky, like talking to a ghost. I mean, not that ghosts are real."

He chuckled. "Boy, have I got some news for you. I've seen shit you wouldn't believe."

"You curse too much, Jupiter."

"Don't get prudish on me now, Lett." He knew the second he said it that she wouldn't be happy, and sure enough, she gave him the devil eyebrow again. "Look, I didn't call you Letty, so relax. Besides, I'm about to show you something that's going to blow your freakin' mind."

She crossed her arms over her gray vest. "Okay, go on, then. Dazzle me, Houdini."

Oh, he would. He pulled out Priya's sigil from his wallet and dramatically spit on the card. So far, she didn't seem impressed, but she would be. "Priya, come," he said loudly, then to her, "You'd better back up. He needs room to land if he's flying."

"Who?"

"Priya, come," Jupe said louder, and nervously smiled at Leticia.

They stood together, listening to the clock tick on the mantel. He wiped sweat off his forehead. She looked at him like he'd gone fruit-loopy. This was getting embarrassing.

Jupe tried once more, this time with extra spitting.

Tick. Tick. Tick.

Nothing.

"What the hell?" he mumbled.

"Are you seriously telling me you've got a guardian?" Leticia said.

"He's Cady's. But we're connected. It's a long story. But I call him every day, just about. He always comes right away. I mean, *always*. You think maybe I don't have enough Heka to call him? I'm not a magician."

"You might try blood."

Crap. He really didn't want to do that. But he also didn't want to look weak in front of her, so he nicked himself with a knife from the kitchen and bled a couple of drops of blood onto the card. But when he called Priya a fourth time and the guardian didn't show, he knew something was wrong.

"You think he could be mad at me?" Jupe asked.

"Hermeneus spirits are servants. They don't get mad. If their owner calls, they come every time. Well, I take that back. My grandma called her guardian a couple of years ago, and it never came, so that's how she later found out it had died in the Æthyr."

Died? "Oh . . . shit." A terrible fear pricked at

Jupe's nerves. He pretty much hated Priya's guts, but that didn't mean he wanted the guy dead. Cady would freak out, and she already had enough on her plate. Last night, after the big talk, Dad had told him the memory magick was still active, so she still didn't remember she was pregnant or that she and Dad were practically engaged.

On top of all that, if Priya died, who would keep tabs on Cady's mom in the Æthyr?

He took out his phone and started to text his dad but remembered that he had specifically told him not to bother them, that they wouldn't answer his texts. They'd only been gone, what, a half hour? They weren't starting until the Holidays called to confirm they were all safe inside the house, so Jupe still had about thirty minutes.

He pocketed his phone and Priya's card. "We need to go find my dad and Cady right now. This definitely qualifies as an emergency. Come on."

They rushed out into the night air, Foxglove at their heels, and he showed Leticia the back road the pickup truck had taken. If she hadn't been with him, he would have run, but he didn't want her to think he was freaking out as much as he actually was. After a couple of minutes, the Holidays' cabin came into sight, the windows glowing with warm yellow light. "Stay on the other side of the road, and if they spot us, I'll do the talking."

But they didn't come out. And once Jupe and Leticia began hiking down the next switchback turn in the road, more lights shone in the distance. The shed. A metal wall hid the inside from view, but Jupe could just make out his dad's pickup truck parked in the dirt driveway that looped around back. Thank God.

Foxglove started running toward the shed before Jupe broke down and did the same, his sense of urgency outweighing his eagerness to rack up coolness points with Leticia. Then the damn dog started barking, and Jupe couldn't shut her up. No sense trying to hide things anymore; Cady and Dad would definitely know they were coming now.

"Jupe!" Leticia called out, just behind him.

He glanced over his shoulder and saw her pointing up at the sky, then swung back around to follow the direction of her finger. He saw it, too: a black shape falling like a torpedo. It was too big to be a person, too dark to be a falling star. A gigantic boulder? Crap, maybe it was a meteor! Foxglove was going nuts now, heading straight for it.

Jupe saw the light inside the shed, and his mind registered Cady and his dad standing under the utility light that shone down from the roof. But as the falling thing rocketed past the tops of the trees, he realized what he was seeing, and he couldn't stop himself from crying out.

30

The summoning circle was fully charged. Everything was ready. We'd wait until the Holidays called to confirm that they were safe inside the house with Jupe, and then all I had to do was call down my mother.

Lon had swapped the Lupara for a full shotgun. We'd both already transmutated. "Whatever you do, don't use your moon power until she's inside the binding," he warned. "Don't give her any opportunity to connect with you during the summoning, or she might end up outside the trap."

"I know," I said testily. We'd gone over this a million times. I'd call her into the circle, and the second she manifested, Lon would shoot her. If for some reason he missed, I would burn her to a crisp, just as I'd burned Dare. Brutal, but what else could I do? She was beyond redemption and a threat to everyone around me. A rabid dog who should have been put down a long time ago. I wanted to skip the shotgun and do the deed myself, but Lon said a child should never have to kill her own parent.

"You already have enough blood on your hands," he said, reading my second thoughts. "You don't kill. I kill for you."

"How can I ask you to do that?"

"You don't have to. I'm volunteering. Besides, you don't even know how to use a gun, and now's not the time to learn. You summon, I execute. This is just like that green Pareba demon that chased you down the cliff the first night you came to my house. Just call her. I'll do the rest. I can't say I'll take pleasure in it, but I won't be lying awake regretting it, either. So don't worry about me."

I flicked my tail and exhaled slowly. No use pretending that I wasn't worried, because I was, and he knew it. My own empathic ability was gone when I awoke from the too few hours of sleep we had managed earlier in the day. I missed that connection to Lon, but at the same time, I already had enough crazy emotions jumping around inside me, so I supposed I didn't need his, too.

And I definitely didn't need another random knack to replace the empathy, so thank God I hadn't noticed one.

"It all seems too easy," I said, checking the summoning circle one last time. Even though she'd be coming from the Æthyr, she wasn't a demon, so I seriously doubted I could trap her in a binding triangle.

But I charged one inside the circle, just in case. "I don't trust it."

Lon didn't, either, but he remained silent.

A distant sound caught my attention outside the workshop. Something approaching? The road leading up to Lon's house was heavily wooded, so it could be any number of animals—foxes, rabbits, deer. Lon said he'd even seen a bobcat on his property a couple of years ago. But we were outside the house ward, and I was already in freak-out mode, so when the sound changed from something approaching to something racing, I rushed out of the shed to see it.

"What the hell is that?" Lon said, striding behind me.

Barking.

"Foxglove," I said, recognizing the dog's glow-in-the-dark purple collar bounding down the road toward the shed.

"What the hell is she—" But Lon never finished, because between the Labrador's sharp warning barks, Jupe's voice carried in the wind. He was shouting at Foxglove, then answering someone. A girl's voice. As she cleared the trees and came into sight with Jupe, both of them running as if the devil himself was at their heels, I heard what the girl was shouting.

"Up!"

Up? I swiveled around and tilted my face to the sky. A black shape was falling, picking up speed, getting bigger and closer and—

"Lon!"

The shape knocked him sideways and hit the ground hard enough to shake the soles of my shoes. As Lon scrambled to right himself, I rushed to help him and cried out when I spotted what lay on the ground a few feet away.

"No, Jupe! Get back!" I shouted as his long legs picked up speed and carried him straight for what had fallen out of the sky. But he wasn't listening, concern for his father giving way to horror as he skidded to a stop behind the fallen shapes.

Two figures, one female, one male, untangled their limbs as Foxglove barked furiously, hackles up. The female was riding on the back of the male. She unwrapped her arms from the choke hold she had around his neck and squatted next to him.

"Get up!" she shouted at him, and my heart shriveled inside my chest.

Priya whimpered and pushed himself up. Blood streamed down his face and chest. One of his wings was broken and wouldn't retract. He cried out in pain when the woman jerked his arm to pull him in front of her like a shield.

Her hair was tangled and wild; the toga-like gown she wore was bedraggled and dirty. Dark symbols were painted over every inch of her bared skin—magical armor, glowing softly with Heka. And from the way the symbols dripped in places, I had a feeling she'd used Priya's blood for paint.

"*Ma petite . . . lune,*" she said between labored breaths. "I got your message, yes? Thank you for being thoughtful enough to send along transportation with your invitation. I've been trying to catch this little bird for weeks, and *quelle surprise!* He appears right in front of my eyes."

"Run, Mistress," Priya said hoarsely. I could barely hear him over Foxglove's barking.

A shotgun racked near my shoulder. "She's not going anywhere."

My mother roughly twisted Priya's head to the side. "*Tsk, tsk*, Kerub. You'll have to kill the bird to get to me."

"No!" I shouted. "Don't do it, Lon."

"I'm sorry," he murmured, bracing the butt of the shotgun against his shoulder.

Jupe took another step closer to Priya, waving his arms. "No, Dad, no!"

"Get back!" Lon bellowed to Jupe. "Run!"

Quick as lightning, my mother reached back and snatched Jupe's hair. His scream shattered my heart as she exchanged hostages, dragging Jupe against her and tossing Priya's broken body to the ground. He yelped in pain and balled up on the ground, clutching one shoulder while my mother jerked Jupe's arms behind him.

"Struggle, and I'll snap your neck," she calmly told Jupe.

"No!" I shouted. "Let him go right now, or so help me God—"

"You'll do what? Use your new powers? *My* powers," she corrected. "Go on, Sélène. Try. I'd like to see them in action. You, too, demon boy. Just know that this symbol will prevent any of you from using your demonic abilities on me."

That's when I saw the truth in what she said: not *symbols* painted on her but one symbol, repeated. I'd seen it once before on Rose Giovanni's signet ring, the one she'd used to deflect Yvonne's knack at Christmas.

Oh, God. She'd made herself invincible? What the hell was I going to do now?

"Dad," Jupe moaned.

"Stay still," Lon said.

"Listen to your father," my mother chirped. "If my daughter had listened to hers, she wouldn't be putting your lives at risk. But now he rots in the Æthyr, and I am forced to fend for myself."

"No one to do your dirty work," I said, trying to waste time as my brain desperately analyzed my options. I could see Lon slinking away from me, trying to get a better angle as he edged toward Priya, but my mother's sharp eyes were noticing, too. She swiveled Jupe in Lon's direction as a warning. "I know you had Dad kill my brother."

"Your brother was a walking corpse. Your father performed a mercy. He was softhearted that way. And now I'm about to show you an even bigger kindness. I will let all of your filthy little friends live, and I'll let you live, too. All you have to do is agree to let me transfer my soul to your body." She grinned, as pretty as pie, behind Jupe's corkscrew curls.

But something in that smile faltered, and a

strange fuzziness blurred her face for a moment. I'd seen that before, when Priya couldn't hold his corporeal body on this plane. She was feeling the same tug. Something must have happened to her when she crossed the planes, which meant . . .

She couldn't remain here without borrowing an earthly body.

All I had to do was wait it out, let the clock run. She'd eventually lose her hold and zap back up to the Æthyr.

And then what? She'd terrorize Priya or some other guardian and catch another ride down when I didn't expect it? Or she'd continue to puppet me until I ended up hurting Jupe or Lon?

No.

I had her now, and this had to end. No more running.

But how could I get to her without Jupe getting caught in the crossfire?

Oh! Of course: our connection. He was still under my protection, with my sigil tattooed on his hip, and a thin spider web of light joined that tattoo to my hand. But Jupe's thread was joined by four others.

One sprouting in his direction, blinking with static and connected to my mom.

A black thread connected to Priya's injured body.

A green thread connected to Lon.

And another white thread piggybacking on it, connecting back to my stomach.

Memories flew back to me like dust being sucked

up by a vacuum cleaner: Lon performing the memory spell on me after I begged him to do it; when I first discovered multiple threads in the alley; Lon kissing me in our bed when I came home from the hospital; Dr. Mick informing me that I was pregnant; me telling Lon I loved him after I killed Dare . . .

On and on, a chain reaction of lost memories filled up my head, each one throwing off the magick that had kept them all hidden.

Lon made a gut-wrenching sound. His hands shook on the shotgun.

I blinked away tears and looked up at Jupe, seeing the fear in his eyes in a different way. He wasn't just a quirky teenage kid, he was mine. All of them were—Jupe, Priya, Lon . . . our unborn child. All mine, and my mother wasn't taking a single one of them away from me.

I held up my hands in surrender. "All right. You can have me. Let the kid go, and you can have me."

"And have your demon lover shoot me in the process? I don't think so. Come here, and I'll release him in exchange for you."

"Cady!" Lon warned. "She's fading. Let her go."

But I *couldn't*.

I began walking toward her, slowly, hands still in the air.

"Don't do it!" Jupe cried, tears streaming down his cheeks.

But I *had to*.

No other choice, really. If I didn't, she'd kill Jupe

before she got yanked back to the Æthyr, when she realized she had nothing to lose. And what kind of life would Lon and I have left if that happened? No life at all.

Three more steps, and I'd be within her reach. Last chance to change my mind.

A movement behind her made me lose my focus. The girl who'd raced down here with Jupe stood in the shadows outside the circle of light beaming from the shed. I'd never seen her before, but I recognized something familiar in her face. This had to be Leticia Vega, daughter of the grandmaster at the lodge in Morella. She was gesturing wildly, pointing at my mother, drawing shapes with her finger on the front of her clothes, tapping her back between her shoulder blades, shaking her head, pointing at my mother again.

I hesitated in midstep, realization sending goose bumps over my arms.

An Achilles' heel. My mother had painted the symbols on herself; she must not have been able to reach her own back. Did this matter or not? I wasn't sure.

I closed my eyes for a moment and tried to still my thoughts. Maybe I was going about this all wrong. When I'd needed my Moonchild abilities in the past, they'd shaped themselves without conscious thought. Could I count on that again?

"Cady!" Lon shouted to me in desperation. He was moving again, racing to get around Priya, and my mom was twisting, trying to shield herself with Jupe without losing sight of me. Or was it that she didn't want to turn her unprotected back on me?

And that's when a strange idea came to me, one I wasn't sure would work. But what did I have to lose?

Trust me, I told Lon in my head at the same time as I told my mother, "Take me" out loud.

And when she released one of Jupe's arms to reach for mine, I avoided her grip, slapped a hand on her back, and unleashed what I prayed was an actual knack and not just some fleeting, fucked-up magical vision.

Everything around me vanished.

31

Jupe felt the grip on his arms loosen, but he was too scared to move—not until he saw his dad's expression change. Spiraled horns and fiery halo blurred toward him as he wriggled out of the woman's stiff hands and propelled himself away.

His dad grabbed his arm and jerked him to his side, and that's when Jupe swung around and got a look at Cady and her mother. They looked frozen in place. Like storefront mannequins or one of those stupid artist hippies in the Village who painted themselves to look like statues and jumped out at people.

And Cady's eyes were all messed up. Her pupils had disappeared. They were nothing but silver.

"Get behind me!" his dad snapped.

But he couldn't, because—

"Leticia!" he shouted, seeing her move in the shadows.

"Don't go near them!" Dad shouted toward her as he steered them all toward Priya. "Circle around this way."

Leticia jogged and met them, Foxglove bounding behind. Jupe grabbed her hand and pulled her behind his dad. "Are you okay?"

She nodded, but he could tell that she was freaking out. And how could he blame her? Dad had gone all Hellboy, Cady had turned into a black and white reptile, a body-painted psychopathic witch just fell out of the sky and nearly broke his arms holding him hostage, and a shirtless boy with a broken wing had crash-landed at their feet.

Sort of put Leticia's naked-altar-sister, racist-grandma family to shame.

Still, Leticia was a warrior. So it shouldn't have come as a surprise to Jupe that she managed to keep a level head in the middle of all this crazy shit. She didn't scream, and she didn't run. She just looked up at his dad and said, "What's happening to them?"

"Cady said she was going to let her mom take her body," Jupe said. "Does that mean her mom's soul is inside her?"

Dad's eyes flicked back and forth between the two frozen women. "I'm not sure."

"Maybe they swapped bodies, like some kind of bad '80s movie," Jupe suggested.

Dad shook his head. "Cady looked like this yesterday, when she had a . . . vision."

"What kind of vision?"

Dad held his shotgun as if he wasn't sure if he should be aiming it or not. "Like an out-of-body experience. She traveled somewhere."

"Where?" Jupe asked. "Do you think she took her mom back into the Æthyr?"

"She is still on this plane," a pained voice said at their feet. "I can feel her, but I cannot hear her anymore. I cannot verify exactly where she is or whether her mother has control over her, and I am not sure if I can locate her in this state of injury."

Jupe bent down to inspect Priya. "Dude, are you okay?"

"I need to heal, or I won't be able to fly again," he said through gritted pointy teeth.

"We know healers. I can call one," Jupe offered.

Priya's skin crackled with static. "I can find a healer in the Æthyr, but I cannot stay here much longer. And if I leave, Enola may return with me."

For a moment, Jupe thought this was the best idea in the world. But if Cady's mom returned with Priya, she might kill him. Or torture him and use him to fly back down here again. Or if she was inside Cady's body right now, she might try to take Cady's soul along with her.

Crap. There were too many possibilities. But he suddenly thought of one that might be the answer to all of them.

"Shoot her mom's body," Jupe said to his dad. "You have a clear shot—just shoot her."

Leticia shook her head. "I don't think you should. If you destroy the mother's body while the soul is inside Cady's body, will the soul be trapped?"

"Crap," Jupe said. She might have a point.

"And what if they've swapped bodies?" she said. "You might be killing Cady's soul."

"When magick is present, anything is possible," Priya mumbled.

Okay, now Jupe was right back to being overwhelmed by possibilities. "What do you think, Dad?"

He didn't answer. Just stared at Cady with a helpless expression.

Leticia shook her head as if she was unsure about all of it. "This is strange magick."

"It's not magick," his dad said. "It's one of Cady's knacks."

"She's not human," Leticia said, flicking a glance from his dad to him.

No use denying it now. Not in the middle of all this. "We're Earthbounds," he said. "I'm sorry I didn't tell you, but it's not something we usually talk about with, well, you know—"

"Humans," she finished.

He nodded. When she didn't look at him, he felt a fresh burst of panic in his gut. Because they couldn't see halos, most humans didn't believe Earthbounds really existed. Cady said half of her order didn't, which was stupid, because they were all about summoning demons from the Æthyr. Leticia had never mentioned the subject, so he didn't know how she felt about it.

Or how she felt about him, now that she knew the truth.

But what could he do? She either accepted it or

she didn't. Knowing this didn't make him feel any less anxious; he liked her way too much.

Exhaling heavily, he studied Cady's frozen scaly body, partly scared, partly worried, and a little bit amazed. It was so quiet. Even Foxglove had stopped barking. Was that a good sign? He wanted to ask about the baby, what with all this talk of soul swapping, but he didn't want to worry his dad. Dude was already on edge.

"She sort of looks like a dragon."

Jupe glanced at Leticia, heart thudding in his chest. She flashed him the tiniest, quickest smile he'd ever seen. But it was just enough to give him hope—about her, about him and her together, and about this whole damn mess.

"Oh, Mistress," Priya moaned. "I have failed you again."

Jesus, what a whiner. Jupe glanced down at the guardian, who was still struggling to stay on this plane. Then Jupe turned to his dad, who looked as if he was seconds away from a heart attack.

"Come on, people, have a little faith," Jupe told them. "I mean, it's Cady. And she's pretty damn strong. She survived that fight with Dare, and she's rescued a lot of people. She pulled me down off that roof last fall, and she went girl-on-girl with Yvonne at Christmas. Oh, and she beat the crap out of that girl magician with the school desk—and that was before she could shift into a dragon." He flashed Leticia a little smile of his own and waggled his eyebrows at her, because just saying all this out loud made him feel a million times better.

"If she can do all that," he added, "surely she can handle one crazy mother."

32

White walls surrounded me. I stood next to a perfectly made double bed, which would have perfectly tucked hospital corners if I lifted up the plain bedspread to check. His-and-hers closet doors were both shut, but no doubt the space behind them contained neat rows of perfectly pressed clothes.

The blinds were tightly shut, just as they were in the rest of the house, to hide dark secrets from snooping neighbors. On the surface, they wouldn't have seen much if they'd been able to peep inside: no decorations, no paintings, no framed photos—not in here. Those would be out in the living room, to prove to visitors that we were a Normal Family and that there was nothing to see here, move along.

But not at the back of the house. No need for them. Because we weren't a normal family, and there was no need to keep up appearances behind closed doors.

I never was allowed in this bedroom, so naturally, I always tried to sneak inside. And I'm sure I was successful a time or two, but the memories I had of this room had likely been wiped away by magick. And I'm sure that when I did make my way in here, I would have noticed the only thing of interest, a set of closed curtains on the inner wall.

That's exactly where my focus was now. Until a confused moan drew my attention.

My mother looked a thousand times more disheveled in this light, a thousand times more feral when contrasted against the tidy cleanliness surrounding her. And in bringing her here, I felt as though we'd switched places: she was now the one panicking, and I felt as if I were standing in front of a wildcat that had been defanged and declawed and had just had its balls chopped off.

"What is happening?" she said, looking around wildly. "Where are we?"

I forced a smile. "Why, this is your bedroom, don't you remember? It doesn't exist anymore, as I'm sure you know. Plowed down with the rest of the houses on this block to make way for condos. Miami real estate waits for no one."

She tentatively took a step before reaching out for the bedpost. "*Mon dieu*. What have you done?" A quick anger flared behind her eyes, but the rumble of a truck passing by on the street outside made her flinch.

Putting some distance between us, I headed to the curtains on the inner wall and wrenched them open to reveal what lay behind. Built-in bookshelves lined the wall below my waist. The lower shelves near the floor were filled with occult books—mostly first-edition copies of my parents' greatest hits—and on top were a velvet cloth and several ritual items: a chalice, a ritual dagger, a salt cellar, a caduceus staff, and a carved wooden box for red ochre chalk.

Innocuous stuff found in every magician's home. I kept far more dangerous things in Tambuku.

But it was the thing above those supplies that drew my interest. A small two-way mirror let me see into the room beyond. A child's room with a small bed, bookshelves, a toy chest. A picture map of the constellations on the wall and plastic stars pressed into the ceiling.

And on the floor, in the middle of a round rug with a woven man-in-the-moon design, sat a slightly older version of the Sélène I'd glimpsed in the winter home. Perhaps four or five years old, she lay on her stomach, engrossed in a picture book, lazily kicking her feet in the air.

"Did you watch me through here all day?" I asked. "You could've played with me instead. Or were you trying to keep your distance so you didn't develop any pesky maternal feelings?"

My mother walked up to the window and drew in a sharp breath, a look of amazement on her face. But when the shock wore off, her shoulders dropped as she quietly stared at the child in the other room. I could practically feel her guard drop. "This . . . is an incredible ability."

"Useful. It's good to see the past as it really was. Especially since you stripped so many of my memories."

"Enjoy your stroll down memory lane. I will find better uses for this ability."

"'Better' is subjective, but I don't doubt you would use it for something more ambitious," I said. "This is exactly what you wanted, isn't it? I'm sure you stood here watching that child in there, dreaming of having access to powers like this."

She tore her gaze away from the glass long enough to give me a once-over. "I certainly did not dream of commanding them in that ugly reptilian body you're wearing, but now that you have made a hash of my dreams, I suppose I will learn to tolerate it."

"Hey, you're the one who mated with a serpent, not me."

Oh, the look she gave me. I wouldn't have been surprised if it burned right through my eyeballs and out the back of my skull. In the past, that look would have been enough to make me cower but not here. Not now. And when she saw this, the fire fizzled and was replaced by something less sure. She scratched at the bloody symbols drying on her arm and refocused on the mirror. "At least your body is still young."

"And I'm not a notorious serial killer wanted by the FBI, so you wouldn't have to duck security cameras in airports anymore."

She cocked a brow. "When I get possession of

those powers, every camera in the world will want to take my photograph."

That sounded about right. She was always happy when she was commanding attention.

"Can she hear us?" my mother asked. I didn't answer—I honestly didn't know for certain—so she tapped on the glass with a knuckle. Five-year-old me jerked her head to the side and stared up at the window, which I remembered looking like an ordinary framed mirror above a desk from her point of view. "She hears us," my mother whispered.

More than heard us, apparently, because little Sélène pushed off the rug and warily walked toward the desk below the mirror. She pulled a chair out from beneath it and stood on top of it, peering right at us. My mother stared back at her. No one spoke. After a few seconds, little Sélène gave up and headed back to her book.

"Extraordinary," my mother murmured. "You could always see things no one else could."

"Maybe it's not just me. Maybe you should walk to the kitchen and say hello to *your* younger self."

A small laugh bubbled from her mouth. "You have no idea how to wield this power."

"And you do?"

"Darling, I know things about your powers you couldn't fathom." She lifted her chin to the mirror. "In your head, you are still that little girl in there. Naive. Submissive. And only breathing because I've allowed you to live. Would you like me to show you the fruits this ability can yield?"

"I don't need any more magical instruction from you, thank you."

"Oh, I'm done teaching. And I'm done waiting. I'm ready to take the reins now."

"And you really believe I'm so submissive that I'm just going to allow you to slip inside my body without a fight?"

A slow smile spread across her face, cracking the dried blood on her skin. "*Ma petite lune*, you already have."

I snorted, ready to hurl a retort, but there was something about the absolute confidence on her face. It tripped me up. Made me doubt.

"Use your brain, Sélène," she said in a low voice. "How do you think I am here with you? We are not flesh. We are observing a moment in time constructed of memories. *Your* memories. You opened the door and guided me through."

Was that true? Was this just a piecemeal reconstruction of a series of memories? The first time I'd experienced this, when I saw Dare talking to my parents back at the cabin in California, was that a dormant memory, something my parents had hidden with magick but not stripped away completely?

"Dare," my mother mumbled. "I couldn't be happier that you burned that devil up."

All my muscles turned to stone.

My mother's smile widened. "Surprised? Yes, I can read your thoughts. I can see all of you now. Aren't you listening? You invited me inside. We are sharing the same body. You, me, and that monstrous child growing in your belly."

Oh . . . God.

"Three souls cannot inhabit one body," my mother said. "Let me show you what power looks likes when the person wielding it knows what she is doing."

The white walls melted like spring snow. Floorboards fell away. Nighttime swirled around us, and the musty scent of my childhood home in Florida was replaced by damp earth and trees and the mineral scent of red ochre chalk.

Trees. Night. A clearing. A rocky hill in the distance.

Panic shot through me as cool night air chilled my skin. I tried to move, but my hands and ankles were strapped to a post. The metal of a sacrificial oracular bowl cooled the bottoms of my bare feet, waiting to catch my blood.

Bound in Balboa Park. Last September. We were back where my parents had tried to sacrifice me and steal my power. The worst night of my life. Only it was just the two of us here now in the dark. No elemental creatures bound in the great circle before me. No Frater Blue. No father.

"*Victoire!*" My mother's laughter echoed off the rocky hill as she spun in a circle with her arms outstretched, face tilted up to a full moon.

I struggled against my bonds as hysteria blotted out reason. Rope bit into my wrists and made my fingers tingle. I tried to rock the post and the heavy oracular bowl and only managed to draw my mother's attention. She halted her swirling dance and stalked toward me.

"This is how you wield power," she said, getting in my face. "You are in my memories now."

But it wasn't a memory—not exactly. Things were missing. I wasn't naked and covered in a red veil. The ritual circle wasn't charged.

"Why do I need protection?" my mother answered, reading my thoughts. "Your devil lover isn't coming to save you this time. After I kill your soul, I will take control of your reptile body and lay waste to him with fire, exactly as you destroyed Dare. Then I will use magick to snuff out the life of your child."

I snarled and strained to bite her cheek, but she jerked out of my reach, laughing.

This wasn't actually happening, no matter how real it felt. I had to get control of myself and think. But how could I, when she was listening to my thoughts?

"Not just your thoughts," she said. "I see *everything*. All your mistakes. All your fears. And all your weaknesses. Your friends and so-called family, the mundane life you've cobbled together from the scraps I left you and the misplaced loyalty you've given away freely. I see it all, Sélène."

Unbidden images of Lon and Jupe popped into my head. I tried to shake them away, but it was impossible. My thoughts were tangled, tripping on her words. But when she sighed and closed her eyes with a look of deep satisfaction settling on her face, I remembered Lon telling me how to keep him out of my thoughts when he was transmutated.

If we were really inside my body, then why was I giving her control?

My mother's eyes snapped open.

I immediately put up a barrier in my head.

"Go on," she said, "if that makes you feel better. I don't need your memories."

"Are you sure? Because it seems pretty barren out here. Why did you choose not to remember Dad?"

"Alexander is dead. He was weak, and I am strong."

An oblong shape glinted on the ground between us. She stooped to pick it up and showed it to me: the ceremonial dagger she'd tried to use on me the first time I'd been tied up here. The blade gleamed in the moonlight beneath the white of her smile.

"That's not how I see it," I said, ignoring the fear gnashing at the edges of my thoughts.

"See what?"

"You said Dad was weak and you're strong. But all I see is a middle-aged woman whose life is filled with failure. You failed to create a Moonchild when you had my brother. You failed with your stupid idea to unite all the occult orders. You failed when you tried to take over all the orders by force—double fail, really, because you got caught by savages instead of ruling over the occult world like some kind of pope."

Defensive anger flared behind her eyes. "I am not in jail."

"No, but you're a wanted felon who had to leave the order in disgrace and abandon your home to live like a rat. What else? You failed to sacrifice me and siphon my powers last year. You failed to keep your husband alive in the Æthyr."

"But I slaughtered the demon who killed him."

"Who cares? What do you have now? The shoddy clothes on your back? You have no family, no friends, no roof over your head. Where's your occult army? No one's here to defend you. No one's got your back. Everything you've tried to accomplish has backfired. Hell, even your stupid publishing career was a flop— you never had a single book hit the bestseller lists."

"That is—" She tried to finish but ended up huffing.

"But you know what was your biggest failure? Me." I stretched against my bonds to lean closer and spoke in a low voice. "You had all the power you wanted in the palm of your hand, but you couldn't control me. Not when I was a child and not now."

In a blink, my bonds fell free. I was standing where she stood, holding her dagger. She was tied to the post. Her shoulders jerked as she fought to free herself, a string of French curses spewing from her lips. Feral eyes pinned me as she tried to calm herself, chest heaving with labored breath.

I could almost see her mind working; even now, she was cocky enough to think she was still winning.

It was the same conceit that had buoyed her through her killing spree of the occult leaders and that made her keep pushing forward in the Æthyr to find another way to get at the Moonchild powers, even after my father was dead.

The entire world revolved around her. If she hadn't possessed the magical talent she did, if she wasn't the lunatic bound before me, it was still easy to picture her using all that selfish determination to accumulate wealth or status or fame. A dirty politician. Head of some shady corporation. Amoral scientist. Enola Duval could have been any of those things. She would have been married to her job, obsessed with success. And even without a bloody trail of bodies, she still would have screwed over her coworkers left and right, stepping on their backs to climb up some other kind of ladder.

And I still would have grown up in a sterile, lonely house with a mother who didn't give a damn about her daughter.

I glanced down at the dagger in my hand. "I just want you to know something," I said in a voice that was surprising calm.

"And what would that be?"

"That even though you were an insane monster who treated me like a science experiment, even though you never truly loved me or even thought of me as more than an inconvenient stepping stone, even though you considered selling me like a slave to Ambrose Dare when you suspected I wasn't your real

Moonchild, even when you abandoned me at seventeen with the FBI on my trail—because of crimes *you* committed—even when you tried to sacrifice me, I still loved you."

I brushed away angry tears and stared her down, waiting for a reaction. She didn't even blink. She simply said, "Then perhaps I am not the one who is insane."

"Maybe not," I murmured, sliding my fingers to the handle of the dagger. "But I wanted you to know that. And I also wanted you to know that I forgive you for all of it."

She stared at me as if I were an unsolvable puzzle or a pet ape that had suddenly developed the ability to use sign language. As if she could *almost* summon enough humanity to pity me.

Almost.

The dagger's handle fit in my grip like it had been made for my hand—just the right length, just the right weight.

And maybe I did have some of her crazy genes bubbling inside me after all, because I felt nothing but dizzying relief when I sank the blade under her ribs.

33

Silver eyes squinted in front of my face. I shifted down from my transmuted state, and within a blink, the silver turned to green. Lon. No horns, no fiery halo. Just the man.

The dagger was gone; I'd dropped it before I transported back. But any doubts about what I'd just done dissipated when I caught a glimpse of my hands; they were roughly fisting Lon's shirt, one of them staining the cotton with blood.

"Is she . . . ?"

I pulled back and spotted the fallen body next to us. The relief I'd just been feeling melted into a slow, humming sadness. Not regret, though. It was just my mind getting accustomed to the sudden weight of this burden: I had killed my own mother. Never mind that I didn't have a choice. Just because *she* felt nothing for me didn't mean I was an emotionless machine. I was sad that I had to do it, sad that she was truly, irretrievably gone, and sad that I couldn't save her—not from herself or from me.

But like most things, it would pass. And I'd grieved for her too many times already.

What mattered now were the ones I'd saved by doing this, and they surrounded me.

"Cady?" Jupe said, eyes big and wary. "Are you in there?"

"Yes, I'm here." I grabbed him and fell against Lon's chest, embracing both of them. Happy tears streamed down my cheeks as Lon kissed the top of my head over and over, nearly squeezing the breath out of me. Even Foxglove tried to get in on the action, standing on hind legs to paw at Jupe.

"Get down, you dumb dog," Jupe said cheerfully. "You just ruined a happy moment, congratulations."

"Are you okay?" Lon asked, eyes glassy with emotion—which, knowing now exactly how strong that emotion could be, was probably barely contained.

"I'm fine." My hand slid to my stomach, as if I could tell something. "Everything feels okay. Priya?" I asked, pushing away to search for him.

"He couldn't hold on," Jupe explained. "He said he'd find a healer in the Æthyr. And he's pretty torn up about what happened, thinks he failed you and all that junk. So you should probably be nice to him next time you summon him. He's got some self-worth issues."

"Thank God you don't have that problem," Lon mumbled, and I wanted to hug them both all over again. But the crunch of gravel behind Jupe made me remember we weren't alone.

I peered around his mass of curls and spotted the girl. She was pretty, now that I could see her better. And she held herself as if she was slightly uncomfortable but would die before she admitted it. I liked her immediately.

"Hi," I said.

She held up a tentative hand. "Hi."

"Thanks for the heads-up earlier."

"No problem."

A slow grin lifted Jupe's cheeks, and his eyes went a little squinky. "*This* is Leticia Vega."

"Nice to meet you, Leticia." I gripped Lon's hand like he might dry up and blow away. "I'd apologize that you caught us on a bad night, but this is pretty much the everyday circus sideshow for this family." Dead body. Pig's blood summoning circle behind us in the shed. A great first impression.

"Her sister gets naked in front of the entire lodge every week, and her grandmother's a racist," Jupe volunteered happily. "She's used to weirdness."

"Well, then," I said, giving her a sympathetic smile to ease her through Jupe's gift of oversharing. "I think we'll get along just fine."

EPILOGUE

August, three and a half years later

I lounged on a wide wicker chaise in the backyard. It had been dark for an hour or so, and a pretty good fire still crackled in the round stack-stone fire pit Lon had built this spring. It felt fabulous on my chilly feet.

Behind me, a few hundred yards below our cliff, the dark Pacific crashed on the beach. In front of me, beyond the fire, Mr. and Mrs. Holiday hauled away the last of the plastic cups and paper plates to the garbage before they drove back to their cabin. And beside me, a lingering party guest shared my lounge chair.

"I swear, it's a good ten degrees colder out here than in the city at night." To prove her point, Kar Yee shivered dramatically and hugged her sweater tighter.

"You say that every time you come out here."

"It doesn't stop being true. It's summer, for the love of God."

"I don't mind when there's a fire. Where's Hajo tonight?"

"Working some police case in the foothills. A missing girl."

"Another one? Damn, he's really helping them out a lot lately. Not half bad for a former junkie." I wanted to add *and the biggest jerk I know*, but the last time I joked about someone "pulling a Hajo," Kar Yee and I had a huge fight and didn't speak for almost a week.

"Thank you," she said, taking full credit for his miraculous turnaround from Death Dowser/Drug Dealer to Death Dowser/Halfway Decent Person. "He's cleaned up nicely. And if he quits smoking, he can move in with me."

I chuckled. "Crack that whip, Kar Yee."

"Gross. You know how I feel about black leather and vinyl."

"S'pose there's no need for riding crops when you're wielding that fear knack of yours."

She tucked the tips of her bobbed hair behind her ears and grinned. "Oh, I almost forgot. Glen texted me to say he got the snafu with your business license smoothed over. I told you he would."

"Thanks for that."

"No problem. You need me to help you with anything? Spreadsheets, organizing . . . ?"

"Think I'm good. Everything's squared away now. Grand opening's on Friday."

"I'll drop by after closing to see if you need help counting all the cash."

I laughed. "Deal."

Although Kar Yee and I were still co-owners of Tambuku, I hadn't bartended since I buried my mother. Kar Yee had promoted Amanda to head bartender and hired two assistant managers and three new servers. Back in May, I signed a lease on a shop in the Village between an art gallery that sold Lon's signed prints and Three Dwarves Pottery, which made all the Tambuku Tiki mugs.

And my new demon-friendly business? Arcadia's Garden. Yep, I was now the proud owner of a rare herb emporium and tea shop and the only magical apothecary in town. I figured making magick medicinals was one of my better skills, and it was something I enjoyed. And it damn sure could be put to better use helping locals in La Sirena than pacifying drunk-ass bar patrons.

Karlan Rooke and I had kept in touch since my visit to Pasadena, so he was supplying most of my rare herbs. And although I'd be selling some of them loose—a fine selection of valrivia, rare teas, and few obscurities for the magick-minded customer—the majority of my business would be in medicinal teas and drinks. Depressed? Need energy? Trying to detox? Need to calm your nerves? I had you covered.

And it didn't hurt that my old buddy Bob would be sending patients my way; he'd have his medical license next year and was interning under Lon's BFF Dr. Mick at the hospital here. If I could just get Kar Yee to move to the beach, the whole gang would be back together. As it was, Auntie Kar Yee was driving out here at least once a month, and I did the reverse, popping in at Tambuku on occasion.

"Well, I hate to eat and run," she said, staring at her phone. "But Hajo found the body. Which is gruesome, but it means I have a date, and sex trumps children's birthday parties."

I gave her a fist bump. "Thanks for coming. Your gift was a big hit."

"Clothes are better than toys any day. She'd do well to learn that early on." She blew Jupe a kiss across the yard and marched up the steps to the patio, black bob swaying as she ducked under party streamers and strings of carnival lights, and left through the house.

A dark male figure blocked the light from the fire pit, sparks glittering around his shoulder-length hair as he stoked the wood. When he was finally satisfied, he plopped down next to me and slung an arm around my shoulders. "Peace and fucking quiet," he said. "No more birthdays. Ever."

I sniffed the wood smoke clinging to his shirt. "Next time, don't say 'Daddy is going to throw you a big party' and expect her to forget it."

"Mmm."

I poked his side, smiling when he flinched and made his I'm-too-manly-to-be-ticklish noise. "By the way, thanks for telling me you invited Ben Waters. He had his hand halfway up Mrs. Dutton's skirt every time his wife turned her back. That man is not family-friendly."

"You'd think he would be. He's fathered enough bastards around town to start his own baseball team. Anyway, it was a goodwill gesture and a reward for not breaking our truce."

Truce. I guessed that's what it was. Although Lon was officially not active in the Hellfire Club, he turned out to be the only remaining member trusted with the club's bank account. And that included Dare's son, Mark. Dare's wife had long ago moved to Europe, but Mark and his family ended up staying to run Dare Enterprises. Now, make no mistake, I still hated Mark Dare. But as long as he stayed away from my family, I tried not to hold his father's sins against him. Mark might be an ass, but at least he wasn't an evil overlord. And if he ever knew what his father did to me, I had a feeling he'd be pretty sick about it.

So Mark got to play leader of the club, Ben Waters was his second in command, and Lon controlled the money behind the scenes. Which meant no more Hellfire-bought drugs at the monthly parties, no more demon fight club, no more Incubus and Succubus sex circles in the Hellfire caves. That didn't mean the parties were G-rated. I had no doubt plenty of the members were still banging each other's brains out in the back caves and snorting every drug they could pass around.

"I'm just saying, if his wife comes into my shop asking for something to cure her husband's roaming eye, I'm telling her to toss his ass out and get a divorce. Maybe give her something to rot off his boy parts."

A slow smile spread over Lon's face. "God, this town doesn't know what it's in for."

No, it totally *did*, which was why Kar Yee had to send me the guy who helped her fix legal stuff at Tambuku. Someone at City Hall had messed with my license paperwork, and when I found out who was behind it, they were in for a world of hurt.

A screech shot across the yard, immediately followed by maniacal, tinkling laughter and excited barking. Two halos raced across the lawn under the carnival lights. One spring-green, the other silver and gold.

"Oh, *really*," Jupe called over his shoulder. "That's how it's going to be? After I helped you smash that piñata and all that candy I picked out of the grass for you?"

More laughter and some serious huffing and puffing.

"Jesus, she's going to have a heart attack," I mumbled, feeling mildly panicked myself.

"She's fine," Lon assured me. "Let her run off all that sugar."

Jupe stopped several yards away and turned around. "Come on and get me, Tabby-cat. That cape of yours is slowing you down."

And God, it really was. Kar Yee would faint if she saw her gift, a sparkly robe, tied around my kid's neck by the sleeves. It looked like it was practically choking her, but she didn't seem to care. Orange dress, paper pirate hat, sparkly pink cape waving like a flag as she bobbed toward Jupe like some crazed fruit bowl.

Jupe lunged to one side and skidded in the grass, and that's when she tagged him on the leg.

"Ow! Shit, Tabby, that hurts!"

"Shit!" she cried out triumphantly. "Shitshitshit!"

Great. Now she'd be busting that out at the grocery store.

Jupe rubbed his leg. "You shock me again, and—"

She got him in the arm.

"Goddammit!"

More batshit laughter followed.

"Hey, no shocking. Stop egging her on, Jupe!" I called out as he sidled around her as if they were opponents on a soccer field. He jumped back one more time, moving too fast for her to follow. And in her sugar-hyper, overexcited, past-her-bedtime state, she miscalculated and tripped over her own feet. The fruit bowl went down, face-planting in the grass.

The piercing cry that followed knifed right through my heart.

Lon's hold around my shoulders tightened before I could scramble off the lounge and run to her. "She's okay."

And although that was probably true, it didn't stop that heart-squeezing wail from jumbling all my insides. Nor did it stop my eyes from transmutating from human to serpentine. I focused on her with moon-powered nocturnal vision that gave me a sharper, silver-tinged view of her body.

Jupe bent over her and hauled her into his arms. "All right, I'm sorry. Enough playing." He walked her over to us and peeled her arms from around his neck. Lon was closer, so he got the pass. She fell on him in a fit of quivering, jerking sobs.

"Da-a-a-ddy," she cried. "Jupe hurt me."

Jupe's mouth fell open in mock offense. "I didn't even touch you."

"Shhh," Lon said, rubbing her back as she clung to him. "You're going to live."

I sat up and inspected her as she cried her eyes out all over Lon's chest. One barely skinned knee and some grass stains on her dress and palm. Switching knacks, I pushed my senses a little further into her body to make sure nothing was broken. Everything seemed to be in order, so I rubbed my fingers over her knee to heal up the scrape.

"All better," I said.

Lon pushed her hair back. "See? Mommy fixed you. It's all fine."

She wasn't ready to stop crying, so I reached over to heal up any other scrapes on her other knee, and that's when I found the weapon locked in her plump grip.

"Who gave her the pencil?" I said. It wasn't sharpened, but it served its purpose well enough. She'd started with the shocking a few weeks ago—without any prompt from me, I might add—and I'd been freaked out that she was going to hurt herself. So I showed her how to release Heka through pencils.

Huge mistake. Last week, I had to round up every pencil in the house.

"Jesus, Jupe," I complained. "She could've poked her eye out when she fell."

"Come on, it's not like they were scissors."

"It's my fault," a girl's voice said.

Leticia strode up behind Jupe. "Jupe's art teacher left her present next to the grill. She tore into it before I could stop her. It's an art kit with a bunch of crayons and stuff, but she went straight for the pencil." She handed me an unopened birthday card.

I stuffed it into my sweater pocket and made a mental note to add it to the thank-you list. "She can sniff out graphite a mile away," I said, tugging the knotted sleeves around her neck and slipping off her impromptu cape. "But don't let her run with stuff in her hands, okay, Jupe?"

"Got it—my sister is clumsy."

She raised her head and stopped crying long enough to say, "Am not!"

Jupe grinned and rubbed his arm. "Well, nothing like electrocution to end a party. We're out of here."

The tears suddenly shut off as if she'd turned a spigot. "Don't go!" she pleaded.

"I have to," he said, mussing up her hair. "Movie starts in half an hour, and I want to get a good parking space before the drive-in fills up."

"What are you seeing?" I asked as she pouted, burying her face in Lon's shirt.

"*An American Werewolf in London*. From 1981,

directed by John Landis." Jupe pretended to bite Leticia on the neck. She punched him in the arm where his sister had shocked him, and he feigned injury.

Looking at him now, I was amazed at how much and how little he'd changed since I first saw him standing in Lon's doorway. He was still long and skinny, but the seventeen-year-old was all lean muscle now, thanks to two seasons of being the top midfielder on La Sirena High's soccer team.

And although he'd somehow sprouted up several inches and morphed from a boy to almost a man while I wasn't looking—a painfully good-looking man who attracted stares wherever he went—he was still the same old cocky, overly optimistic, filterless Motormouth.

"Be back by one," Lon said

"One? It's Saturday, and I have to drive a half hour to take Leticia back to Morella, then a half hour back. That's an hour right there, and the movie doesn't let out until midnight. I'd have to speed to get home in time."

"I'm not paying for another ticket or a jacked-up insurance bill," Lon said. "Figure it out."

I held up two fingers.

Jupe grinned while his dad mumbled under his breath.

"No later, okay? And please don't speed. I don't want to sit around here worrying about seeing a smashed purple GTO showing up on the late news." He'd finished fixing it up two months before he turned sixteen and then promptly dented the back end—the tree next to the garage "looked farther away after it got pruned" and several other ridiculous defenses. It took him three additional months to fix the damage; the tree still had electric purple paint wedged into the scrape marks on the bark.

"I'll never speed again," he promised. A lie if I'd ever heard one. I pointed to my lips. He leaned down and kissed me, mumbling, "Thank you."

"Good night," Leticia said.

"Thanks for helping me with the decorations."

"Anytime. See you on Wednesday at the shop."

I grinned and gave her a thumbs-up as she ran to catch up with Jupe. Turned out Leticia was a surprisingly good apprentice and wasn't half bad at making medicinals.

As the GTO rumbled to life in the distance, the bundle in Lon's arm let out an exhausted sigh. Laughing, crying, and now fast asleep, all in the span of five minutes. He carefully removed her cardboard pirate hat and set it on the grass, then tucked his chin to his chest and picked a stray piece of confetti out of her hair.

She looked a lot like him, with her long body, high cheekbones, and wavy hair that was almost exactly the same length as his. Green eyes, too, so apparently, someone on my side of the fence carried a green-eyed gene.

And she might have Lon's waves, but it was dark brown like mine, and she definitely had my nose. Everything else blended together in that weird, unique way it does with kids—part of you but not you—including the silver and gold halo swirling above her frizzy dark hair. She was born with it, no waiting and wondering, and its metallic swirls almost looked like moving stripes.

Tabitha Rose Bell Butler was born two weeks early, after fifteen grueling hours of labor. And three years later, even through the postpartum depression and the nights I sat awake scared out of my mind that I didn't know what I was doing—or that she was too good to be true and something horrible would happen to rip her away from me—it was worth every second.

Tabby likes collecting shells, coloring on the walls and floor, clementines, birds, and building sand castles down at the beach. Every Saturday, she watches cartoons with Jupe. And every Sunday night, we call up her favorite bird of all, Priya, who shows her all the threads that connect us together and how big his wings expand.

She loves to tell wild stories, so when she informs the checkout lady at the grocery store that Mommy can turn into a dragon lady and Daddy has horns, we just shrug and smile.

And as for horns of her own? The verdict's still out on that, I suppose. Apart from her halo, there's nothing unusual about the way she looks. But she can already kindle Heka, as Jupe knows all too well, and although we haven't seen any definitive proof of an early knack, Lon and I have been a little on edge.

This past Christmas, Jupe rushed downstairs in a frenzy to tell me that Mr. Piggy wasn't waking up. He was already on the far side of normal life expectancy for a pygmy hedgehog, so I knew the day would eventually come. And he might not be the coziest of pets, but it still broke my heart.

However, after I raced back upstairs with him, we found Tabby in Jupe's room, sitting in the middle of the floor with Mr. Iggy, as she calls him. The hedgehog was sniffing around her shoes, looking perfectly normal. Tabby smiled up at us and said, "I woke him back up."

Maybe it was nothing. But it sure freaked Jupe out. Hell, it freaked me out, too. I'd experimented with a lot of my own knacks over the last few years, but reviving the dead sure as heck wasn't one of them. Lon said we were both crazy, but I could see the fear in his eyes. Kid with a persuasion knack? A headache. Kid with the power to reanimate dead things? A waking nightmare.

But I'm no walk in the park, either. I still didn't completely know the outer limits of my own abilities. The rotating smorgasbord of random knacks stopped after Tabby was born, thank God. Turns out maybe it was a side effect of my pregnancy and not a sign that I was losing my humanity. And although I could still access some minor knacks when the sun was out—mostly sensory-based ones, such as empathy and clairaudience—they were nowhere near as strong in the daytime as they were after dark.

For the past year, I'd been seeing Jupe's old psychiatrist, Dr. Spendlove, the Earthbound doctor who specialized in knacks. Naturally, I was his favorite patient, and not just as a curiosity—he said I was helping him better understand the limits of demonic abilities. I'd definitely done a lot of experimenting in his office. Most of it was harmless.okay, maybe I'd set a few things on fire and accidentally transported his desk out of his office. Where it went, I'm still not sure. Maybe I'll find out one day.

A tiny snore erupted from Tabby's open mouth. Lon and I stifled laughs and watched her twitch her way into dreaming. His fingers twined with mine over her back. The sliver of his halo glowed as bright as ever in my engagement ring.

Our wedding was no-frills, just us, Jupe, Kar Yee, the Holidays, and the Giovannis—minus Yvonne, who may very well be going on two years of sobriety in Miami but is not invited to family functions. Father Carrow, the retired Earthbound priest who played Cupid by introducing us, performed the ceremony right here in this yard.

A couple of months later, Lon, Jupe, and I went to his adoption hearing and made Jupe officially mine. A piece of paperwork wasn't half as binding as my tattooed sigil on his hip, but you wouldn't have known it from all the crying he did that day. Granted, I might have shed a few happy tears myself. Lon, too, although both of them would deny it if you asked.

Lon and I haven't had time for a honeymoon, but

he's promised we're still going to France alone this winter. I might have to work my way up to it. Right now, I was struggling with the decision to send Tabby to day care. It was only a block away from the shop, so I could be there in two minutes if I ran, but it felt like a bigger step than starting a new business.

"How about you put her in bed while I bank this fire?" Lon said. "Jupe won't be back until two—"

"You're welcome."

"—and she'll sleep like the dead."

That she would. Until exactly seven a.m., at which time she'd bang around in her room or sneak into ours and whisper, "Mommy, wake up," until I gave in.

"We still have that bottle of wine," he said. "And we can clean the rest of this up tomorrow."

"Or never."

"And Rose and Adella will be here next weekend."

"And Adella's new boyfriend," I reminded him. I was a little excited to meet him. Sexy professor, she'd said. He taught at her university in a different department. And—scandal of scandals—he was two years younger.

"If people don't stop coming to visit, I'm going to build us a separate cabin out here."

"A sex cabin?"

"The floor will be nothing but one big mattress," he promised. "No, I take that back. It will have everything built just the right height for every imaginable position: the counters, tables, holes in the walls—"

I laughed and had to cover my mouth not to wake the kid.

"It'll be an Olympic training room for sex," he said, waving his hand through the air as if he was envisioning the whole thing.

"We might need that chair, too," I said. He knew exactly the one I was talking about.

"Hell, we might need that chair right now."

"I'll meet you upstairs in two minutes," I said, pulling Tabby off his chest to settle her against one hip.

He kissed the top of her sleeping head and then leaned closer and kissed me, tickling my lips with his pirate mustache; clean-shaven Lon had only lasted for a few weeks, thank God. "Make it three," he murmured against my lips, "and be naked by the time I get up there."

"Dragon lady or beguiling witch?"

"Surprise me," he said with a sexy grin.

And I did . . .

ACKNOWLEDGMENTS

This series would not have been the same without Brian Bennett, Laura Bradford, Jennifer Heddle, Adam Wilson, Julia Fincher, Wendy Keebler, and Anne Cherry. Thanks to all the folks who work behind the scenes at Simon & Schuster, and to Tony Mauro for the great covers. Gigantic sloppy hugs to the writers who offered advice or a kind word when I needed it most, including Karen Chance, Carolyn Crane, Ann Aguirre, Karina Cooper, Lauren Dane, Donna Herren, Bree Bridges, Kevin Hearne, Kelly Meding, Sierra Dean, Sandy Williams, Marta Acosta, Delilah S. Dawson, Suzanne McLeod, and Jaye Wells. I don't have the space to list all the bloggers and reviewers who took the time to read and review Arcadia Bell over the years, but your support has always meant the world to me (and still does). I especially want to thank *Romantic Times*, who gave me a fair shake and jumpstarted my fledging writing career when no one knew my name.

My biggest thanks, however, go out to all my

readers. You are a delightfully vocal bunch, and thanks to fan mail, Twitter, and Facebook, I know so much about you. Some of you are students, wives, parents, teachers, grandmothers, activists, and even priests. A few of you live in California, Ohio, Canada, France, Africa, Sweden, New Zealand, Brazil, and Greece. Many of you are wonderfully strange, witty, loyal, and smart, and you come from every manner of social class, race, religion, philosophical background, and political persuasion. How amazing is that? It's never easy to say goodbye, but Cady, Lon, Jupe, and Tabby now belong to you. Please take good care of them.